Totally Bound Publishing books by Jayce Carter

Collections
Sun, Sea and Sinful Delights

Dark Sanctuary

BURIED BY DESPAIR

JAYCE CARTER

Buried by Despair
ISBN # 978-1-80250-977-9
©Copyright Jayce Carter 2022
Cover Art by Fiona Jayde ©Copyright August 2022
Interior text design by Claire Siemaszkiewicz
Totally Bound Publishing

BURIED BY DESPAIR

Dedication

To all the people throughout my life who wanted
me to be more normal.
Kindly fuck off.
Repeatedly.

Chapter One

This isn't right at all.

Frustration caused Kat to toss her pen across the desk. After six different attempts at the same cartoon, she'd hit her limit.

She needed to get something new up on her store, since she'd kept up with a biweekly schedule for over two years without fail, but nothing had come to her. Somehow, all those cute little ideas she normally had, the quips, the humor, the adorable characters with large eyes and charm, sat just out of reach.

Kat folded her arms on her desk and dropped her head onto them. Her back ached from the hours she'd spent staring at her sketch pad, from all the attempts that had led to nothing. She kept thinking that if she started drawing, some idea would come to her.

It always had before.

The problem?

Each time she tried, her brain went AWOL, and she found herself back in that damned hotel room. A flash of pain, the memory of a smirking face —

"Knock it off!" She stood, shaking her hands as if that would dispel the memory she'd been running from for the past few weeks.

It didn't work, but what other option did she have?

Kat paced, then reached to smooth her hands over her hair. She grimaced at how oily it was. How long had it been since she'd washed it?

Days. Maybe longer?

The sensation grossed her out, but the idea of stripping down, of taking a shower, that seemed far worse. She hadn't been willing to attempt it, choosing instead to use clean wipes on the important areas.

Fox Asher, the doctor who had taken care of her at the hospital, had said no baths anyway.

Fine by me. What does it matter?

Kat sighed and shook her head. She'd never been a coward before, so what was wrong with her now?

The ringing of her phone made her jump, her fingers clutching the front of her button-up pajama top, as if holding it closed made it into some sort of armor. Once it filtered through her head that it was only her phone, Kat cursed herself and picked up her cell from the desk.

Sunny's name flashed across the screen, and the desire to ignore it hit her.

Then again, if she didn't answer, Sunny would show up with Garrison, Connor and Trent in tow. Kat had ignored calls for days, having no desire to talk to anyone, but that sort of understanding only went so far.

Not only was Sunny sweet, but the Doms of Sanctuary, the BDSM club that felt like the one place in the whole world where Kat belonged, were both protective and tenacious. The last thing she needed was for any of them to show up and disturb her hiding.

She sighed and answered the call. "Hey, Sunny."

"Kat..." Sunny's voice was exactly what Kat *didn't* want to hear. It was pity and worry.

At least it was Sunny and not Ell, though. Sunny was sweet and worried, but Ell had *been* there. Kat couldn't handle seeing that knowledge in Ell's face.

Kat forced some levity into her voice, faking a smile she didn't feel. "What's with that voice? Did you make the mistake of taking my advice and hiding Trent's paddle?" The last word caught in Kat's throat.

Something that would have made her laugh before felt like swallowing rusty nails, and that same memory of pain hit her.

"I just miss you," Sunny said, ignoring Kat's statement. Damn, it would have been so much easier if Sunny was carefree. Instead, she had that *'I really care'* tone of voice.

"I've been busy with work," Kat lied.

"Uh-huh. Well, I thought maybe you could come over soon? We could have dinner. I'll cook something you love."

"I'm swamped right now. It's not a good time."

Sunny sighed. "You can't just hide away from the world."

"I'm not."

"I know how you feel, but you don't have to go through this alone."

Kat squeezed her eyes shut and trapped the words she wanted to scream inside her head. She wanted to tell Sunny that she had *no* idea what Kat was going through, that she didn't need sympathy, that what she needed was to get back to regular life and forget the whole thing as soon as possible.

Yet...when offered a chance at regular—meaning dinner with her friends—Kat couldn't stomach the idea.

"There isn't anything to worry about," Kat said. "I really need to get going, though. We'll talk again soon, okay?"

Sunny's voice echoed through the line, but Kat didn't want to hear it. She hit the End button, her head pounding, her breath racing. She all but collapsed into her office chair, her knees weak and her hands trembling.

The ringing of the phone made her squeeze her eyes shut as she dropped her head into her hands and ignored the sound.

Her life had changed so much but she couldn't move forward.

And each time she shut her eyes, all she could see was the face of the man who had done it to her, who had turned her into this, and she wasn't sure if that would ever go away.

* * * *

Dean smiled at the happiness on Ell's face.

Fuck, how long had he wanted that for her? How many years had he spent watching over her, wanting nothing more than for her to get the life neither of them had had growing up?

And here she was, looking right at home helping Sunny at the women's shelter Sunny ran.

"Well don't you look happy?" Dean asked as he took a seat in Sunny's office.

A flush to Ell's cheeks said life with the three men she'd somehow ended up with suited her.

It certainly wasn't what Dean had expected from her. Ell was tough as they came, so he'd always figured she'd end up with some spineless man that she could run around all day long. Of course, as seemed normal for him, he had no fucking idea what women wanted, as evidenced by her ending up with three Doms.

"Stop it," Sunny said, that edge to her voice when she was protecting someone else.

"It's fine," Ell said. "If Dean isn't causing problems, someone should probably check him for a pulse."

Dean set his hand over his chest, feigning hurt.

"Now," Ell went on. "Why are you here? You didn't come all this way just to drop off these." She held up a stack of his business cards.

"Of course I did."

No, I didn't. Dean could have dropped those off anywhere, or even just given them the information over the phone to hand out to women at the shelter who might need a lawyer. He handled mostly divorce cases, some custody as well, so it made sense for him to help.

Ell lifted her eyebrow, silently calling him out.

Dean let out a loud sigh. "Fine. I wanted to see if you'd heard from Kat."

Ell's smile came on quick, as if she'd suspected as much, but she didn't keep that smile for long. It fading gave Dean his answer.

Sunny spoke up. "I talked to her this morning, but she got off the phone fast. I tried to get her to agree to coming over, but no luck."

"I went over to her new place," Ell added on, "but if she was in there, she didn't answer and there weren't any signs of her. She moved after…" Ell trailed off for a moment, and that old anger surged inside Dean at the tremble in her voice as she skipped over what they all knew. "But I don't think anyone has gone inside her new place. Well, except for Toya."

Dean snorted. Toya did as she damned well pleased as the owner of Sanctuary. No doubt she'd hired the movers herself and ensured the new place was up to specifications, especially for Kat, who had been the heartbeat of Sanctuary for years. "How is she?"

Ell and Sunny exchanged a loaded look, but it was Sunny who answered. "I don't know. Going through something like that, it takes a toll. It doesn't go away all at once."

Dean lowered his voice to a whisper, as if that made it better. "What exactly happened?"

Ell shook her head. "I don't know. Fox couldn't tell me, of course, because he's her doctor, but I know it wasn't good. His face gets serious each time she gets brought up."

Dean slumped forward. It was about what he'd expected, which was a whole lot of nothing. No answer, no understanding, no information. He hadn't reached out directly to Kat because he didn't think he had any right. They'd been acquaintances—nothing more.

Ell tilted her head as if trying to figure something out. "Are you two…?"

"No. Nothing like that. We never even played together. She's just a sweet girl, and I hate to think of her suffering."

Boy, was that one hell of a whopper. Sure, they weren't like that, and yeah, they'd done nothing sexual together, but he knew damned well there was something there. Or, maybe it was better to say he felt something, and he wanted more.

He still remembered seeing Kat as the detective, Olin Ramiz, had escorted her from that motel room. He'd known Ell was fine, had already seen her, but to watch Kat wince as she walked, to see how her broken gaze remained on the ground, how a sheet stained in blood was wrapped around her, how she flinched when Fox had reached for her, it had broken him.

Or, perhaps it was better to say it had woken a part of him he'd tried to destroy. That old part of him, the one that had survived his childhood, that had helped him to make it through what would have killed so many others, it had roused when watching Kat.

Which was dangerous.

Dean had worked hard to smother the old him, to bury it beneath layers of charming smiles and well-made suits and spot-on small talk.

He let out a long breath, trying to release the memory, trying to quiet the part of him that still wanted to exact revenge for what had happened.

"No word on the asshole who did it either, right?"

Ell gulped but answered anyway. "Nothing. Jerry's off the radar for now, it seems. He probably took off because he realized it was only a matter of time before he got himself caught if he hung around here."

Dean tried to hide his disappointment. Sure, it was good that Jerry wasn't around, wasn't looking for revenge or another shot at Kat, but fuck...Dean wanted the chance to get his hands on that man, *personally*.

He thought back to so many years ago, to the way blood had stuck to his hands, to how Dean could watch someone gasp for breath and not give a single fuck.

He shook his head then swallowed hard, trying to cage that part of him in the deepest hollows of his soul. He plastered on his perfect, charming smile, the one that hid what he was capable of. "Well, I should get going. If you hear anything, let me know."

Sunny and Ell both agreed, and as Dean left the shelter, his mind spun. He wanted to see Kat, to ensure she was okay, but another part of him? The one that ached for the chance to get hold of Jerry, to punish the fucker for what he'd done, it wasn't fair to subject Kat to that.

Dean was a lot of things, but the word good only fit with the fact he was good at fooling others.

Kat was better off without him around her. She'd suffered the actions of too many monsters already.

* * * *

Kat tried to breathe deeply as she sat in the exam room at Fox's clinic.

Fox—or Dr. Asher, as other patients knew him—didn't normally treat adults since he was a pediatrician. However, given that she knew him, and he'd already treated her wounds, he made her more comfortable than anyone else.

The last thing she wanted was to have to explain the situation or bare herself to some total stranger.

Still, sitting in the room, waiting for Fox to arrive sucked. She wore one of those damned cloth gowns and the cold air made her shiver. Each minute that passed allowed her anxiety to grow.

Finally that door opened, and Kat had no idea if seeing Fox made it better or worse. She hated that he knew what had happened, that he looked at her with pity in his eyes. Kat had always been the life of the party, the brat who no one could tame, but now he looked at her as if she had broken.

"Sorry for the wait," he said as he shut the door behind him. "I had an emergency case come in and it's thrown my schedule off."

"It's fine," she said as she tried for a smile she was sure looked strained. "Gave me time to break into your office and hide everything you might need."

She hadn't, of course, but the threat alone felt like something she would have done if she was still her instead of whatever she'd turned into.

14

Fox gave her a gentle smile, but it didn't hide the pity there. "Any problems since I saw you last?"

"Nope. Been doing fine."

"Pain level?"

"Good."

Fox lifted an eyebrow. "Good isn't a rating."

Kat blew out a slow breath. "It's low. One star? And only when I move too much."

"Good. Are you taking the meds I prescribed you?"

"Sometimes," Kat lied. She hadn't touched them, but she knew if she said that, he'd lecture her, and she wanted to end this little exchange as soon as possible.

Fox pressed his lips together into a tight line, then shifted so she was looking right into his eyes. "Kat, I know you don't want to be here, but I need you to be honest with me. I'm on your side. I'm not judging you, but I need to know the truth, though."

The eye contact was too much, and Kat dropped her gaze the second she could. "I haven't used them because I don't want to, but the pain hasn't been that bad."

"Okay," Fox said. "Can I see?"

Kat took a deep breath, then undid the ties of the gown. The nurse had said she could keep on her bra and underwear, which helped her nerves.

And wasn't that stupid? Fox had seen her naked — everyone at Sanctuary had — so why did this make her so damned nervous?

Because this *was* different.

Still, with trembling hands, Kat parted the fabric and locked her gaze on the ceiling tiles. She hadn't looked at herself since it happened, and she wasn't ready to yet.

Fox's gloved fingers moved over her skin, clinical and professional, following the long cut she knew was there. "It's healing well. No signs of infection or any issues. You've been keeping it dry?"

Kat nodded. "No baths, and I've worn loose clothing like you said."

"Good. You can start with scar cream if you want in another month or so. I doubt there is anything cosmetically a doctor could do given the length of the injury, but it will fade with time. It's closed well, so you can start with normal bathing again and clothing depending on your comfort."

The burning in Kat's eyes intensified, but she blinked it away. She would *not* cry in front of Fox. She hadn't cried yet, and she wasn't about to start now like some damsel.

"All done," Fox said as he moved back, and that was all Kat needed to hear before she yanked the gown closed, her knuckles aching with how tightly she held the fabric.

And of course, Fox noticed.

No matter how hard she tried to hold it together, to be the old Kat everyone knew and tolerated, she just kept falling short.

He opened his mouth, but Kat knew exactly what he was going to say. He was going to reassure her that it would take time, that she'd been through a trauma, that she needed to give herself a break. He'd hand her the card to some therapist and tell her to seek help.

She didn't want to hear any of that.

"Why don't I get dressed?" she interrupted to head him off. "I mean, I don't normally get naked unless an orgasm or two are in the cards." The joke fell flat.

What had she become a joke killer?

Fox didn't even bother with a pity laugh. He shook his head. "Plan a night to come to our place for dinner."

"I'm really busy—"

Fox dropped his voice into that commanding tone she used to love. "This isn't optional, Kat. We've all given you time, but you can't keep sulking. You think I didn't see that you've lost ten pounds in the last few weeks? You think I don't see those bags beneath your eyes? You either get something on the schedule to visit or you're going to find out just how invasive your friends can get."

Kat let her shoulders drop, knowing when he had outmaneuvered her. "Yeah, okay. I will."

Fox nodded, as if pleased. "Good. Set up another appointment in a month with me, but if you have any issues before then, I expect you to call." He didn't wait for an answer—probably knew that if she did answer, it would just be snark—before he left.

Kat dressed slowly, pulling the sundress over her head. She wasn't normally a dress person, but the fabric was loose, and it didn't bother her wound. Hopefully she could go back to her beloved leggings soon.

A knock on the door as she slid on her boots had her calling for them to enter, figuring Fox wanted to lecture her about something else.

Except, when the door opened, when she saw who it was, she froze.

She had hoped to never see that face again.

Chapter Two

It had only been a few weeks since Olin had laid eyes on Kat, yet it felt as if years had passed. She sat in one of the extra chairs in the small exam room, frozen as she stared at him, a shoe in her hand.

Right, she probably wasn't all that happy to see him.

At least, he figured that given she'd refused to answer his calls.

"Detective Ramiz," she said, her voice breathy and unsure.

"I told you before—call me Olin."

She swallowed hard, and when she spoke again, her voice was impossibly softer. "Olin. What are you doing here?"

"You've been ignoring my calls."

"I've been busy."

Olin crossed his arms and leaned his back against the door, just staring at her to call her a liar. She wasn't busy—she was hiding. There was a hell of a difference.

She shook her head, as if she didn't want to have the fight. "Was my statement not enough? If you have more questions, ask them."

A sharpness in her tone made him want to smile, but he was pretty sure that wouldn't go over too well. Instead, he kept his expression blank. "I wanted to give you an update. We're still looking, but for now, the suspect seems to have gone to ground."

"That isn't an update—it's a lack of an update. You didn't come all this way for that."

No, he hadn't. He'd come all this way because he'd wanted to see her, because something inside of him had kept him up late at night wondering if she was okay. He recalled how he'd helped her walk from the motel to the ambulance, how she'd stumbled, almost numb to the world, and he'd wanted to know she was doing better.

But is she?

That numbness still rested in her eyes. From what he'd heard, she'd pulled away from everyone in her life, had closed herself off in place as if she could pretend nothing had happened.

"I also wanted to give you this." He pulled a card from his pocket. "Victim advocacy group. They help with medical and mental health bills for victims of violent crimes and, when we catch the man—and we will catch him—they help you with that process as well."

Kat didn't reach for the card. "Thanks, but no thanks."

"Kat..."

"I have great insurance, so medical bills aren't an issue, and I don't need a therapist. If you catch him, then that's all on you. I don't need an advocate."

He sighed but set the card on the exam table beside her. Arguing wouldn't do either of them any good, and he found himself reluctant to go down that route when he wouldn't have long with her. No doubt Kat was already looking for an escape.

She leaned forward to slide on her boot, but a sharp inhalation stopped her.

Olin reached for the door, ready to call the doctor back in, but Kat gave him a withering glare that rooted him in place.

"You're hurting," Olin argued.

"I'm fine. I just forgot my body doesn't really like that whole bending thing yet."

Because that asshole had taken a knife to her. Olin hadn't seen the damage, since they'd wrapped a sheet around her before he'd gotten into the room, but he'd never forget the red that had seeped into the white fabric.

It had been like a horror movie, except all too real.

"Then let me help," he answered. At her hard look, he went on. "I'll help you get your shoes on or I'll call Fox back in. Your choice."

Color blanched from her lips, but finally, she held the boots out.

They were the type girls often wore, with some sort of soft fur on the inside. Olin dropped to his knees in front of her, groaning slightly as he did so because his body didn't much like doing that anymore. He tapped the top of his thigh, and Kat followed the request, setting her foot there.

Her foot looked so small against him, and again it reminded him that she should have never been at that fucking motel. It never should have happened. From all he'd heard, Kat had been a hellion—sweet and fun and tenacious.

Look what that asshole had done to her...

He tried to push that away and lifted one of the boots. She slipped her foot inside and he worked it up until it fit, then repeated the motion on the other side. By the time he'd finished, it was impossible to ignore the way she trembled.

It made him look up and meet her wide gaze. Her eyes were a strikingly bright gray, which was odd given her light hair and pale skin. She looked almost ethereal.

"Stop it," she whispered.

Olin sighed and dropped his hands to his side, trying not to crowd her. "I'm not doing anything—just helping you with your shoes."

Kat all but jumped out of the chair and away, as if terrified at being close at all. Then again, he couldn't blame her, not after what she'd been through.

Olin had submitted the report, knew what happened, had taken her statement. The only blessing of the whole damned thing was that she hadn't been raped. No doubt Jerry would have gotten there eventually, but he hadn't had time. Instead, the sadistic bastard had just taken a knife to her, leaving a long cut from chest to pubic bone with a few others on her lower stomach.

It made Olin swallow, but he remained on his knees. The last thing he wanted was for her to look at him with that same fear.

"You didn't come here just to tell me that. I don't know if you're hoping something will happen or if you just feel bad, but I don't need you to hover."

"I don't think seeing you once since it happened is hovering."

She offered him a side-eye that said she didn't find him amusing. "I'm fine, okay? I get it—everyone wants me to break down and cry and lose my shit, but I really am okay."

"Oh yeah?" *I should shut up. I should just let it go.* Sadly, Olin hadn't ever been good at that, and the words kept coming. "Because from what I heard, you haven't gone back to Sanctuary, haven't been talking to your friends, have all but fallen off the map. Are you trying to tell me that before this happened, you would have shaken like this? Would have jumped away from someone helping you put your shoes on? You can pretend all you want that nothing happened, but trust me, these things have a way of sneaking up and biting you in the ass if you ignore them."

Kat stared right at Olin, and he wondered if he'd ever been on his knees in front of a woman before.

Probably, but never like this.

Finally, she shook her head. "How about this? I have to be fine, because the other option is not being fine, and that can't happen. So I either keep moving forward or I collapse, and I *can't* collapse." She said the words with so much force, Olin almost regretted what he'd said.

She was hanging on the only way she knew how, but it still felt like watching someone drinking seawater when thirsty. He could tell her all day long that it would do more harm than good, but that wouldn't change a thing.

So Olin nodded. "When you're tired of pretending, just remember you've got friends, and I'd like to be one of them."

Kat gulped then ran from the room, leaving Olin there, kneeling and alone and all the more confused.

He doubted she'd call him, but fuck, he wished she would…

* * * *

How was it that Kat's house seemed even quieter than it had before? Maybe it was the difference between the noise of the doctor's office, the sound of Olin's voice—the general clatter of the outside world that made her recognize just how silent her house was.

And she *hated* it.

She had never liked silence or quiet houses. Maybe that was why she was used to talking so much, to filling the space with prattle. Silence was deafening and dangerous. It was impossible to judge how a person felt or thought if they were quiet.

However, no matter how badly she wanted to call someone, just the thought made her stomach churn.

The conversation with Olin replayed in her head, the way he'd looked at her. Why was it that no matter how much she told herself nothing had happened, she couldn't stop her reactions?

Kat had faced down countless Doms without the slightest bit of fear. How many times had she stood toe-to-toe with men far larger than her, both in Sanctuary and outside of it? She *never* flinched.

And now? When Olin had helped with her shoes, she'd trembled.

Her anxiety had grown until it sat like a ball of electricity inside her stomach, writhing and impossible to ignore. It had her going into her bedroom and reaching for the cannabis drops a friend had given her months before. They were supposed to help a person relax, and while she hadn't ever indulged before, was there a better time than now?

Maybe they could take the edge off and help her sleep. Wouldn't that be something? Sleeping through the night without waking up with a gasping scream?

The directions said to start with a quarter dropper, but Kat rolled her eyes. This wasn't some average anxiety, so she needed a full dose. She placed it beneath her tongue and held it there for thirty seconds, then swallowed.

It tasted somewhat like s'mores, but had a bitterness that wasn't quite right. If it worked, she didn't care—she'd lick dirt if it made her feel a little better.

Kat paced, waiting for the drops to take effect, to feel that loosening of her muscles and slight fuzziness to her thoughts she needed. However, as the minutes ticked by…*nothing*.

Maybe she just had a high tolerance? She placed another dropper full beneath her tongue, repeating the process from before. After another ten minutes, when she was sure it wasn't working, she tried yet again.

Then the drops caught up with her…

* * * *

Bradley rotated his arm as he rubbed his shoulder. He'd been giving one of his mares a shot, but the horse had figured out that if she pinned him to the side of the truck, he couldn't give it.

Thankfully, one of the ranch hands had been there to help deal with the unruly mare.

She was one of his favorites, of course. He'd named her Brat, and he'd had her for five years. She'd come to him when her old owner had abandoned her, moving and thinking she was more trouble than she was worth. A horse rescue who he'd worked with before had reached out, and Bradley had always been a sucker for a hard case.

Five years later, and he couldn't help but smile at the spirited girl.

Of course, his shoulder wasn't smiling.

His phone rang, and he let out a loud sigh. He could always just ignore the call. It was late and about his whole life was on the ranch, which meant emergencies didn't really happen.

The ringing stopped as Bradley turned on the shower. Heat would soothe his muscles, then he could turn on the television and fall asleep watching some dumb show he didn't give a damn about.

Except, the ringing of his phone went off again. He left the water going so it would warm, then answered the call, a number he didn't recognize there. "What?"

"How dare you send me to voicemail."

Bradley frowned at the voice, his brain not working fast enough to identify it.

Still, the person went on. "I sucked your dick, and that should give me immediate answer status."

And that tells me exactly who it is...

There was only one woman who would ever dare to call him and say such things.

"Charming as always, aren't you, Kat?"

Chapter Three

Kat groaned as she woke to a horrible sound echoing through her place. Was that a fire alarm? She had a moment where she wondered if she was in school, if there was some fire drill?

No, wait, I'm an adult. I'm a long way past school.

The sound stopped, so Kat pulled her blanket over her head to avoid the daylight, wanting nothing more than to go back to sleep. The night before was a blur, but she did recall ordering enough food for a party of twenty, then trying to invite the delivery woman in to eat some when she realized how much food there was.

The rest of the night was blank.

A bang made her bolt upright, and it was accompanied by another.

Knocking? She pulled herself out of the bed, her head fuzzy as she tried to wake up. The glowing red of the digital clock above her desk read eight in the morning.

Who the hell has the audacity to show up at this ungodly time of the morning?

When she grasped the doorhandle, ready to give whoever it was a piece of her mind, she froze. Fear spread through her, a memory of waking up to some man grabbing her at Ell's place, when she'd fought with everything she had and still lost.

It felt like a shadow behind her, reaching for her, breathing on her neck.

Kat let out a pathetic sound when the person on the other side hit the door again.

No. I will not be a coward.

Kat shook her head and undid the deadbolt, pulling the door open to find the last person she would have expected there.

It was like the past slapped her across the face, a sharp pain in her chest as she laid eyes on Bradley.

For one moment, she struggled to pull herself out of the memory — Bradley's demanding lips, his strong hands, the way he always made her feel safe. He looked just as he had before, as if the years hadn't touched him. He had his head shaved still — perfect for a man who didn't give a damn about appearances. His skin held a deep tan from him working outside, and he had the sort of muscles a person got from hard daily work rather than a gym. Worse? Those brown eyes were so familiar, she nearly fell into them.

He woke her from the past when he didn't wait for an invitation to enter, when he walked into her house without so much as a word, a bag over his shoulder.

Kat swallowed hard, then finally made herself speak. "What are you doing here?"

He didn't answer right away, dropping his bag by her couch before he peered around the living room. The way he used silence had always unnerved her, especially since she'd never learned to counter it. Silence was easily her biggest weakness.

"Just in the neighborhood?" Kat tried to use her old tone, one full of snark.

Bradley took that moment to stare directly at her, the weight of that gaze heavier than a 747. "You were the one who called me."

"I did not."

"Not a shock you don't remember, since you were high off your fucking ass." He reached into the pocket of his jeans and pulled out his phone. A few clicks to the screen, then he turned it toward her.

Sure enough, there was her number in his recent calls.

I called him? Talk about taking a bad situation and making it far worse. Why was it that Kat seemed so skilled in doing exactly that?

"What did I say?" she asked, a nagging fear growing inside her. What if she had blurted out more than she should have?

"You said a hell of a lot." His gaze dropped to her chest, making Kat take a step backward.

That answered the question, didn't it? Bradley wasn't looking with lust, but with knowledge. It meant Kat must have told him what had happened. A part of her was glad she didn't remember it, but another hated that he knew.

It was worse for Bradley to know. The asshole had always been confident, sure of himself, so him finding out she'd been at the mercy of another, hurt and scarred by that person, seemed unreasonable.

Still, anger at the audacity of him to show up helped keep the shame at bay. "Well, you can't hold what high me says against sober me. Thanks for coming, sorry for the inconvenience, you can leave." She went to walk past him, her chin held high.

"Not so fast, Kat." The tone took her back, the way he said her name so much like the one he'd used in the past, when he'd all but growled it into her ear.

It drew her to a stop. "Please, don't do this," she whispered.

"Me?" He let out a soft laugh, then crossed his arms. "What am I doing other than coming over because clearly you needed me to? You called me, you dropped this shit off on my doorstep, so you're the one who started this."

Kat swallowed hard, her shoulders dropping, her old confidence seeming so far away. "I'm sorry. I didn't mean to call you."

"Course you didn't. Kat actually asking anyone for help? God fucking forbid." He snorted and peered around. "One bed or two?"

"One." As soon as she answered, she cursed herself for falling so easily into Bradley's trap. He'd always made her mindless.

"I'll take the couch, then."

"Excuse me?" *That* got her brain working. The idea of allowing Bradley into her space at all was a lot, but then the fact he seemed to think he'd be *staying* was entirely too much. "You better mean that you're stealing it, because you sure as hell will not be sleeping on it here."

"Good to see your bite isn't gone. Be a pity if someone defanged you." Bradley didn't argue with her—he never really had before.

Some Doms stomped their feet and yelled. They felt the need to prove they were in control. Kat had always enjoyed that type, had mostly played with them. They were easier to manipulate, easier to get what she wanted from.

Bradley had *never* been that type. Maybe it was what had ended them, the fact that he stood firm where he was. He didn't budge, didn't raise his voice, never had to prove anything.

"You can't be serious," Kat finally said. "You can't just show up after all this time and think you get to tell me what to do."

Bradley faced her directly, and the weight of that gaze was crushing. He reached out slowly and caught her chin, forcing her gaze to his dark eyes. It took her back, made her remember and get lost in the times she'd stared into those eyes before. And on the tail of that, the memory of how happy she'd been tore through her.

"What's happened between us doesn't matter, Kat. You're hurting, and your stubborn ass is trying to deal with it all on your own, and you're suffering. Did you really think I'd just stay away when I found out? That I'd hang up the phone and ignore it?"

"What about your ranch? You can't just drop everything."

"Being the boss has some benefits, including that I've got plenty of help to handle the place while I'm here."

"This is stupid," Kat muttered softly, easily recognizing the set of Bradley's jaw to tell her he wasn't budging.

He stroked his thumb along her jawline, softening his grip. "Yeah, it is, but I'm still here and I will be until you're back on your feet. Argue all you want, bitch all you want, but it's never deterred me before."

Kat let out a slow breath, knowing he spoke the truth. She had never won against him, and that was really the end of them, like it always was for her. Not that he scared her—she wasn't afraid of him.

If Kat safe worded, he'd back off. He'd still want to help, still do what he could, but he'd never force her into something she couldn't handle. That almost made it worse, though. It made her accept that while he was being pushy and annoying, he wasn't really forcing her into anything.

"How long are you going to stay?" she asked as she gave in.

"That's up to you, Kat. I'll be here until you stop needing me." And damn it, that did *not* make her feel better at all.

* * * *

Walking into Sanctuary was so much harder than it should have been. Kat drew her hands into fists as she forced one foot in front of the other.

The place looked different—it always did when it was empty during the day. Kat was one of the few with access anytime she wanted it, mostly because she'd gotten her hands on a key one time and Toya had never taken it away.

At night the place was lively, had a heartbeat all its own. During the day it seemed dead, like a husk left behind after something terrible had happened. She struggled to recognize it at all, to feel any connection to the building that had been her source of safety before.

Damn Jerry.

Even thinking his name made her shiver, but she forced herself forward, refusing to give everything up to that asshole.

Not that she'd planned on going anywhere. Bradley had been hovering all day, taking up space in her house, silent and judging her.

At least, that's how it felt.

In reality, he'd had his e-book reader and had planted his ass on the couch. When she wanted to pace, to lose her shit, his presence had put her on edge.

So after a few hours of that nonsense, she'd needed to escape. The only place she could think of going was Sanctuary. At least she'd get some privacy since it should have been empty.

Or so she thought, until she walked through a doorway and nearly ran right into someone else.

The fear that swept through her shamed Kat. She, who had never had the good sense to be afraid of *anyone*, cowered on instinct.

The man took a large step backward and lifted his hands to the side as if to show he wouldn't grab her. And wasn't that yet another kick to her pride?

It took a moment for her eyes to clear, for her head to quiet enough for her to recognize the man.

"Sorry," Kat apologized to Dean, rubbing her palms over her thighs to wipe away the sweat that had suddenly sprung up there.

"It's fine. Bet you didn't expect to find me here."

"I didn't think anyone else had keys."

Dean offered her a charming smile, one he wielded like a weapon, one she'd seen too many foolish women fall for. "Toya gave me a set because I help with permit issues that come up. I was dropping off some paperwork for her to sign."

Kat swallowed hard and nodded, giving herself a moment for her heart to stop racing. This was Dean, for fuck's sake. She knew him, had for a few years, and while they weren't close at all, she knew he wasn't some monster who would attack her.

"Haven't seen you around," he said, and although his smile didn't slip, she could *hear* the pity beneath it, the meaning.

"Been busy." The lie slid from her lips as easily as it always did.

"Right. Well, what gets you out today?"

"An unexpected houseguest. My place didn't feel quite so relaxing anymore."

A hardness set in Dean's blue eyes, one Kat wasn't sure she'd ever seen before. "Are you all right? Do you need me to—"

She shook her head quickly. "Nothing like that. It seems I called up an old friend when I wasn't feeling quite myself. They're just trying to keep an eye on me." She forced herself to laugh, to sound like her old self even if she didn't feel like that at all. "He thinks I'm not doing so well."

"He's not the only one," Dean muttered, his words so low she wondered if he'd meant for her to hear them.

Dean was odd when it came to the Doms. Most of the ones Kat had dealt with were self-assured but quick to try to force everyone around them to dance to their tune. Even when they meant well, they were used to taking control. Dean had always struck her as rather sweet and vanilla.

Well, that was the way he seemed, but the rumor mill at Sanctuary said differently. There wasn't any doubt he was a Dom, and there were plenty of heartbroken but satisfied women in his wake to say he knew what he was doing.

"Well, I'm about done here anyway," Dean went on. "So I'll get out of your hair soon."

Guilt tugged at Kat. Was it fair to send someone else running from Sanctuary? It wasn't *her* place. That damned sense of fairness had her speaking up. "It's fine. How about a drink?"

"Toya gave you keys to the good stuff?" Dean lifted one of his dark eyebrows, reminding Kat just how handsome he was.

He was the sort of man a person might assume was an actor or model. His dark hair was slicked back without a strand out of place, and his facial hair was neatly groomed. He dressed impeccably, in a three-piece gray suit with a black and white polka-dot tie. If she'd heard of such an outfit, she'd have figured it would never work, but somehow Dean pulled it off perfectly.

He looked smart and wicked and as charming as ever.

It was only when his tempting lips pulled into a smile that Kat realized her mistake—she'd been so focused on how he looked that she'd missed her question. She moved past him, trying to regain her normal attitude. "*Allow* implies Toya gave it to me. I just like to collect keys when I can then don't mention it, so no one takes them away. What's your poison?"

Kat slid around to behind the bar as Dean took a seat at a stool.

"I'm going back to work after this, so let's just go with a Shirley Temple."

Kat froze, furrowing her brows. "What?"

"What's wrong with that?"

The unexpected drink took her off guard, but quickly enough, Kat let out a laugh and shook her head. "Nothing. I'm just used to the Doms here ordering the manliest drink possible, as if they were doing a testosterone check with it. Didn't figure you'd order something an eight-year-old girl would."

As soon as Kat spoke, a slight tremble started through her. That sounded like her, like her old self, the one who teased and bratted to everyone around her. Still, after Jerry...

Dean didn't look bothered at all by the exchange, however. He grinned. "Maybe other men feel the need to prove their masculinity, but I figure I have plenty of other things that prove I'm a man without having to drink things I don't like."

His response helped her regain her own footing, helped her remember this was Dean she was talking about. She let out a soft laugh, then went about making him the drink. Lemon-line soda, grenadine and extra cherries to rib him over what he'd picked.

Not that it seemed to matter. Dean took the drink as if it were everything he could have wanted and sipped from the red straw. "Perfect. You should bartend more often here."

"I tried. Apparently, bartenders are supposed to be *professional* and give people what they ask for. My way is a bit more free-spirited. Toya gave me one night, then fired me."

"Was that the fastest you've ever been fired?"

"Oh, god no. One time, I showed up to work at a vet's office as a temp receptionist in a shirt that read, *Need Bacon?* I didn't make it past the front door."

Dean let out a laugh, as if he could perfectly imagine that happening. Which, to be fair, seemed pretty on-brand for Kat. "Anything for you?" he asked.

Which reminded Kat that she hadn't made herself a drink. She pressed her lips together, then shrugged. "I guess I'll have the same." After making one of her own, she considered moving around to the other side, and taking a seat beside Dean.

However, the thought of doing so was much too far. No matter how much she tried to pretend nothing had happened over the past few weeks, it just wasn't true.

So, instead, she grabbed a chair behind the bar and pulled it over so she sat across from Dean, giving her the distance she needed.

His expression screamed he knew what she'd done and why, but he didn't comment on it. Instead, he took another sip of his drink, then asked, "How's work?"

Terrible. Kat recalled how she'd been unable to create a new image for her shirts, something cute and funny and irreverent. Instead of admitting that, however, she forced a smile. "Like it always it."

"You're an artist, right?" At her nod, he went on. "What kind of art? Painting, sculpture, graphic art for marketing?"

"None of that. I do cartoon work and sell it in my own shop."

"Oh yeah?"

Kat nodded, then pulled her phone out. A few swipes brought up her shop, and she handed it to Dane. He took the phone and scrolled through the images.

However, Kat didn't really feel any nerves. She never did, not with this work. It was easy, almost mindless. Draw an animal or person with large eyes to make them adorable, then create some joke to go with it. Rinse and repeat.

Still, Dean nodded as he looked. "These are good. I've *seen* this image, in fact. Never realized it was your work." He handed the phone back.

Despite Kat not caring what people thought normally, she couldn't deny a small rush at the way he spoke, the pleasure at his praise. She slid the phone into her back pocket. "Yeah, well, it pays the bills. Not a lot of people get to do what they love for a living, you know?" She not-so-subtly looked at Dean, who as a lawyer couldn't possibly be all that happy with his own work.

He let out another warm laugh. "Hey now, maybe I grew up dreaming about wasting my years nose deep in law books. Maybe I was a very boring child."

"I doubt that."

"Really?"

She nodded, taking another drink as she peered at him, trying to fit together what she knew. "You weren't a book sort of kid. You're the type who gets bored easily. I bet you were a handful, causing problems and being wild. You got into more than your fair share of trouble." She said it with a laugh, imagining a young Dean — probably just as charming and perfectly dressed — running around some mansion he probably grew up in and causing trouble for the help.

Except, Dean's expression hardened in a way she wasn't sure she'd ever seen before. Even his smile faded. As quickly as it happened, he blinked it away. "Excuse me, won't you? I need to check in with the office." Without another word, he rose and headed toward the staircase that led up to the offices, leaving Kat alone.

That was weird…

The ringing of her own phone interrupted her thoughts, though. Without thinking, she lifted the phone to her ear, answering it while her gaze watched where Dean had gone. "Hello?"

"Hello."

The voice sucked the floor from beneath Kat's feet. It was smooth and clear and burned into her memory. It was the one she heard at night when she closed her eyes and couldn't fall asleep, the one that haunted her.

Jerry.

Kat didn't respond — what was there to say? The still healing marks he'd left on her burned as if they reacted to his very voice.

"I've missed you," he said. "It turns out your screams are hard to forget."

Kat's breath sped, turning shallow. A part of her wondered if she'd snapped beneath the pressure of dealing with what had happened, of burying it down and pretending it hadn't happened. Maybe this was her brain giving up the good fight.

Except, it didn't stop. A cold laugh came through the line. "No fight left? Don't tell me that's true. You were far too much fun. Maybe you're just surprised to hear from me. You did move, after all. I don't mind you playing hard to get."

"How did you get my number?" Kat asked.

"Do you really think that is so difficult? Finding someone's number takes little work."

"What do you want?"

"Isn't that obvious? You." At Kat's silence, Jerry let out a dark chuckle. "Don't worry, I'm not going to come and get you. What fun would there be in that?"

"You didn't mind doing it before."

"You were a happy accident last time. Now, though? Now you're more than that. I am a very patient man, Kat, and I'm more than willing to wait you out. When you're ready, you'll make the right choice and come to me."

Kat shook her head, and despite the tightness in her throat, she forced herself to speak. "I won't."

"You will. I haven't made it as far as I have in this world by not being able to read people and knowing how to get what I want. You will walk, on your own, to me. You will choose to give yourself over to me. I don't care if it takes weeks or months or years, but you will. Until then, Kat, make sure no one else gets to hear those pretty screams of yours. They're only for me." The call ended, leaving Kat holding the phone, her heart pounding so fast she became lightheaded.

He was wrong, right? Kat would *never* return to him.

Yet…the way he'd spoken, the absolute certainty in his voice, the memories of how he'd dragged that knife over her skin and laughed as she'd screamed, it all made her unable to be sure.

And before she knew what was happening, the world started to fade out around her.

Dean hadn't had a call to make, but the way Kat had decided who he was had driven him away to collect himself.

Which made no damned sense. Dean had always prided himself on looking exactly like Kat saw him. He wanted to be that charming man, the smart one, the one who no one looked too closely at. So why was it that when she saw exactly what he put forward, it bothered him?

Why mattered little, however. He'd stepped out, given himself a few minutes to rebuild his façade, then walked back into the bar with a smile, ready to play his part as always.

Except, he didn't see the Kat he expected. She stood by the bar, but her normally pale skin was even whiter, as if all the blood had leeched from her face.

"Kat?"

She didn't respond as he came closer, his steps slow so he didn't further startle her. He moved around the bar, repeating her name, trying to get her attention to no avail.

Then it seemed whatever was going on in her head went too far. She wavered on her feet, giving him only a moment of notice before she toppled. It was just enough time for him to reach for her, to capture her before she hit the ground.

She trembled, her breathing sawing in and out of her lungs, and her body felt so damned fragile in his arms.

What the fuck is going on?

"Hey now, take some deep breaths for me." He pulled her against him, then all but carried her over to one of the seating areas. He set her down and kneeled in front of her.

The girl was panicking *bad* but over what? He hadn't even been there when she'd lost it, so he didn't think it was him.

Or maybe it was? Had he frightened her with his attitude? She had just been through a lot... Maybe his annoyance at her guess had shown on his face and reminded her of Jerry?

Dean struggled to decide how to proceed. Maybe he should call Sunny... If anyone knew how to handle this sort of thing, if anyone was equipped for it, it was that woman.

However, when he reached for his phone, Kat seemed to come out of it a bit. She grabbed his hand, her eyes wide as she shook her head.

"This is a bit out of my league, Kat." By which he meant that while he held some strange desire to take care of Kat, he knew his emotional depth wasn't near enough to deal with scraped knees let alone whatever Kat was suffering.

She gripped his hand tighter, and he dropped his gaze to the touch. His skin turned white where she held him, where her nails dug into him as if she needed the touch to keep herself together.

While he had no idea what to say, he'd happily bleed for her if it helped.

After a moment, her breathing slowed enough that he didn't think she'd pass out. She whispered out a soft, "sorry," as she stared at the floor instead of at him.

"What happened?" He paused, not wanting to ask the next part but unable to stop himself. "Was it me?"

She furrowed her eyebrows as she looked at him. "What?"

"I walked out, and maybe I wasn't in the best of moods, and I thought maybe…" He let the words trail off.

She let out a sigh, then shook her head. "No— nothing like that. You're a lot of things, Dean, but scary isn't one of them."

He released a long breath he hadn't realized he was holding. Damn, he really had been worried about that, hadn't he? The thought of her seeing that other part of him, the one who was capable of some terrible things, it made his chest tighten.

Dean offered her his normal, practiced smile. "Good. So what was it?"

"Nothing." Boy, that was a lie, wasn't it? Still, she went on. "I was just…having a moment. I should get home." She stood, but the moment she did, she wavered and another quick move from Dean led her back down to the couch again.

"You aren't driving anywhere, Kat."

"I'm not staying here."

"Well, the answer is obvious, right? I drive you home or we call someone else to do it." As soon as he said it, he knew he'd won.

She pressed her lips together, and it screamed that she didn't want to bother her friends, that she didn't watch to reach out. He'd already figured that, because she'd all but disappeared from her friend's lives. There was no chance she wanted to let anyone else get this glimpse of her.

"All right then, Kat, let's go. I'll get you home."

She let out a shaky breath, and Dean tried to ignore just how right it felt when he lifted her—it was easy to say it was because of the way she still wavered but knew damned well it was more because he just wanted to. Still, he ignored the way it warmed him, the way she fit against his chest, the way she all but melted against him.

He knew this was a bad fucking idea, but it didn't stop him from clutching her to him just a little tighter.

Chapter Four

Of all the things Bradley was expecting when someone pulled up to Kat's house, her getting out of the passenger side of a man's expensive-looking town car wasn't anywhere on the list.

The man was tall and well-dressed, not someone who worked with his hands for a living, that much was clear. He had on a suit and wore it in a way that said he was accustomed to it.

If Bradley were younger, he might have felt threatened by it. The man who walked around and spoke to Kat was all the things Bradley had wanted to be at one time—clearly rich, intelligent, the sort of man who didn't do much physical work for a living.

Was this someone Kat was involved with now? Bradley tried to ignore the growing jealousy inside him, reminded himself that he didn't have any claims to Kat, not anymore. They'd been apart for years, so what did he expect? That she'd write off the whole idea of relationships as he had?

He tried to bury the discomfort deep inside him. There was no reason to think too much about it—he was here to help her, not to start up anything again.

He might still love her, but his heart couldn't take that crash again.

The front door opened, and Bradley went back to slicing the bell peppers for dinner. Nothing like a good chili to warm a person up, and he wasn't a man used to sitting around idly.

When Kat lifted her gaze, however, all those doubts left him. The girl always had trouble hiding her feelings well, at least to anyone who really knew her. A fear in her eyes said something had happened, and the paleness of her skin backed that theory up.

"What happened?" Bradley asked as he set the knife down.

The other man stared at Bradley for a quick moment before offering a smile that seemed forced. "You must be the friend who's babysitting."

"And you are?"

The man pressed a hand against Kat's back to get her moving. "Go on, honey. Go wash your face and take a few minutes, huh?"

Kat did as she was told, and *that* seemed like one hell of a new trick. Had she ever done as she was told in Bradley's experience?

Probably not.

Still, once the door to her room closed, Bradley brought his gaze back to the new man who looked significantly less friendly once Kat had gotten out of earshot.

A long, tense moment passed before the other man spoke. "My name's Dean. I'm a friend of Kat's."

"Friend, huh?" Bradley shook his head and went back to cutting the bell peppers, wanting something to do with his hands that kept him busy. "And why exactly is she worse off than when she left?"

"No idea. We were having a drink, and I stepped out for a moment. Came back to her having a panic attack."

Bradley brought the knife down harder than needed, the thump of it against the wooden cutting board like a spotlight to his feelings. "Damn it. I didn't realize she was having panic attacks. She's as closed-lipped as a person can get."

Dean walked forward until he stood on the other side of the kitchen bar. "So you know what happened?"

At least that let Bradley take a bit of a breath. He didn't have to dance around anything if Dean already knew.

"Not exactly. Girl called me high off her ass, in tears. Said someone attacked her, but I can't say I got much more than that."

"And you came running?"

Bradley's gaze drifted to Kat's closed door. *Of course I did.* "Kat and I, we were…something quite a few years back."

At that, Dean's eyes opened wider, as if pieces had just fit together. "That must make you Bradley, right?" He let out a soft laugh and shook his head. "Word travels around Sanctuary fast."

"You know her from Sanctuary?" Bradley wasn't sure if that made it better or worse. On one hand, Dean appeared to be a part of the life that Bradley had once lived, a connection to his old friends. On the other, it made it feel even more like Kat had replaced him, like she'd upgraded from him to this new version. Still, Bradley wasn't a man to wallow.

"Yeah. We don't know each other well, but that's where I saw her this morning. I was over at the club taking care of some paperwork for Toya when Kat showed up. We had a couple sodas before I found her hyperventilating. Told her she was in no condition to drive, so I brought her home and called my office to have my secretary bring her car here."

Secretary. Yet another example of how little this new man was like Bradley.

Still, Dean had taken care of Kat, had brought her home safely, so Bradley reminded himself to go easy on the other man. What did their relationship matter? As soon as Kat was back on her feet, Bradley would be gone again, retreating to his ranch where he didn't have to see hide or hair of her or endure the pain that always came with doing so.

"So if you know what happened, how is she *really*?" Bradley asked as he dumped the sliced peppers into a large pot on the stove. They sizzled as they hit the hot oil at the bottom and released an immediate wave of delicious scent.

"Hard to say," Dean answered. "She's tried to drop off the face of the earth. I'm close with a few of her friends, and according to them, she just hides out here by herself. She hasn't come to Sanctuary, hasn't seen any of the people in her life. She just lies if anyone asks her and says she's busy."

Bradley nodded, that sounding exactly like the stubborn woman he knew and loved. "Seems pretty much out of Kat's playbook. I remember years ago, she got the flu bad. She kept telling people she was fine, blowing us all off, and when I got sick of it and showed up at her place?" A slight tremor ran through Bradley at the memory, at how pale and fragile she'd looked when he'd finally all but broken into her place. "I called the ambulance immediately and it took her nearly two weeks before the hospital would release her. Turns out she ended up with double pneumonia. My point? Kat lying to people and pretending to be fine right up until she collapses is exactly what she does."

Dean didn't respond right away. Did he dislike that Bradley and Kat had a past? If that was the case, he said nothing, moving on as if the tense moment had never happened. "Yeah, I guess she is a hellcat, isn't she? Is that why you're here?"

"Pretty much. She and I, we may have ended, but there are some ties that no number of years can cut. She called, and I knew I had to do something. Figured I'd come, spend a bit here, help her get back on her feet."

"Does she listen to you?"

"Kat listen to anyone? I'd like to see that. No, she doesn't do what I say, but I've dealt with her long enough to know how to handle her at least. I mean, one day of me here and she left."

Dean laughed, though that sharpness in his blue eyes never faded. The man was *far* more dangerous than he let on—that much was clear. "That sounds about right. So you're planning on staying here until she gets her ass in gear and stops hiding?"

"Pretty much. And you? What's your plan?"

Dean set his arm on the counter and stared at Bradley without a hint of fear. "I'm not a relationships sort of man, so if you're worried about that, don't be. Kat and I, we're just friends—nothing else. I want the best for her, and I'm willing to do whatever that take. It means if you need a break here, let me know and I don't mind taking shifts." Dean rose, as if the conversation had suddenly gotten too awkward. "I'm going to head

Jayce Carter

out. I bet she'll hide in there for a while anyway. Nice to meet you."

Bradley said nothing back as the other man left.

Dean's words ran through Bradley's head, the declaration that he had no intentions toward Kat, but Bradley could read people with ease. Dean wanted those words to be true, maybe, but he didn't quite believe them himself.

Which just made this whole thing even messier...

* * * *

Olin took a deep breath as he walked onto the crime scene and pulled his gloves on. There was always this heavy sense when he went to a crime scene in the moments before he knew all the details, when there were only questions and tension.

It was his job, and he loved it every bit as much as he hated it, but that didn't make it any easier.

This one was probably the same as so many others. They liked to throw anything in the shadier areas of town to the gangs division, as though if it happened between Oak St. and Fifteenth, it *had* to involve gangs.

It was just a bad area of town, though, a place where gangs had power because people lived in too much fear to stand up to them. Worse, the citizens were just as scared of him, of the other officers. It made even coming down to this area a risk.

And for today? Beneath a sheet rested the body of a young woman. Olin didn't know much else about it, would find out when he got to the scene, but he'd been at this so long he wasn't sure he needed to know much more. The girl was probably a sex worker, had taken a client who thought he had the right to do whatever he

48

wanted to her, and the yellow crime scene tape was the result.

Those were the worst cases for Olin, the reality that he couldn't save everyone, that there were people who, even if they were in danger, wouldn't ever come to him for help.

Like Kat...

The unwelcome thought was nonetheless true. No matter what he did to reach out, it never made a bit of difference. Kat had made it perfectly clear that she wanted nothing to do with him.

It wasn't like he was looking to go start up anything serious, but he wanted her to at least know she could lean on him.

Focus. This isn't the time to be daydreaming about women.

"So what do we have?" Olin asked as he walked up to the officer who stood watch a few feet away from the covered body.

"It's...bad."

The tone made Olin face the officer. Ah, that explained it. He was young—maybe on his first such case. It wasn't something anyone ever got used to, but they learned to deal with it, eventually.

Or at least learned to hide their reaction.

"Anything else?" Olin asked, not wanting to draw attention to the officer's discomfort.

The officer nodded, as if woken from his stupor. "Sorry, sir. Young woman, no identification, no purse, no clothes. Time of death estimated as sometime late last night. The garbage man discovered the body as he was doing his rounds this morning and called it in."

"Cause of death?"

"Undetermined. There are a lot of wounds, so probably blood loss, but the medical examiner will have to look to be sure."

"Weapon?"

"Knife seems like."

That took Olin back, made him remember Kat and the blood on the comforter of that motel room. He swallowed hard, trying to push down the fact that this could have been Kat if they hadn't been fast enough.

There was a lot of evil in the world, people who wanted to hurt others just because they could. Olin had gotten a front-row seat to that sort of thing enough times, but it hit differently when he knew the victim.

"Thanks," Olin said, letting the officer off the hook from anything else. It wasn't because he was being nice—the man looked green, and Olin didn't want to have to explain why one of his officers had thrown up on the crime scene.

He crouched beside the body and moved the sheet. He wasn't prepared, even with the officer's description. Blood sat everywhere, so many wounds it was difficult at first to see a body past it.

At least, until he focused on the woman's face—well what little was left of it—and noticed her hair.

A blond so pale it was essentially white.

A tightness he couldn't help gripped his chest. It couldn't be...

He moved the sheet but seeing more of the body didn't clear anything up. Pale skin—it was hard to tell much more with so much blood and so many deep cuts—a body type that could have been her.

He yanked his cell from his pocket and dialed, terrified that he'd hear the ringing of Kat's phone somewhere nearby him.

Nothing, though. Straight to voicemail.

He dialed again and again, the pressure around his heart increasing each time.

However, on what had to be the fifth time, a voice that made him nearly sag to the ground answered. "It's creepy to call so many times in a row."

Olin pulled in a shaky breath as he rose to his feet, trying to calm himself.

"Olin?" An uneasiness in her tone woke him up. He didn't need to frighten her further.

"Sorry," he said, having no idea if he'd calmed his voice enough to reassure her. "I, uh, wanted to see if you'd taken care of calling the victim's advocate."

"No. I said I didn't need to."

"Right, right." His gaze drifted down to the body on the ground, the girl who could have been Kat's twin. It felt like staring into a mirror of what things could have been like, what could have happened, and it shook him to his core. "Sorry. You be careful, okay, Kat?"

She didn't answer right away, and when she did, her voice was soft. "Are you okay? You sound weird…"

"Yeah. I'm fine. Just a hard case, I guess. I'll talk to you later." Olin hung up before Kat could respond, needing to get off the phone and get his mind back on the case at hand.

Yet, each time he stared at the body, each time he looked at the woman whose life someone had snuffed out so cruelly, he couldn't focus. He couldn't think about what had happened and his brain just kept looping back around to Kat, to how easily this could have been her.

It was foolish to pretend that woman meant nothing to him, wasn't it? But… Olin had about lost everything once before, had seen how the world liked to crush those who didn't quite fit in.

Kat was a bad bet any way he looked at it. A brat, a troublemaker, a woman healing from a traumatic experience, and a sub entangled in the Sanctuary scene. None of those things made her a viable option for him.

So why was it that he couldn't stop thinking about her?

And why had he never felt fear like he had when he'd thought that body might just have been her...?

* * * *

Kat woke with a scream already tearing from her throat. The dream had felt *so* real. Jerry had been there, that fucking knife of his in his hand, and he'd laughed.

She'd never forget that laugh, the one full of confidence and some twisted form of affection. The memory of his call plagued her, too.

She'd told no one about it because she needed to pretend it hadn't happened. If he was telling the truth, if he wouldn't ever abduct her, then she wasn't in any danger. Why open old wounds?

Though the way she panted on the bed, her throat raw, said the wounds weren't really closed.

Her door flung open, making her jerk her gaze up to find a shirtless and mostly asleep Bradley there.

And the sight of him half-dressed was just about enough to distract her from the panic at a man rushing into her bedroom—especially after her nightmare.

He blinked, looking around as if ready to fight anything that might have frightened her. Too bad that didn't include dreams, huh?

Eventually, he met her gaze, the fog of sleep drifting out of his dark brown eyes. "Nightmare?"

Kat nodded, gripping her sheet and keeping it at her neckline. She'd worn one of her nightgowns to bed, changed into it only after she was safely in her room, because it would show the top of the mark Jerry had left.

Bradley let out a soft sigh, then turned to leave. It made Kat frown, at least until she heard noises in the kitchen. She would have followed, but the reminder of her mark made her stay put. The last thing she wanted was him to see that.

A few minutes later, he returned. He turned her lights to low when he entered, then handed a cup to her.

Warm milk with cinnamon.

It took her back to years ago, to when he'd make that for her after...

She dropped her gaze to the cup and took a sip, trying to shove away all the past. Mindfulness said to stay present, and she knew nothing in the past would help her.

"You having a lot of nightmares?" The bed dipped as he sat on the edge of it, facing her.

Kat shook her head. "Not really." She almost went to say she wasn't sure why she had one today, but that would have been a lie and Bradley had always seen through hers.

"Maybe it's because I'm here..."

She opened her mouth to make a smart-ass joke, but it died in her throat. She swallowed hard, then took another sip to ease the way her heart still pounded.

"No comment?" He lifted an eyebrow. "I don't know if you've ever let the chance to insult me go before. You really aren't doing well, are you?"

"I'm doing fine," she argued but still didn't rise to his jabs.

"What happened, Kat? What really happened? I know you were attacked, I know you got hurt, I know you have marks from it you don't want me to see but tell me what happened." His tone was low, pleading.

Had he *ever* begged her for anything before?

No, that wasn't Bradley's way. He'd always been the type to never ask for anything, to just work harder at whatever it was until he secured what he wanted. It meant that the soft request broke some of her resolve.

"It wasn't that bad, not really. Women go through some awful things—I've got friends who have been through hell. This wasn't like that."

"Comparing pain won't heal a wound," Bradley said. "Doesn't matter what anyone else went through, doesn't change a thing about what you went through. I just want to help you carry it."

"No one can carry things for someone else. If I tell you, my weight isn't lightened, but you become burdened, too. How does that help?"

A weight on her knee made her jerk her gaze up to find he'd set his hand there, and despite all the reasons she should shove him away, the touch eased her.

"Let me help, at least a little."

She blew out a long breath. If it had been anyone else or anytime else, she'd have never uttered a word. Maybe it was her still waking up, or the memory of the nightmare, of the years of history between her and Bradley, but she spoke softly. "I don't know what I said before, exactly, but he didn't rape me or anything. It wasn't like that."

Bradley's thumb rubbed her knee through the sheet, as if coaxing her to continue. It was one of the good things about Bradley. He knew when and how to shut up.

So she went on. "The man, Jerry, wanted something from my friend Ell, and I was at her house drinking our sorrows away. I got caught up when he abducted her, but I guess he took a liking to me. When he got what he wanted, he took me into the bedroom of the motel."

She trembled but forced herself to keep going, to spit it out like rotten food, as if she could expel it and it wouldn't hurt her anymore. "He said he liked my fight, my spirit. He's a sadist, I guess. Mostly, he liked my screams." She squeezed her eyes closed as she recalled those screams. "I hate myself for making a sound. I told myself I wouldn't, that I wouldn't give him the satisfaction, but the knife—" No other words would come out, and she didn't understand why at first.

"That's enough," Bradley said and took the cup. Wetness covered her hands, and it took a moment to realize she'd shaken so hard the milk had spilled over the edge.

Her breath tore through her so rapidly she couldn't draw in enough air to speak.

Warm arms came around her, and the familiar scent of the man she'd loved so long ago soothed her. He made a soft humming sound, a deep one she remembered falling asleep to in the past. She remembered how he'd used that sound to soothe his horses, the way even the flightiest of animals calmed from it.

He'd always called her his wild mare, had laughed at how the same tricks he used on the horses worked on her.

She squeezed her eyes closed tighter to ease the sting.

"You don't need to say anything else," he whispered against her hair, his hands strong, clutching her to his chest. "I didn't mean to make you go through that again."

She shook her head. "It's over. It doesn't matter anymore."

He pulled away just far enough to stare at her, and she forced her eyes open when it seemed he wouldn't speak until she did. "It matters. It matters to me and to all the other people who care about you. You don't have to act like you're all right."

"I am all right."

"You haven't been as feisty as usual. The jokes you would have made, the little revenges for me being here, you haven't done any of them."

Which was true... She'd thought about it, considered the ways she could get back at Bradley, the way he'd frown at a prank and the tiniest lift at the corner of his lips that showed he wasn't as annoyed as he let on. However, each time she considered one, this fear took her over.

"That man made you afraid, made you worry about what someone might do, didn't he?"

She nodded before she could think better of it. That was *exactly* what had happened. She couldn't get the feeling of that knife out of her head.

"*This* used to be fun," she said, knowing he could keep up without her having to spell it all out. "I've dealt with shitty men before, but never like this. I always trusted that I had control at the end, but Jerry taught me that isn't true at all."

Bradley shook his head and shifted around until his back was against the headboard and his legs stretched out in front of him. He gathered Kat up and pulled her closer, so her cheek pressed against his bare chest. The rise and fall as he breathed felt like a metronome to the conversation and helped calm her more.

"I can't tell you there aren't shitty people in the world, Kat. You know there are, and now you've been forced to get a personal lesson in it. The thing is, there have always been shitty people. Always will be. There are good people too, though, so you can't let the bad ones take everything from you."

Kat sighed, knowing this was dangerous. Maybe more dangerous than Jerry. Jerry could kill her, but Bradley had nearly destroyed her before.

He made a soft sound, and Kat lifted her gaze to his.

Except, he wasn't looking at her, at least not her face. Instead, his gaze had locked onto her chest.

To the top two inches of the still healing wound.

It felt as if the injury reopened under his gaze, the first time anyone other than Fox or the medical staff had seen it. She reached for the sheet, wanting to cover it, to hide.

Bradley caught her hand before she could. "Don't hide, Kat, not from me."

"I hate it," she whispered back.

"Doesn't mean you should hide it. I've seen you at your worst, at times when you wish no one had, so don't act like nothing happened, not with me."

Kat sighed but stopped trying to cover it. Bradley had already seen, so what was the point?

He ran his fingers through hair, the touch gentle and familiar. From there, he went to stroking over her throat, the touch making her shiver.

How many times had she slept with Bradley in the past? Countless. Probably more than any other person in her life. He knew every inch of her, and she knew his body instinctually. It was so easy to fall prey to what had always been between them.

And why fucking not?

Kat twisted her head and pressed a kiss to his bare chest, to his warm skin that smelled like it always did — like leather and something masculine. How could it feel so much the same even after so long?

He groaned, his fingers pausing on her throat. "Maybe that's not so good an idea."

She huffed softly but kept leaving kisses, moving over the hardness of his chest, over his pectoral muscle. It felt so good, so familiar, like not everything in her world had changed.

He slid his fingers into her hair and used a tight grip to turn her face toward his. The sting in her scalp made her moan.

He sighed. "How can I resist you when you make sounds like that?"

Kat licked her lip, unable to help it when she stared into his familiar dark eyes. "Please."

"Please what?"

"I need…" She trailed off.

He traced his fingertips over her cheek. "What is it you need? Because I showed up to help, to do what I can for you, so tell me what you need."

"You."

"Why?" He must have seen her frown, because he went on. "If you can't even figure out why you want this, then you aren't ready for it."

Kat twisted slightly, then slid her leg over him so she straddled his waist. "You say ready for it like I'm some fragile thing. I'm not. I already told you he didn't—"

"Just because he didn't put his dick in you doesn't mean there aren't still things you'll need to work through."

The way Bradley spoke both amused and mortified Kat. It was funny, because most people would say the same thing about her, about the way she phrased everything. She often was the one others had to shut up before she made everything worse. Where she was blunt and funny, Bradley was just blunt.

Still, she understood his point, and he wasn't wrong. Jerry might not have raped her, but that didn't mean she wasn't still suffering aftereffects.

Yet, that wasn't enough for her to not want him. Bradley had always been unmovable, impossible to push, to force into anything, and the grip of his hand in her hair said he wouldn't give in until she did as he said.

It reminded her how frustrating life with Bradley could be. He never let her get away with anything. "I want to feel like the old me," Kat admitted. "I want to feel like I'm still the same person even after everything feels different."

He tilted his head, his expression softening. "Kat, you're about the toughest person I know. If nothing else you've been through has broken you, some two-bit asshole won't be the one to do it." He tugged at his grip in her hair, pulling her closer.

Kat placed her hands on his chest to brace herself but didn't push, didn't fight him at all. "So you're saying yes?"

He exhaled and rested close enough she could feel it blow across her lips. "How about I say we'll see. We aren't playing, though."

That was fine by Kat. She wasn't ready to play with anyone yet, but the idea of losing herself in the familiarity of Bradley's kiss and his touch and his body sounded like exactly what she needed.

She nodded, rewarded when Bradley pulled her in the last few breaths and kissed her. It was like taking her back years ago, to when she'd been too idealistic for her own good. His kiss was comfortable in the way her favorite meal was. Familiar but exactly right to hit the spot.

Kat moaned and curled her fingers in to grip him. This was everything she wanted, this wash over her of sensation that told her she could still feel something normal.

And Bradley sure as hell had the skills to help her forget everything beyond how he touched her. He kept the one hand in her hair, that edge he couldn't hide even if they weren't playing. He was a Dom through and through, and even if he wasn't going to fill that role, he was still an aggressive lover.

He proved it as he deepened the kiss, as he used his grip and tilted her head to take her harder, to slip his tongue past her lips. Fire surged through her, made her reckless and hungry and drunk off him.

Bradley slid his free hand up her side, and even through the silk of her nightgown, the touch seared her. She wanted more.

No, it was deeper than that—she *needed* more.

Kat ground herself against his lap, a gasp leaving her when his hard cock stroked her through the fabric of his pajama bottoms.

The fact he even *had* pajamas was a miracle. "You never wore pajamas before," she whispered breathlessly against his lips.

"Like I was going to be sleeping naked around you when I didn't know what exactly had happened."

The care charmed her as it always did. Bradley seemed like a dick so much of the time, but then he had moments like this where he went out of his way for her wellbeing or comfort without saying a word. He wasn't the type to need praise or accolades, to want to point out what he'd done so she'd give him credit.

And more than anything else, that made her comfortable. Sleeping with Bradley felt like coming home.

He rucked up her dress in his hands, pulling it so it bared more of her. Fine by her. She wasn't ashamed of her body and having been naked in front of so many people at once, it didn't bother her at all, especially because she knew the best was still to come.

At the first touch of his fingers between her thighs, when he found her without underwear, she let out a thin, hungry sound. He stroked through her folds with the confidence of a man who knew exactly what he was doing. He went slowly but surely, teasing her body with every kiss and every touch. Kat rolled her hips, wanting more, wanting him to pull his pajama bottoms off and fill her. She craved that burning stretch, that moment of closeness, the way she could pretend for that time that everything was okay.

There was nothing better than that, than the way the world slowed to a stop when she entangled her body with someone else's.

The fact it was Bradley made it more complicated, but more powerful.

Bradley groaned and pulled his hand away, muttering, "Impatient as ever, aren't you?" He didn't seem all that annoyed when he wrapped an arm around her waist and flipped them, putting her on her back beneath him. She kept her legs spread around him, not hiding anything from him.

He broke away enough to stare down at her, his gaze hungry. He gripped the hem of her dress and dragged it up until his expression changed. He furrowed his eyebrows, and Kat looked down to see what it was.

Oh.

He had his gaze locked onto the bottom of the long cut mark Jerry had left behind, at the place where it neared her pelvic bone. Right, he'd known she had a mark, but he obviously hadn't realized just how far it went.

All the lust inside her disappeared. It didn't just drift away, but felt like water boiled down to nothing, where she felt like a pot left on long after everything inside it had evaporated.

Kat scooted backward, then yanked her gown to cover herself. Not her pussy—what did she care if he saw that?—but the evidence of her suffering.

He didn't stop her, didn't do anything but frown. "Fuck," he whispered, his gaze locked to her as if he could see it even through the fabric covering her.

"You're right—this was a bad idea."

He swallowed hard before nailing her with a hard look. "Just how bad did he hurt you?"

"It's nothing."

"That is sure as fuck not nothing." The harshness of his words made Kat move away more. Bradley didn't get mad often, but the fury in his voice came through loud and clear. He took a deep breath as if to calm himself, but the sharp edge to his words remained. "I didn't realize..." He trailed off, looking unusually unsure of himself.

Kat rose from the bed, shaking her head and unable to put herself back together. Maybe if Bradley hadn't stared like that, maybe she could have ignored the new marks. Maybe if he were anyone else, someone who wouldn't realize that those marks were new, that they had changed her, she could have kept going.

Having him see them, though, having him freeze at the sight, it was too much. "Leave."

He met her gaze at that. "What?"

"Exactly what I said. We're done. This was a bad idea, like you said to start with. I've changed my mind."

He pressed his lips together for a long moment. "So you're going to just keep running, huh?"

"I'm not running. I just don't want this. Are you going to ignore that?"

He sat up straighter, as if she'd thrown a challenge to him he couldn't ignore. "You know I'm not going to pressure you into anything, Kat."

"So you'll leave?"

"Not a fucking chance. I'll leave you alone tonight—believe it or not, I didn't come back for this—but I'm not going back home, not until you're better."

"What if I'm never better?" Kat whispered, the question so hard to ask.

Bradley paused by the door and offered her a sad smile. "Then I guess you've got yourself a permanent roommate. As soon as you want to be free of me, when you're sick of me hanging around, all you've got to do is stop running." He didn't wait for her to respond before walking out of the room, leaving Kat alone in the room, her body heavy and unsettled and sleep nowhere close.

Her gaze settled on the cup of warm milk, and she sighed.

Better, huh?

Better is a fucking fairy tale, and I'm too old to believe in that anymore.

Chapter Five

Kat sighed as she leaned against the counter at the phone store. After the call from Jerry, she hadn't been able to hear her phone without another rush of panic.

No matter how hard she'd tried not to think about it, about Jerry's confident tone, she couldn't get it out of her head, either.

Her only option was to change her number and her phone. Until she did that, it felt as if Jerry had a straight line to her, and she struggled to even look at it without a sickness in her stomach.

The salesman worked on setting it up, leaving Kat to stand there awkwardly and wait without even a phone to doom scroll through.

"Well, well." The male voice made Kat tense, her body always on high alert anymore.

Plus, the man who owned this voice made her nervous.

"Olin," Kat responded, turning as she gave him a forced smile.

His smile in return showed tension at the edges, proof that he saw through her façade. Still, he didn't call her on it. "I was going into the coffee shop next door and noticed you."

The way he offered up the information made Kat suspect he wanted to make sure she knew he hadn't been following her.

The truth was that the town wasn't all that large. There were a lot of people who came and went, tourists who stayed in short-term rentals to see the local national park, but when it came to residents, there just weren't all that many. Running into someone wasn't all that uncommon.

"New phone?" Olin asked as he peered around the shop.

"Yeah. Figured it was time for an upgrade."

He frowned. "It's not because you're having problems with anyone, right?"

Kat forced herself to stay calm at the right guess. "Nothing like that."

He paused, then asked even more quietly, "And it's not because I've called you?"

That broke the grip fear had on her. The question was sweet, honest, and Kat couldn't let Olin worry that she was changing it because of him.

"No." She went for the closest to the truth as she wanted to risk. "I changed apartments, but I kept feeling like *he* might have my number. I couldn't shake the worry, so I figured I'd sleep better if I changed that, too." Guilt pricked at her for the lie. "Fresh start and all that."

Olin nodded, his expression making him appear tired. "Well, I'm going to get a coffee. You want one?"

She opened her mouth to tell him no—the idea of spending time with anyone felt like more effort than she had in her to give—but something stopped her. Maybe it was the way he'd asked if it were him, or the discomfort she still carried from the night before with Bradley.

The idea of sitting down with Olin wasn't as objectionable as she thought it would be.

"Okay," she answered, her voice shaky. "Yeah. It's going to take them a while longer here."

Olin's eyes widened, a sign he'd expected her to reject the offer. Still, the way his lips curled into a real smile afterward warmed her.

Kat ordered a double latte, wanting the warmth and the caffeine and sugar to sooth her. Something about a hot drink could turn around any day.

Olin ordered a cappuccino, the drink coming in a small cup with fluffy white foam on top. The scent was heavenly, but Kat knew it wasn't for her. In fact, it impressed her to see Olin drinking something so strong.

"You look like you could really use the coffee," Kat said.

Olin chuckled. "Insulting me already, huh?"

Discomfort washed through Kat, like a scream in her head to be cautious, to remember that Doms weren't as safe as she'd always felt before. Being a brat carried a risk that Jerry had taught her.

No. You can't put that on everyone else.

Even as she scolded herself over the thought, she tried to play it off, to hide it all from Olin. "Dark circles happen when you don't get your beauty sleep. So, what's keeping you up?"

He lifted the drink to his mouth and sipped slowly at it. When he lowered it, a bit of foam stuck to his lip, captured by his tongue in a way that made Kat feel warm in *all* the best places.

When he met her gaze, his eyebrow raising, Kat quickly averted her eyes.

Still, Olin went on as if he hadn't caught her ogling him. "Difficult case. Some of the time I can go home and sleep like nothing happened, but other times? Other times the faces stick with me, especially until I can catch the person behind it all."

Kat nodded, understanding that. She wasn't a cop or anything like that, but she held grudges with the best of them. Even when the crime was as small as being rude to her friend, she had a strong sense of justice that required retribution.

When dealing with issues like murder and gang violence, Kat could understand how he might lose sleep. In fact, it would bother her far more to find out he slept with no issue after seeing such horrors. "I'm sorry."

"It's part of the job." Even that statement made her feel like he was holding something back.

But it did bring up another thought, something Kat had heard around but had trouble believing. "I heard a rumor about you."

"Yeah? Were you asking around?"

Kat rolled her eyes. "Don't flatter yourself. I'm just a humble keeper of knowledge."

"Uh-huh. Well, sacred keeper of knowledge, what's the rumor?"

Kat ran her finger around the rim of her cup as she forced herself to ask. "I heard that you used to go to Sanctuary."

Part of her expected him to furrow his eyebrows, to ask what she was talking about. Sanctuary wasn't the best kept secret, but most people in town knew little about it unless they'd been.

He laughed softly, breaking some of the tension. "Yeah, I used to go."

"Used to?"

"It's been..." He paused, as if doing math in his head. "Damn, it's been seven years maybe?"

"What happened? Did you settle down or something?" She left the other part off, the question of if he'd settled down with someone vanilla. Few people entirely left the lifestyle, though life could easily get in the way and make it so participation wasn't always possible for a person. When they just stopped coming at all, it was often due to a partner who didn't care for the place or some other issue that happened there.

"Me? Settle down?" He made a derisive sound, as if the idea were preposterous. "No, nothing like that. Sanctuary just stopped being a good fit for me. It's like a pair of pants—they can be great at first but sometimes, after a while, they start to chafe."

Kat thought about her own feelings and understood what he meant. At least, to some extent.

"I heard you're not going either." Olin broached that carefully, as if he knew it was a hard question.

"I guess you could say it's chafing a little for me, too. I used to love being there—it felt like home."

"And now?"

"Now it's like...like in those amusement park rides where everything is dark except for what they want you to see. That's how it was before. Then someone turned the lights on, and I saw all the wires and the gears and now the ride doesn't feel so magical." As she spoke, Kat frowned. That sounded like some poetic bullshit, like something she deserved to be laughed at for saying.

Except, Olin wasn't laughing. He stared at her, his face impossible to read, his expression intense. Finally, he nodded. "Yeah, I get that. Still, don't let something you love slip away just because it doesn't feel so safe anymore."

"I could say the same about you."

"You could," he said with a laugh. "But that doesn't make me wrong—just bad at taking my own advice."

"Well, when I see *you* there again, I'll go." Kat threw out the ultimatum like a joke, wanted Olin to realize just how stupid it was to tell her to go when he wouldn't.

"Deal."

That stopped Kat cold as she jerked her gaze to his. "Excuse me?"

"Deal. You said you'd go when I do. How about Saturday?"

Kat's mouth dropped open, the turn of events one she couldn't have predicted or readied herself for. The fact was that she often made such flippant remarks— she sure as hell hadn't expected him to call her on it. "That isn't such a good—"

"You were the one who threw down the gauntlet— or are you all talk?" The sexy curl of Olin's lips made Kat's cheeks heat, made her struggle to remember why it was such a terrible idea.

Olin was handsome, apparently a Dom from what she knew, and he knew little about her. It felt like a restart to her life that she desperately craved. She could go with him, pretend like nothing with Jerry had happened and maybe find something she felt like she'd lost.

"O-okay," she said. "I'll have them put you on the guest list."

Olin waved her off. "No need. I'll call Toya this evening."

Toya? If Kat needed any proof as to if Olin were telling the truth or not, there it was. He had to be in some sort of contact with the owner of Sanctuary to speak of her so casually, to know he could just call her up to be put on the list. Just how connected to Sanctuary had he been?

What was she getting herself into? Her fears and wants swirled together, entangling, making it difficult to pull one from another, to figure it out. The happy times at Sanctuary mixed with her memory of Jerry. The pleasure she'd felt, the times she'd fallen so deep into subspace that she never wanted to leave, they competed with that crushing loneliness the place held when she left alone every night.

Sanctuary was a place of extremes, and Kat wanted to go back just as much as she wanted to avoid it.

A weight on her hand made her realize Olin had set his over hers. She lifted her gaze to his, to find a comforting smile. "It's just a trip there. I'm not expecting anything."

Him voicing exactly what she'd feared helped her pull in a deep breath and nod.

Right.

Because trips to BDSM sex clubs with attractive Doms always ended innocently…

* * * *

Kat couldn't bring herself to go into Sanctuary. She'd done it so many times before, yet somehow, she struggled to find the strength. Instead, she sat at one of the tables outside, far enough away from the main walkway that no one would notice her.

Why was she being such a coward?

Because they'll all see that I'm different.

That kept running through her head, that they'd all see right through the part she played. She'd spent so long creating an image of herself, and the idea of it shattering terrified her. Sanctuary was a place where she'd always felt comfortable, yet now? Now they'd see she was jumpy, now they'd either see the marks if she stripped or notice that she refused to.

Either way, everyone would know.

This was a horrible idea.

Yet…she couldn't seem to just leave, either, to bail on Olin who she was sure was already waiting inside.

Kat had left without telling Bradley where she was going. Maybe she should have felt guilty about that, but they'd said all of nothing to each other in the days since she'd kicked him out of her room. The memory of how he'd stared at the cuts on her still burned, still made her want to bury herself in a pile of blankets and never come out.

Which meant she had no plans on inviting him.

"Never figured you for a coward." Dean took a seat beside Kat. "It's already been twenty minutes that you've been out here."

"It's a nice night—just enjoying the ambiance."

He let out a soft laugh. "I know hiding when I see it. I mean, I'm happy that you're here, but are you sure you're ready? Because sitting out here doesn't scream ready."

Kat sighed, unsure how to answer. "I need to be ready. How is that for an answer?"

"It's a very Kat answer, at least." Dean peered to the side, his lips curling up. "Nice outfit."

Kat looked down at herself, at the bodysuit she'd picked. The coat she'd left in the car had hidden the outfit from Bradley. No doubt he'd realize something was up if she tried to walk out in this.

Plus, most of those would reveal her chest or stomach, and she couldn't handle that. Instead, she went with a bodysuit cut high to show off her legs but with long sleeves. It prevented a chance of anything moving or showing marks she wasn't ready to bare to people.

On her feet were a pair of fuzzy boots. She could have gone with heels, but she just couldn't bring herself to do so. Instead, the softness of the inside of them made her comfortable and steady, things she desperately needed.

"So, are you going to come in?" Dean asked.

Kat wanted to say no, but she wouldn't stand Olin up, not after he'd come because she agreed. "I can't run. I made a bet, and I always follow through."

"A bet, huh?" Dean frowned for a moment, his gaze shifting toward the door. "Who exactly is that bet with?"

Kat forced herself to her feet. "A friend." Best to leave it vague, to not offer anything specific. "I guess I better get in there."

Dean rose, once again reminding Kat just how tall he was. He'd always made her take a second look, the way he filled out those slacks he wore, the way he managed to look put together no matter how disheveled he should have been. "Sure. I'll see you in there."

Dean probably knew Kat needed another minute to herself, since the observant Dom could easily read most people.

Still, once she took a deep breath, the chilly night air cooling her cheeks, she figured it was time to go in.

The check-in process was familiar enough that Kat hardly paid attention. She already had her cuffs on, the ribbons tied there to show what she was interested in and what she wasn't. A part of her had considered changing that, because even the thought of allowing anyone to inflict pain on her had her stomach clenching in fear.

She'd stared at the cuffs at home, doubting this whole damn idea, but had ended up deciding to leave them as they were. She didn't want anyone to notice that she had changed them, that anything was different than it had been before.

Instead, Kat plastered a false smile over her lips and wrapped herself up in the idea that nothing had happened, that nothing at all had changed. She was the same old happy Kat she'd always been. After signing in, she passed the entry space and entered the actual club.

The music was loud, and somehow the movement of people felt different from before. Kat sighed, rubbing one hand against her other to dispel the anxiety inside her, to ease the desire to turn around and run right the hell back home. She'd thought this was better than dealing with Bradley, but now she wasn't so sure.

"You came." Olin's voice felt like a lifebuoy thrown into the sea of noise and movement, something for her to grab onto and hold for dear life.

Kat turned slowly to find Olin standing behind her, and it only took one look to derail her train of thought.

She'd only seen him dressed for work so far, which had meant slacks and a white button-up shirt. As it turned out, he could dress down and look amazing.

He had a pair of jeans on and a black T-shirt, but his auburn hair was as unruly as ever.

He moved his gaze over Kat, a heat there telling her that he hadn't invited her there as some sort of platonic thing. It warmed Kat, made her feel a rush like she had before, a desire to throw caution away and lose herself in another person for the night.

Except, he didn't come closer, didn't make a move. "You look nice. You strike me as the sort of girl who likes to dress up."

"I like fun." *At least, I used to...*

Olin's smile softened, as though he could read the thoughts on her face. "You'll find your feet."

Kat wasn't sure what to say back to that. She normally always knew what to say, how to act, yet she suddenly had no idea.

Olin let out a soft laugh, then nodded toward a table in the back room. "Go grab a seat. I'll get you a drink."

Kat nodded, following the direction without complaint, which wasn't *at all* like her. Still, she just couldn't seem to get her bearings, to feel normal. A glance around the place didn't help at all.

People danced and laughed and kissed, and all looked so carefree. That used to be Kat, too. It felt like a lifetime ago, like someone else. As she took her seat, she struggled to come to terms with why everything had to change.

She picked one of the booths that sat out of the way. She didn't normally care about a private corner, but for some reason, tonight seemed like a better choice. She didn't want to feel exposed, to have others watching her. Hell, she'd be happy if no one realized she'd even come.

The idea of facing Sunny, Ell, Toya or any of her other friends made her draw her shoulders in and try to look smaller.

It seemed that even when she returned to Sanctuary, nothing was the same.

Bradley narrowed his eyes as he spotted Kat sitting at a back table at Sanctuary. She'd walked out of her place with a tight smile and a bad lie—which told Bradley he should follow.

He had to admit, seeing her at Sanctuary eased him. At least, it did until he watched the way she all but hid in that booth.

He struggled to understand her, to know how to pull her from the pit she'd fallen into.

"Surprised she came."

Bradley turned to find Dean standing there, no jacket on, his sleeves rolled up his forearms, his gaze locked over on Kat.

The jealousy Bradley had had the first time he'd met Dean didn't rear up again, which was odd. Maybe it was the fact that he knew Dean was looking out for Kat, that even with Dean's stupid jokes and jovial attitude, it was clear he cared for the woman.

Since Bradley was sure he'd go back to his ranch when Kat recovered, it seemed stupid to get upset about someone else moving in. He really did want Kat happy, even if it wasn't with him.

Dean gave a side-eye to Bradley. "Surprised you came, too."

Bradley nodded toward Kat. "She snuck out with some lie about going jogging. The Kat I know doesn't jog, and she sure as hell doesn't jog in fuzzy boots and a trench coat." Just saying it made Bradley chuckle. Kat really was a bad liar, probably because she lied all the time so didn't put any effort into it. It really shouldn't amuse him, however.

"Sounds about like Kat. Seems that Olin made a bet with her—he'd come back if she did."

"Olin?"

"Detective Olin Ramiz. Good guy, worked on her case, seems smitten."

"This isn't the sort of place people go on a first date." Of course, what Bradley meant was that vanilla people don't come here on first dates.

"Seems Olin is an old member who knows Toya."

Bradley frowned, thinking about the name. After a moment, he nodded, recalling hearing the name around Sanctuary back in the day but not thinking he'd ever met him. That meant he must have been from a long time before.

"So, you just going to stare creepily or go say hello?"

"No. There's no reason to bother her. If she sees me here, she'll just get even more stubborn."

Before Bradley could turn around and leave, as if she had some sort of sixth sense, Kat lifted her gaze and landed her gray eyes right on him.

Dean laughed. "Guess we're both caught. So, run or face the music?"

Bradley moved his gaze to the door, the temptation to head out strong. Still, when he looked back, when he saw the way Kat nibbled her bottom lip, the anxiety on her face, he sighed. "Better to face her now. Worst thing a man can do is give Kat time to think up a good payback."

Olin had two drinks in hands—lemon-lime sodas because some sugar but no caffeine sounded like the best idea. While some alcohol would have been nice to calm down, he understood why Toya had the no-alcohol rule there.

People got stupid too often when alcohol was involved, and that made for a bad mix when it came to BDSM. Consent tended to get messy when people started to drink.

However, when he spotted Kat, he paused. She wasn't alone at the table, instead sitting between Dean and a man he didn't recognize. Then again, with how much time Kat was here, it wasn't a shock that she'd know about everyone.

He approached, then set Kat's drink before her. The action made her jump, as if she'd been so involved in whatever she was talking about that she hadn't noticed him.

"Olin," she said, a slight uncertainty in her voice as if she was afraid he might be angry.

Angry at what? That she was talking to others? The realization made Olin grin. "Hey, Dean," he said before turning his gaze to the other man. "You are?"

"Bradley Smith," the man said. "I'm staying with Kat to help out."

That fit the pieces together. Olin had heard something about Kat's ex having shown back up, though he had to admit, Bradley surprised him. Kat was all fire and light, but Bradley seemed as down to earth as a man could get. He was the sort that Olin could see on the back of a horse, in a cowboy hat, on some advertisement with a piece of wheat hanging from his lips.

"Good to meet you," Olin said as he slid into the booth beside Dean.

"I didn't invite them," Kat said.

"I don't need an invitation," Dean responded with a grin. "It's just a happy accident that I spotted her here."

"She didn't invite me—I followed her."

"Stalking is rude," Kat muttered.

"So is lying to the person trying to help you. If you had just told me you were coming here, we wouldn't have had an issue," Bradley said with a shrug.

Kat let out a long sigh, as if she were over the other man's hovering. Then again, Kat no doubt would prefer to keep hiding from the world if possible. It was probably for the best that Bradley was helping to keep her from doing so. She took a sip of her soda before offering Olin a smile. "Thanks—it's good."

"Wish I could take credit, but it isn't like I made it." He took a drink of his own before peering out toward the rest of the room, the sounds so familiar despite the years away. There was something about the moans, the cries of pain and pleasure that took him back.

This place had been so important to him at one time. He'd come in the way Kat did, like walking into his own home, filled with friends. He hadn't thought about it in so long, hadn't planned to ever return, yet now that he was…

He wasn't sure how he felt. Nostalgic, sad, excited. It all mixed together until he just felt on edge. Still, if it helped Kat, it was worth it.

"Sunny got herself in trouble," Dean said with all the excitement of a high school girl, spreading rumors. Then again, it seemed like the perfect bait to draw Kat into a conversation.

"What happened?" she asked.

"Apparently *someone* told her it was a good idea to play games with Connor. When he wanted to gag her, she told him she wasn't one of his animals to muzzle."

Kat covered her mouth as her face turned red. "Well damn...never thought Sunny had that in her."

"You are a bad influence. When she can't sit for a week, you better take responsibility for corrupting her."

"She'll be thanking me," Kat assured him. "Everyone needs a little trouble in their life. Without that, it's just long and boring and quiet."

"Is that why you're always acting up?" Dean asked.

"Of course." A shadow passed through her eyes. "At least, it's why I used to."

That hurt. The look of fear, the way Kat swallowed hard. Olin wanted to wrap his arms around her, to pull her into his lap and press a kiss to her temple. There was this fire inside her that still shined through her eyes, but fear had diminished it.

It made Olin all the more determined to find Jerry, that he'd make sure that bastard paid for what he'd done. He wanted Kat to smile again, to see those shadows lit up because she trusted again.

No one spoke at first, as if none of them knew exactly how to respond.

"Used to?" Dean asked. "Seems to me you slipped your babysitter to go to a sex club. That doesn't sound like model behavior to me. Doesn't matter what you say, you're *always* trouble."

Kat said nothing back at first, her gaze narrowed as if she was deciding how she wanted to respond. That was the thing—when met with sorrow like that, there were two ways to respond. A person could offer pity or humor. Pity would have pissed Kat off, but humor?

She smiled after a moment. "And yet no one seems to rise to the occasion. Maybe I've managed to make everyone realize I'm just too difficult." Even with the joke, Kat's words held some deeper sadness, as if she truly believed it.

Dean set his arm on the table. "If anyone gets scared off by a little backtalk, they aren't worth your time. Trust me, taming brats takes a real man willing to put in the time."

"This coming from you, who almost never lasts more than a week with the same woman?"

"Maybe I'm just too much for them."

The back and forth between Dean and Kat was fascinating, really. It was like a chess match, with the two of them standing there toe-to-toe. Better yet, it seemed like Kat needed it. She leaned in toward Dean as if drawn by the verbal challenge.

"I doubt that," Kat muttered. "Maybe you play with the newer girls because you know you can handle them."

"Or maybe you like telling yourself that so you don't have to try."

"So try me," Kat said.

With that, the whole table froze. Dean's words had been playful banter, but Kat sounded serious. She'd called his bluff.

"What?" Dean asked, sounding surprisingly unsure for the normally confident man.

"You think I can't handle you? Fine, let's see."

Olin swallowed hard, watching the exchange, wanting…something. He wanted to touch her, to feel if her skin was as soft as it looked, to taste her breath as he kissed her. However, he'd already sworn to himself before coming that he couldn't, that it wasn't possible.

That doesn't mean I have to leave, though…

Dean stared back, as if trying to figure out if Kat was serious. She sure sounded serious…

Kat didn't look away, didn't laugh and say she was joking. Instead, she stared right at Dean as if to challenge him, to see if he'd admit defeat or not.

Finally, Dean let out a dark chuckle before grasping Kat's hips and pulling her over, into his lap, so she was pinned between him and the table. "You want to throw down the gauntlet, Kat? Well, I don't mind at all if I pick it up."

Olin might not be able to touch, but if watching was the closest he could get?

Well, he'd take it happily.

Dean grinned at the woman in his lap. Fuck, when had a woman last been this much fun?

Sex was always fun, but in a different way. It was a time waster, a way to shut his mind up for a while. This wasn't that, though. It wasn't something he could walk away from easily if he wanted, but something that called to him.

Kat's weight in his lap was perfect, and the warmth of her body soaked into him.

He didn't bother to resist, sliding a hand behind her neck and pulling her closer for a kiss. She tasted like the soda she'd drunk as she melted against him, as she returned the kiss with the same passion he felt.

After a moment, he woke himself up. As tempted as he was to slide her bodysuit out of the way, to roll a condom on and plunge into her warmth, he wasn't ready for this to be over that quickly. He wasn't sure he was even ready to actually fuck her.

Kat had pushed him, challenged him, delighted him with their back and forth. The girl deserved him to take a little time with her. He grasped her hips and lifted her until she sat on the table in front of him, her feet planted on either side of his legs.

"Talk about a feast," he said as he stared at her, as surprised as ever by the immediate shot of lust she sent through him.

A glance to the side reminded him they weren't alone. Bradley sat to his left and Olin to his right. It wasn't a problem for Dean—he had no issue with sharing something as wild and marvelous as Kat.

Bradley's dark eyes were filled with want, and Dean lifted his eyebrow in question. Bradley danced his fingers over Kat's thigh, drawing her eyes to him. "This okay?"

Kat dragged her tongue along her bottom lip before nodding. She turned her head to look at Olin.

And who exactly could turn down a woman with an expression like that?

"I don't think so," Olin said.

So…apparently Olin can.

Kat frowned, and it was hard to see the hurt on her face. "Oh, I just thought…"

Olin offered a slight shake to his head before a smile spread across his lips, though the smile seemed more like a consolation prize. "This isn't really my scene anymore," he explained. "But, I'd like to stay if that's okay with you."

Red sprang up on Kat's cheeks, but that wasn't a shock. She nodded once, a quick jerk of her head to agree.

Dean stopped resisting and slid the palms of both his hands up the insides of her thighs, bringing her

Jayce Carter

attention to the fact she was sitting in front of him, her legs spread. "You like being watched, don't you, Kat?"

"I don't mind it," she said without admitting anything. "It's not my fault people think I'm worth looking at."

Dean laughed at her bratty tone, even though she had an edge to it, as if unsure how it would go. It reminded him that despite her wanting this, despite her playing the game, she wasn't entirely back to normal.

Which was okay with Dean. He'd prefer to keep things lighter, because something about Kat drew out his darker side and he didn't need to tempt that any further than he had to.

"I think that you like being the center of attention," Dean said before brushing one of his fingers up her cunt, through the fabric of her bodysuit that covered her. The heat of her pussy made him want to drown in her. "I think you get off on knowing everyone is looking at you, wanting you. You have no idea how to actually *ask* for what you want, so you behave the way you do to make it impossible for people to ignore you."

She straightened her back, telling Dean he'd hit the nail on the head.

At her startled expression, he grinned wider. "I'm a lawyer, Kat. Part of the job is figuring out what people are thinking and why they do what they do. If you were hoping to play games where you get to hide, I think you'd better pick easier partners than a lawyer, a detective and a man who deals with livestock for a living."

Bradley scooted closer, then ran his hand up her side so he could tease his fingers over her breasts. Her chest rose and fell quicker, delighting Dean at how despite all her experience, she was still that sensitive.

Then again, this might have been her first time since Jerry.

The memory of Jerry hit Dean, dragged him backward to how Kat had looked afterward, to the way she'd cowered.

She hissed softly, making Dean drop his gaze to realize he'd accidentally tightened his hand around her thigh. He let go immediately and rubbed his palm over the spot to sooth it. Instead of apologizing, he leaned in and pressed a kiss to the spot.

He needed to focus, to not let his mind drift to what had happened. That woke those parts of himself he was trying hard to smother.

Bradley reached for the neckline of her top, but Kat lifted her hands to stop him. She said nothing, just stared as if trying to get him to understand.

Bradley sighed and shook his head. "Really?"

Kat remained still, her fingers grasping the neckline of her top so tightly, her knuckles had gone white.

Bradley set his hands over hers and squeezed. "I'll let you off the hook this time." He leaned in and pressed a kiss to her hands until she let go.

Which sounded like Bradley had had this talk with her before. It made Dean frown, made him want to strip her to nothing to see what she was hiding. He knew she'd been hurt by Jerry, but had no idea the extent of it. It seemed it bothered her, too, which was likely why he wanted to see them. He wanted to get her past it, to show her he didn't give a damn what anyone had done to her, that it didn't change her or how he saw her.

But they didn't have that sort of relationship. He could offer her some fun for the night, but that was about it. Helping her any more than that was up to Bradley, it seemed.

So Dean did what he could by taking his thumb and slipping it past the crotch of her bodysuit. He felt the fabric of a thong, but burrowed past that as well until he could touch the wet heat of her pussy directly.

Kat reached forward on a gasp, as if surprised by his sudden movement.

"Hands behind you," Bradley snapped, his voice low and rough.

Kat gulped but did as told, setting her hands behind her, causing her to lean away. It arched her back, pressing her chest out, and it seemed Bradley was only too happy to take advantage. He leaned up and in, sliding his tongue over one nipple, the thin bodysuit not nearly enough to hide the hard buds.

Kat's moan filled the space, hungry and desperate.

Dean twisted his hand so he could sink two fingers into her pussy, enjoying the way it welcomed him, the way it seemed to pull him in. Still, he was a man who liked a good show…

He used his other hand to hook two fingers into the crotch of her bodysuit and tugged it to the side, to bare her to him. "You have such a pretty little cunt," he told her as if talking about the weather. "Next time, you should wear a short skirt with nothing beneath. Not sure anyone could resist that, especially because you're the bratty sort of sub who would purposely bend over, giving everyone a peak of the heaven beneath that skirt."

He groaned at the thought of it, of how that teasing would drive him nuts. He pumped his fingers into her hard before using a finger on his other hand to rub against her clit. "Hell, maybe you should do that somewhere else. Maybe go have a fancy dinner somewhere, you in a little scrap of a dress with no panties. Sit nice and close so your date can sneak his hand under the table and fill your needy pussy up in a room full of people who don't have a clue. Would you come on those fingers, Kat?"

Her pink lips parted on a sharp cry, her eyes closed as she let her head fall backward. "Yes," she answered, as if automatic, before shivering. Had she realized she was being *far* too obedient? "I mean, as long as it wasn't you, since I don't think you could get me off."

Dean laughed, unable to help it. She really was a handful, wasn't she? It didn't annoy him at all, didn't make him angry. Instead, it was like a game, like a challenge he wanted to live up to. "Guess we'll see about that, won't we?"

He stopped playing around, stopped teasing her, choosing instead to focus on her clit with hard strokes of his thumb. Her pussy gripped him in tight waves, telling him she was close.

Good.

He was *far* more into overstimulation rather than denial. Any asshole could manage *not* to get a girl off. It was so much more fun to watch her come over and over again.

Bradley released her breast from his lips, his hand cupping her other one, teasing the pointed tip of her nipple. He blew a stream of air over the wet one before speaking in a low voice. "Eyes on me, Brat."

She jerked her head up and looked Bradley in the eyes just in time for him to lower his head again and close his teeth on her nipple.

Kat went wild, though her hands stayed put. She made the sexiest sounds Dean had ever heard, ones that sounded like a rubber band snapping, as if she finally were able to release the tension inside her. Her pussy tightened around his fingers as she came, but Dean didn't stop. He kept thrusting into her, though he lightened his touch to her clit.

When she sagged back, her hands sliding until she lay flat on the table, she shivered.

Dean's cock was hard, and he *really* wanted to slip into her. He still had her bodysuit pulled out of the way, could see the flushed lips of her inviting pussy, knew he could put on a condom and be inside her in moments.

But...something inside him refused to let him. It felt wrong, and he was terrified that doing it would cross a line he couldn't come back from. She already occupied too much of his mind.

Yet, when Kat whimpered, when he brushed her clit again, when it was so damned clear she wasn't done yet, Dean grinned.

"Guess I can get you off," he said. "And in case once wasn't enough to prove my point, you better hold on, Kat."

The flash of uncertainty on her face was lovely, and Dean grinned wider. Nothing better than a worried sub...

Kat couldn't believe the way she trembled before Dean. This was hardly her first orgasm, so why was it that she felt different, like this was something new?

Maybe it was Dean's mouth, the way his words reached inside her. Maybe it was Bradley's demanding tone or the familiarity in his touch. Maybe it was Olin who had said nothing, who watched her with an intensity that made her nervous.

Whatever it was, Kat was in so far over her head.

And she *loved* it. They gave her no time to worry, to remember things she didn't want to remember, to be anywhere except in the moment with them.

"My turn," Bradley growled out before grabbing Kat. He helped her to sit up, then lifted her off the table. Before she knew what happened, she rested in Bradley's lap, her back pressed to his chest. He danced his lips over the curve of her shoulder, over the side of her throat. His breath warmed her skin, and his touch warmed her body once again.

Dean moved, using his foot to push the table out, away from the booth, to make room. Before Kat could ask anything, Dean dropped to his knees in front of her. His blue eyes met hers, lust swimming there, his lips quirked into a grin.

Bradley shifted behind her, and when she rose a bit with the help of his hand, she realized just how they'd exhausted her body. Dean tapped her feet until she inched them out, then hooked his fingers around the crotch of her bodysuit again. He tugged it to the side, but that wasn't what got her.

What drew a gasping moan from her was when Bradley tugged her back again and his thick cock slid into her. She must have been so distracted, she hadn't even noticed him putting on a condom. She'd had threesomes before, but never with men who seemed to actually work together. Normally, the Doms she'd slept with together had both been out for themselves, had seemed to use her without any consideration of the other man.

That wasn't Dean and Bradley, clearly. Instead, the two men worked together, each of their touches driving her crazy, as if they were focused more on outwitting her, on overwhelming her than they were on getting what they wanted.

It made her feel out of her element. Handling just one Dom was an easy task, but trying to stay on top of two—or, worse, three—was a whole different thing.

And the sensation of Bradley filling her was intense. It felt like it had years before, made her struggle to remember all those times when she'd said she was different. She didn't feel different.

Bradley groaned in her ear. "You're so damned tight. Fuck, I missed you like this, missed those sounds you make, missed the way you just lose control."

Kat jumped when lips pressed against her bare thigh, made her look down to find Dean teasing her. It wasn't like she didn't know exactly what he planned—there weren't a lot of reasons for a man to be on his knees in front of a woman.

And Kat was all for the only reason she could come up with.

Dean smirked, his expression full of confidence. Then again, he'd already proven his skills, hadn't he? Still, it didn't fully prepare her for the moment he leaned in close, when he used his tongue to stroke across her clit. With Bradley filling her, it was awkward, but that didn't change that the sensation drove her wild.

Bradley grasped her hips in his strong, large hands, and forced Kat to move. She rose and fell, though not far, which allowed Dean to focus on her clit. The sensations overwhelmed her, the way Dean ground against her, the way Bradley filled her. It all mingled until one ran into the next, until her body burned with the feelings.

"I've been waiting for this," Bradley whispered, like some dirty secret between just the two of them. "Ever since I came back, since I saw you, I've been thinking about this, about having you again. You can drive a man fucking crazy, you know that?" He gripped her tighter, as if afraid she'd run off.

Not a chance.

Kat reached up with her own hands to cup her breasts. She'd have rather been nude, rather have been able to tease her hard nipples directly, but she knew that wouldn't happen. Instead, she brushed her thumbs over her nipples through the fabric.

She'd never been a girl afraid to do her own work, afraid to chip in to get her where she needed to be. If it felt good, why the hell should she worry about *anyone's* opinion?

A glance down made her whine, especially when Dean lifted his eyes to hers, the blue of them almost shocking in the dim room. He stuck his tongue out farther, ensuring she could see as it touched her clit, as he used it to please her. His shoulder moved, and it took a moment to realize he was stroking his own cock.

And *that* was amazingly hot. Kat wished she'd been able to watch properly, that she could have gotten a good look at Dean nude. He didn't undress publicly much, so she'd never gotten the chance to really enjoy the view.

Yet that idea fled when he flicked her with his tongue, a hard touch that made her arch as she resisted the orgasm that threatened her. She resisted to hold off, to let the sensations inside her linger, let them grow. If she came too soon again, she'd be too sensitive.

She'd rather savor the feeling, that growing electricity that zapped through her, that set every nerve ending in her body on fire. She wanted to hold on to it for as long as possible.

When she arched, it brought her gaze up to find Olin there. His eyes seemed darker in the club, the normally honey color now appearing almost amber. He stared hard, as if drawn in and trapped by the sight.

If she'd thought for a moment he wasn't interested, his expression said that wasn't true. His lips were parted, and he gripped the edge of the table with his hand, the knuckles white. It was the look of a man who wanted what he couldn't have.

Which was stupid.

He *could* have Kat. If he came closer, if he kissed her, she'd be lost. She had no idea when exactly she'd started to want Olin like this, when he'd gone from the man who had saved her to one she lusted after, but she couldn't deny it anymore.

Kat licked her bottom lip and furrowed her eyebrows, trying to beg him with that expression.

Olin let out a long sigh before jerking her head side to side once—an absolute rejection.

Kat may have been upset at any other time, but right then? With the want in his eyes, with the way his gaze moved from where her hands teased her breasts to where Dean licked her, she just couldn't find it in herself to worry.

"Fuck," Bradley groaned into her ear, the curse word making it clear just how close he was, just how much he'd wanted this.

It warmed her, and when Dean tilted his head and latched his lips around her clit, she lost the fight. She dove into the crashing waters that had surrounded her, gave into the feeling, the vulnerability, the desperate need.

No matter what happened next, they'd given Kat something she'd thought lost. They'd helped her feel like herself, and that was worth any of the heartbreak that was no doubt to come.

Chapter Six

Bradley groaned as he woke, his shoulder sore. That wasn't uncommon, given working with large livestock could be hell on his muscles, and he wasn't the same young man who had bought the property when he'd barely reached adulthood.

Except, when he opened his eyes, reality fell into place. Blonde hair spread over his shoulder and a familiar sleeping face rested on his chest, her arm wrapped around him.

It made him freeze. Despite everything they had done, the distance they'd crossed since he'd come back, *this* was another level.

For Kat, giving in to a physical relationship wasn't a surprise. She liked to cling to that as a safer alternative to anything else. So the night before, the chance to taste her, to overwhelm her with Dean, that wasn't all that unexpected.

The fact that she ended up in bed with him all night was very different.

It hadn't been a real choice, of course. Kat had been all but mindless when he'd gotten her home, after he and Dean had enjoyed her at the club as Olin had watched. She'd been exhausted, and when he'd gotten her into bed, she'd wrapped around him and refused to let go.

And her sleeping face made him remain still, so he could watch her for a moment without those walls that she'd built up around her. The sunlight that streamed in the window highlighted the freckles on her pale cheeks. Her long lashes cast shadows, and there was a smudge of mascara beneath her eyes — not a shock since she'd been beyond exhausted and ready to sleep by the time they'd gotten back.

Kat shifted, those eyelashes of hers fluttering as her eyes opened. That bright gray met Bradley, took him back when she looked at him with the same old trust.

At least, she did for a split second before her brain started working, before that defensiveness she wore like armor wrapped tight around her again.

Kat pushed herself upright, frowning as if trying to figure out what had happened. A flush covered her cheeks, which told Bradley she'd recalled the night before.

And he sure as hell would not apologize for *that*. He didn't think he'd ever been as happy as when he'd touched her again, when he felt her weight and heard those sounds she made when lost to pleasure.

It had been *way* too long since he'd gotten to experience that, and he wouldn't waste a single minute regretting it.

"Fuck," she whispered softly as she moved her hair from her face.

"Pretty sure we did that," he said.

She pressed her lips together as if she didn't enjoy his attitude.

Funny, given Kat *always* had an attitude of her own. It seemed like a fair turnabout to brat back at her.

"This was a mistake," she said as she pulled herself out of the bed, her nightgown revealing enough of her thigh that Bradley wondered if another go that morning was possible. After so many years apart, he wasn't quite ready to let it all go.

Though, a glance at her face said that wasn't likely.

"You needed it." Bradley sat up, not caring that the sheet fell to his waist and that he didn't have a stitch on. "Nothing to beat yourself up over."

"I didn't *need* anything."

"Course you did. You've been up against a wall for weeks and trying to stand on your own for a lot longer. You needed the chance to just let it go for a while."

"Sure, *you* can say that. You get to leave and run back to your ranch and ignore everything again. You don't have to pick up the pieces. No wonder you wouldn't understand."

"Oh, and of course you act like I just up and left for no damned good reason—like you had *nothing* to do with that. Like I haven't been at my ranch alone because you made it perfectly clear you didn't have any fucking room in your life for me. Don't you try to play the victim here, Kat."

She stood up straight, as if the words had dug down a lot farther than Bradley had really meant them to.

Then again, that was the risk with two people who knew each other so well. It was so much easier to drive in a knife where it would do the most damage, and Bradley always had a sharp tongue and short temper.

He sighed, then rubbed his fingers against the bridge of his nose. "Look, Kat…"

Before he could get anything else out—maybe before he could think of anything else to say—she shook her head. "It's fine. You're right. I'm going to get to work." Kat grabbed clothing from her closet, slinging it over her arm. She paused by the door to her room but didn't look back. "I know I'm not easy to deal with," she said, her voice so soft it almost couldn't carry across the room. "I know I'm a lot. I've heard it my whole damned life, that I'm too much, that I'm extra. I wish I could say that was going to change, that I was suddenly going to be a person others wanted to be around, but if it hasn't happened yet, it isn't going to, is it?"

She sighed, her fingers grasping the edge of the open door as if to hold herself together. "Guess it doesn't matter how old we get—people never really change."

She left, and the sound of the shower running told Bradley she'd finished with their little conversation.

And him? Exhaustion tugged at him despite his sleep. He thought back to the fights with Kat before, to the times when they'd ended up in this exact place, both battling for control, both too fucking cowardly to fix anything or be honest.

Instead, they just chipped away at each other until nothing was left. They picked at one another until love changed into something so much darker. Talk about toxic.

Yet, she never left his head, had lived there the whole damned time they'd been apart.

He rubbed his eyes and wondered just how he'd survive another round of this mess.

* * * *

Olin swallowed as the images from the murders spread across his desk.

They were up to eight women, all tortured and murdered, and all of them with hair just like Kat's...

They were the same general height and weight, the same pale skin. Their hair was often recently dyed, as if someone had wanted them to appear a certain way and was willing to alter them to make it happen.

Each body that had shown up added to Olin's fears, to this nagging feeling inside him he couldn't ignore. The bodies were all found in areas of the city where Jerry had power and they all looked like Kat.

They also all had knife cuts like the ones he knew Kat had.

As much as Olin wanted to believe it had nothing to do with her, he wasn't the sort of man to lie to himself, especially not over anything this important.

Could these be some message?

No, Kat hadn't mentioned anything, and Jerry didn't seem like the type to not personally deliver such a message. If he'd reached out to Kat, the woman would have said something to Olin.

Right? Olin hated that he wasn't sure about it. Kat was difficult to read, but he couldn't imagine she'd be foolish enough to ignore such a threat.

So maybe, if Jerry was behind it, he was simply picking girls who looked similar? Was it some perverse fantasy he wanted to relive?

Olin let out a long sigh before a knock on the door had him calling for the guest to enter.

Olin wasn't surprised when Dean walked in—he'd called him there in the first place.

Dean moved his gaze over the desk, then pursed his lips. Yeah, it didn't take much to figure out the topic.

"Well, that's not good. Heard rumors about a serial killer, but I sure didn't think the victims would all look like that."

Olin gestured at the chair. "So it's not just me."

Dean shook his head. "They all look like Kat. How many in total?"

"Eight bodies so far—all left out in the open. Whoever is behind it wants them found."

Dean sat and blew out a slow breath. "Does Kat know?"

"Not yet. Wasn't sure how to handle that issue."

"How to handle Kat, you mean?" Dean chuckled as if the idea itself were hilarious. "That woman does what she wants when she wants to. I don't know if there's any handling to be done with her."

His words took Olin back to watching Dean *handle* Kat a few nights before at Sanctuary. Kat might hiss a bit, but there was no doubt she melted just as hard.

Still, Olin tried to keep his mind on the task at hand. "Normally I'd let her know, because if this is about her, she could be in danger. However..."

Dean picked up the thought easily. "However, Kat had a talent for doing the exact wrong thing in any situation. I have a feeling if she found out about this, she'd decide to go confront him, and we don't need *that*."

"But we can't ignore it, either."

Dean let out a sigh but nodded. "You're right about that. We need to talk to Bradley and clue him in on what's going on. At that point, we can make sure someone is always watching her."

"Won't she notice that? She doesn't strike me as the sort of girl who is going to just go along with that."

"Fair enough. I think between the three of us, however, we should be able to handle one little girl."

Despite Dean's grin and confidence, Olin wasn't so sure. In his experience, *one little girl* could do a whole hell of a lot of damage, and he had a feeling Kat would give them all a run for their money.

* * * *

Kat stared at her artwork, frowning. The image was nothing like what she was supposed to work on. Instead of the cute, funny things she was known for, this painting was an entirely different style.

It had sweeping brush marks and a surrealist quality. A woman's body was on the floor, as though she'd collapsed, and the outer edges of the painting were black, with light only at the center, making the woman isolated and alone.

Other than the shadows there in the darkness, the ones overlooking her with a sense of menace.

The image had plagued her, refusing to leave her alone until Kat gave in. It wasn't uncommon, to have this need to complete projects. It was as if the picture crawled around in her head, threatening her.

Tiny bits of dried acrylic paint clung to her skin, making her itch, but she didn't mind. Those were like makeup for her, something she often found on herself after she stopped painting.

It was one thing about digital art that always made her sad, the lack of that tactile experience, the scent of the paint, the way she could use her fingers to smudge certain of the colors and soften the shading.

A loud sound drew her attention from the artwork. She blinked, the way she always did, as if she had to wake up from her intense focus.

Right, my phone…

She set the paintbrush in the cup of water and rushed over, grabbing her phone off the edge of the desk to answer. "Hello?"

The second the phone pressed to her ear and a familiar voice reached through it, Kat's head spun.

"Did you really think a new number would change anything? Locating a number is child's play."

Jerry.

Kat wanted to hang up. She wanted to collapse, to give in to the panic beating at her. As it always did, Jerry's voice was entangled in her head with the memory of her own screaming, of the pain that had spread through her, the fear. One couldn't seem to exist without the other.

Had Kat *ever* felt fear like that before?

That was an easy answer. Fuck no.

"What do you want?" she forced herself to ask.

"I've made that clear — you."

"Well, you're not getting that." She wished her voice were strong, but the fact she got it out at all was impressive.

"Have you watched the news recently?"

"I'm not going to talk current events with you."

"You should really check some headlines. I've left a few gifts for you."

Dread slithered through Kat at his words. She didn't think he was lying — what would have been the point? Any *gift* from Jerry was something Kat knew she wouldn't want.

"You're going to get yourself caught. You should just run away while you can."

"Silly Kat," Jerry said, a strange, twisted affection in his voice. "I'm not the sort of man who runs away. I didn't get where I am today by running. I've built myself up from nothing by determination and perseverance. It's how I have everything I have and exactly how I'll get you, too." He let out a breath as if he had lain down. The relaxing sound only put Kat on further edge, as if he were talking to her like some lover. "I put a lot of effort into the gifts. I'd thought you'd hear about it, but it sounds like you don't leave your house all that much. Besides, that detective around you is probably trying to hide it from you."

"Hide what?"

"What fun would it be if I just came out and told you? On Christmas morning, kids aren't told their gifts — they get to open them. I don't want to ruin the surprise. If you want to know, just look at the local news and I'm sure you'll put it together. If you were stupid, I wouldn't be interested in you, after all."

The praise didn't do a damn thing for her. She didn't live for praise, had long before given up getting it, and even if she enjoyed it, she didn't want anything from Jerry.

"You know, I've been thinking about you a lot." Jerry spoke as if he'd intended the conversation to happen one sided, as though he didn't care if she said a word back. "I really thought you would have returned already. Though, if you don't know what's going on, that makes more sense. Still, I spent time looking at your past as well. Your parents are rich and well known. That was the last thing I expected. Given your whole free-spirited thing, I thought you'd come from a line of hippies or some other absurdity. Imagine my surprise to find out you come from well-bred stock."

"Leave my family out of this."

"I can't. I'll use whatever I need to get what I want. However, I wasn't threatening them. Given how little contact you've had with them, I doubt they'd make good leverage anyway. I'm just curious how you could have come from them? Maybe they were disappointed in you and that's what drove you to be the wild one of the family?"

Kat hated that he was right... She didn't like him seeing through her, being able to dissect her so easily.

It made her feel like a cliche. Instead of the free spirit she'd always wanted to call herself, it turned her into every girl rebelling against overly strict parents.

"Leave me alone," Kat whispered. "Whatever you're hoping for isn't going to happen."

Jerry's voice came through the line as she went to hit the End button. "Just check the news."

She clutched her phone in her hand after she hung up on him, his words swirling around in her head. She wanted to ignore him, to believe he was lying, that there was nothing to find. He wanted to manipulate her and playing his game would be foolish.

Still...this nagging sensation inside her wouldn't quiet down. Jerry didn't strike her as a liar, and he was too instant.

With trembling hands, she opened the browser on her phone and went to the local news page. At first, she saw a lot of nothing, a lot of drama she usually tried to ignore. Illegal grow raids, discussion of short-term rentals, road work warnings.

Then an image farther down caught her attention, that of a sheet covering a person. *Eighth Body Found.*

Kat gulped as she clicked on the headline, that fear inside her growing as she took in the details. The blonde hair, the pale skin, the age and body type…

This was what he wanted her to find, right? This was him admitting that he was doing this because of her, that these girls were gone, had suffered, all because of Kat.

Anger took over the fear inside her — or perhaps she just clung to the anger because it felt like she could do something about that. She couldn't call Jerry back — each call had come from a restricted number — couldn't do a damn thing about him, but she knew exactly where to land the rest of her impotent fury.

Right on Olin, who it seemed had purposely kept this information from her.

Chapter Seven

Olin sat at the desk in his office, a headache plaguing him. He'd already down a few ibuprofen, but the pain hadn't gone away. He took a moment and closed his eyes, trying to let the meds kick in. Maybe a quick nap would help—it wasn't as if he'd been sleeping well.

He'd spoken to Dean and Bradley, now, though Bradley handled most of watching Kat. The man was staying at her place anyway, so the only time Dean had to step in was when Kat wanted to go out.

It had worked out fine so far, so Olin had poured himself into the case. He could do more good by solving this thing, by finding some sort of evidence to take down Jerry, than by trying to hover over her.

She didn't need him.

The memory of her at Sanctuary came back to him. He'd watched as Dean and Bradley had enjoyed her, had brought her pleasure, and even if Olin had wanted to join in—and fuck, had he ever—he'd known that wasn't possible. Kat needed that dynamic, craved it, couldn't be happy without it. It was in the lovely way she gave in, the peace that had taken over her, that had stripped away her fears.

And Olin? He couldn't give her that. He'd seen what happened when people found out, and with his job, he couldn't risk it again.

Which meant it didn't matter if he wanted her, or how badly, because it just wasn't possible.

His door opened—no knock, no warning. He opened his eyes, ready to make it clear to whoever barged in that the behavior wasn't acceptable.

Except, rather than a coworker, instead of another detective or uniformed officer looking for information, Kat stood there.

And she sure did short his brain out. She shut the door behind her, and a flush on her cheeks said this wasn't a happy visit. Still...the woman was a knockout. She wore a pair of jeans and a tank top, her hair down and her eyes bright.

Still, it was easy to guess why she was there.

"You heard about the bodies, huh?" Olin remained leaning back in his office chair.

She pressed her lips together for a moment. "So you did know? On my way over here, I'd started to convince myself that I was wrong, that maybe you didn't know about it, maybe it was a different department, and you weren't keeping it from me. Guess that isn't the case."

Olin sighed. It wasn't that he'd thought he could keep it from her forever, but he'd hoped he'd solve it first. Seemed like Kat was smarter than he'd hoped for. He should have expected this. "I didn't want you worrying."

She walked forward and slammed her palms down on his desk. "It's *my* life! I don't need you to protect me from things, to lie to me. How long have you known?"

"From the first victim I suspected."

She frowned. "That day you called me sounding frantic…"

Olin nodded. "I saw the first body, and she could have been your twin. Because of the injuries, I couldn't see her face well, but everything was just like you. I had to call to make sure it wasn't you. I didn't know for sure that it had anything to do with you at that time, though."

"And when you did?"

"By body three I couldn't ignore it anymore. They're clearly a message to you."

"Obviously." Kat let out a slow breath, and Olin shook his head.

This was exactly why he hadn't wanted to tell her. The weight was obvious. Kat blamed herself for it, carried that on her own shoulders as if she were at fault. It wasn't her — Jerry had done this.

He'd never wanted to see that guilt on her face.

"Can you do anything about it?" Kat asked.

"Not yet. There's been all of no evidence for us to pin it on Jerry. He's been careful to make it clear it's him without giving us anything solid. Even if he did, we still can't find him."

"So what? I'm supposed to just sit around and watch women die in my place and ignore it?"

"What other option is there?"

She said nothing, turning away, making Olin hesitate.

"Kat…"

"Jerry called me," she said softly.

"What?" Olin flinched at his own voice, at the sudden anger in it. He tried to rein it in so he didn't upset Kat.

Not that she looked all that fragile in the moment.

Kat turned back toward Olin but didn't meet his gaze. "I've gotten two calls from him so far. The first was just a general call, and the second was earlier today, telling me to check the news for his 'gift.'"

"Why didn't you tell me?" He struggled to keep his temper in check but was pretty sure he didn't manage it at all.

"Because it didn't seem important. He made it clear he wasn't going to come and attack me."

"And you believed him? After everything he's done?"

Kat took a seat in one of the chairs on the other side of his desk and leaned forward. "I think it's an ego thing. He wants me to come to him, to agree to be with him on my own."

"Fucking bastard," Olin muttered, then shook his head. "He wants the power of forcing you to come to him."

Kat sighed softly, looking broken. "What am I supposed to do?"

"We'll figure it out, Kat. He isn't as smart as he thinks and he *will* make a mistake. When he does, he'll get his ass put away for good."

"This was supposed to be over. I was supposed to be done with it."

"Life doesn't work that way. Things aren't finished just because we want them to be."

Kat let out a long breath, as if the answer weren't what she'd wanted to hear. Then again, it was one of those hard truths people eventually had to accept. Olin wanted it over for her, too. He wanted her to be free, to go back to her regular life, to solve this case, but he had to wait for that, too.

"Come on." Olin rose from his seat. "I'll drive you home."

"I can make it there myself."

"You can, but now that you know, I think it's about time to sit down with Bradley and Dean and actually discuss it."

"So you're not going to lie anymore?"

Damn, Olin did like that sharp tongue of hers. "What's the point in lying? You're too stubborn to let it go anyway."

Kat gave him a side-eye, but he was pretty damn sure he saw the corner of her lips curl up.

And fuck him, because no matter how much he told himself it was hopeless, he really wanted to see more of those smiles.

* * * *

Kat sat on the couch between the three men who were now such a large part of her life.

Bradley stood to the side, silent as ever. Dean sat on one of the bar stools, dressed perfectly as if he'd just come from work. Olin sat on a chair across from the couch as he went over exactly what had happened with Jerry and the bodies.

Kat remained silent as she listened. She already knew most of what he'd said—it was generally an update. The only thing she hadn't expected was to find out Bradley and Dean already knew about what had happened.

Jayce Carter

It seemed everyone was talking about her while trying to keep her in the dark.

And Kat did *not* appreciate it.

"You okay?" Dean had his gaze locked on Kat, as if looking for cracks. His worry chafed, especially because it felt like he thought she needed the reassurance, the help.

Kat had taken care of herself for a long time—she didn't need Dean to stare at her like she was some broken doll. "I'm fine," she snapped. "I mean, people who keep lecturing me about being honest have been lying to my face, but what does that matter?"

"Kat—" Bradley started to say.

Kat gave him one hell of a glare. "Don't you start with me. You're the worst, since you're crashing here at my house like some out-of-work moocher. You had every chance to come clean, but you didn't."

"No, I didn't." He didn't sound the least bit sorry about it, either.

Kat narrowed her eyes. Bradley always knew how to pick at her, how to get her temper going. After their time together, he excelled at being able to get beneath her skin.

And Kat *always* rose to that occasion.

"I didn't want you blaming yourself," Olin said, his voice soft. "I was the one who made the decision—no one else."

"Oh, trust me, I have far more than enough anger to go around so everyone gets their fair share."

Olin didn't respond right away, just staring at her. Finally, he shook his head and dropped his gaze to the floor.

Bradley spoke up, no doubt the one who was most used to dealing with Kat's moods. "Look, Kat, be pissed all you want about us not telling you. None of that changes that now that you know, we have to decide what to do."

"What to do? There's nothing to do." She gave a meaningful glare to Bradley. "Except you can move out."

"Not happening. In fact, now that we don't have to pretend like everything is fine, I'm pretty sure you'll have to put up with Dean more often, too."

Kat jerked her gaze around to Dean, who'd said little to nothing since arriving. She almost expected him to side with her, for him to say that the others were being unreasonable.

"He's right."

Bastard.

Dean kept going. "Jerry might have said he wouldn't touch you directly, but men like him don't keep their word, not when push comes to shove. Until he gets caught, you need to make sure you aren't an easy target."

"My house isn't *nearly* big enough for the three of you to stay here."

"We won't," Olin said. "There's no need for all of us to be here at once. We can rotate based on schedules. It gives us the chance to get stuff done but know that you're not on your own."

Kat let out a frustrated sigh. The tone of each man said she couldn't talk them out of it.

Worse? There was a part of her that clung to their offer, to the idea that she wasn't alone. She recalled the weeks before Bradley had come, when she'd been so jumpy and fearful in her own place, especially at night.

No matter how much it annoyed her to have shadows, she couldn't deny that she did feel better knowing he was there, hearing Bradley's bare feet against the wood floors at night when he'd make his rounds, listening to Dean's snarky comments, feeling that sense of safety when Olin stared at her, the way he had the confidence to make her think things would work out.

Sure, she wasn't sure how to deal with them, but it seemed that didn't matter. No one was asking her opinion on the matter.

Kat had just gotten herself three sexy, dominant roommates. What would have been the start to an amazing fantasy just months ago didn't seem so great, now.

It sucked when reality never lived up to fantasy.

Chapter Eight

Kat let out a loud sigh as she paced her living room.

It turned out Dean made for a far more annoying companion than Bradley.

Where Bradley tended toward silence—sometimes loud, judgey silence—Dean commented on everything. He was friendly and seemed comfortable, but that led to him being far too invasive.

He'd asked about her work, had tried to follow her into her studio, had been a shadow with an endless string of commentary.

Worse?

Kat couldn't settle. Each time she tried to breathe, she could only think about those bodies. They'd died because *she* hadn't given Jerry what he wanted. If she only...

"Knock it off," Dean said, his voice coming from right behind her and making her jump.

Kat set her hand over her chest, her heart pounding hard. "You don't need to sneak up on me."

"I didn't—you were just distracted by whatever nonsense is going on in your head."

"It isn't nonsense," Kat snapped.

"You sure? Because the way you're frowning says you're thinking about something unpleasant, and I'm pretty sure I can take a guess at what."

"So you think you know me?" She crossed her arms and glared.

Yet…that little exchange helped. The back and forth distracted her, made her feel alive in a way she'd missed.

"Yeah, I do. Now, sit your ass down before you wear holes in your nice new floor."

"Don't tell me what to do."

Dean lifted one of his dark eyebrows, the intensity of his gaze increasing. There really was no way of pissing off a Dom faster than behaving like this, and it gave Kat a delicious shiver down her spine.

Yes. This was what she craved, that wonderful feeling of defying expectations, of someone who gave enough of a damn to fight her.

Because being hated was far better than being ignored.

"Don't play games with me, Kat." Dean didn't look away, didn't soften his words or meaning.

"I'm not playing." *Of course I'm playing.* "I just don't need some overgrown bully telling me what to do."

Dean didn't react at first, that calmness to him terrifying in the best way. He leaned back, against the bar of the kitchen, his gaze far too smart. Dumb people were easier to manipulate, but smart ones? They saw through her tricks.

Though, that had its benefits… Sometimes playing with fools got boring.

"Overgrown bully? You sure didn't feel that way when I had my fingers inside you."

Heat burned at Kat's cheeks, but she kept her composure. "Orgasms are cheap magic tricks. They can make someone think anything."

"Cheap, huh? Boy, you really are a brat, aren't you?"

"Me?" Kat rolled her eyes. "Not at all. It's not my fault that men think they're scarier than they are."

The chuckle he let out was dark, and Kat suddenly remembered why she'd never played with him before. Dean was the *exact* sort of man who did it for her. He was funny, sweet, but with a harder edge beneath the surface that she wanted so badly to bring out. He might be what she enjoyed, but that was why she'd avoided him.

"Oh, Kat, you are difficult." He advanced on her, forcing Kat to step backward until she hit the wall and couldn't go any farther. He continued until he stood just in front of her, his blue eyes staring down into hers. "So here's the deal—are you pushing me because you're needy and want some attention?"

Kat gulped. She did this so she didn't *have* to say anything, so she didn't have to ask for things she doubted she'd get anyway. Why then did Dean insist on her having to actually say anything?

Because he's incredibly irritating, that's why...

Dean tilted his head. "Not ready to come out and say it, huh? Fine. I'm going to take a step backward, and if you aren't interested in continuing this, just walk away. If you don't want to play, I'll let you go."

"And if I don't leave?"

"Then I'll give you exactly what you're pushing me for right now."

Kat's breath caught in her chest at the promise in those words, at the offer of escape. Her heart beat even harder when he did as he said, when he backed off and gave her the chance to go.

She'd already played with him once, but it had been with Bradley, too. This time it was just the two of them. Was she ready for that? Did she want to risk that? Could she stomach it?

The waves of anxiety churned inside her, unsure if it was part of what she'd felt before or if it was Dean's confrontation.

Still, she knew if she left, if she went back to her room, if she gave in, she'd regret it. She needed a chance to let go again, to unload the bullshit in her head, to set it down for just a moment and nothing had ever worked as well as *this*.

Which meant Kat stayed still, her feet rooted in place, and gave Dean the smallest nod.

His smile widened, a cruel edge to it that made her pussy clench without him even *touching* her.

She might just be in over her head.

"Good answer," Dean said. "Because I've been wanting to deal with that attitude of yours for a long fucking time."

"Good luck," Kat whispered back. "Better men than you have tried."

He came forward and caught her chin, tilting her head so she stared up and into his eyes, his large body crowding hers. "Yeah, they have."

"So why do you think you have a shot?"

"Because that's the secret, Brat. I'm not better — but I might just be bad enough to handle you."

And just like that, Kat knew she was lost.

Dean couldn't believe the way his heart sped at the defiant look in Kat's gray eyes. He'd long thought he'd grown out of that instant excitement, that feeling of uncertainty that came from wondering what exactly would happen.

He'd figured that came with age and experience, that things no longer seemed as thrilling as they had when he'd first started.

Yet...he couldn't deny the sensation running through him as he stared at Kat.

It wasn't *just* sex. Sex was easy to come by, easy to manage. This was so much more. It was the thrill of discovery, of peeking beneath the layers of a person who wanted to hide so much.

And Kat sure as hell hid a lot.

The fact she seemed incapable of just telling him what she wanted was proof of that. Instead of being honest, she'd pushed him, pressed until she thought she'd gotten him right where she wanted.

Poor girl doesn't know me, does she?

He curled his lips into a smirk, rewarded by a sharp intake of breath from her. That nervous edge was a blessing.

Dean reached out, slowly, and wrapped his hand around the back of her neck. He pulled her toward him, not stopping until the front of her body pressed against his. Her chest rose and fell rapidly, proving her whole attitude was nothing more than an act.

She *wanted* him. No, it was more than that. The way she leaned in closer, the way her tongue touched her bottom lip, it was all proof that she craved him.

And he planned to give her all she could take and more.

"Aren't you going to go over the rules?" she asked, a delicious quiver to her voice.

"No. You're hardly some fresh-faced virgin, Kat. You only want me to do it so you can mouth off some more."

She snorted, but her pupils dilated when he tightened his hand on the back of her neck as a warning.

He leaned down, crossing the scant distance between their lips, and took the kiss he'd wanted each time he'd looked at her, each time she'd used that mouth of hers for backtalk instead of things so much more pleasant.

She was fire made flesh — all bite and pleasure mixed together at once. She melted against him, those hands of hers coming to rest on his sides and curling in so she gripped him. Funny how much she could talk and fight and complain and yet how quickly she gave in when she got a taste of what she wanted.

Dean moved his hands down and gripped her ass. *Fuck* the girl had one hell of an ass. It made him want to sink into it, to hear those broken little moans she'd let out when he did.

But he didn't much feel like doing the work at the moment for that — no doubt she had lube at her place, but why find it when he hadn't even gotten to experience the bliss he was sure her pussy was?

He shifted his hands enough to grasp her thighs and lifted her with ease. Kat wrapped her legs around him and moved her arms so they encircled his shoulders, clutching him as if nothing else in the world mattered.

He carried her to her room, then dropped her onto the bed. It gave him his first real look at her bedroom.

It was so much like her — eccentric, a bit wild, but with an unexpected softness despite the bright colors.

"Are you going to stare or do me?" Kat asked with a grin.

"You that needy?"

She narrowed her eyes though her grin never slid from her lips. "No, I just know that men of a certain age need more time to get ready. I thought maybe you were waiting for a little blue pill to kick in."

Dean couldn't help the bark of laughter that escaped him at her barb. If she thought that was all it took to piss him off, she was sadly mistaken.

Besides, Dean wasn't nearly as old as she seemed to think — or rather, as her joke would imply.

"If you want to annoy me, you're going to have to try a *lot* harder than that," Dean said as he unbuttoned his jacket and hung it over a chair near the door. He continued, undoing the vest, then his shirt, each movement methodical and slow to prove he was in no rush. That sort of anticipation could do *wonders* for a sub. "I'm a lawyer, sweetheart. I've been called every name in the book and then some. Your little claws aren't nearly as sharp as you think. Though, that doesn't mean I won't make sure you pay for each little jab you throw."

A moment of fear crossed her features, so fleeting it seemed to dissolve the moment it came together. Still...

Dean softened his tone as he hung his shirt over the back of the chair with his other clothes. "You know I wouldn't really hurt you."

Kat swallowed, then nodded. "I know. Sometimes..."

When she trailed off, he gave her an honest smile. "Sometimes old memories creep up. I get it."

She gave him a smile in return, one that mirrored his, before that mischievous sparkle in her eye returned.

Kat may push for all sorts of reasons—ones he didn't yet understand—but that didn't change that she was a brat at heart.

And it sure didn't change that he liked that about her.

He undid his belt, his cock hardening at the lust in Kat's eyes as he pulled it from the loops of his slacks. "Is that what you need?"

She blinked slowly, then met his gaze, as if she hadn't realized she'd been staring, as if she'd just woken up. "I doubt you know how to use that right."

"Well, maybe I'll practice on you until I get it right, then."

She shivered, as if she couldn't help it, and that only further enticed Dean.

He didn't normally give in to this darker side of himself, but it seemed Kat was hell on his self-control. The idea of not indulging, of not hearing the sounds she'd make, of not giving her exactly what she needed was more than he could stand to bear.

"Flip over," he said, letting his tone drop, his voice going rough and dark.

Kat didn't do it at first, and the movement of her throat as she swallowed nearly drew a groan from him. Eventually, when he said or did nothing else, she obeyed.

She twisted, moving to her hands and knees, giving him a perfect view of her shapely ass.

Thank fuck for leggings... Dean would never understand the people who felt women shouldn't wear the things. They were a gift from the gods as far as he was concerned. The thin, tight fabric showed off her assets perfectly, made him want to lose himself in her.

And there was no good reason to resist. He ran his hand down, over the subtle curve of her back, then over her ass. Her muscles twitched beneath his palm like a siren's call, like a plea she didn't have to voice.

He grinned—not as a game but just because he couldn't help it. He cupped her ass, squeezing the firm muscles there, then released her to land a soft smack.

She gasped, but the sound said she still held on to her control.

And he wanted nothing more than to tear that away.

Dean pressed between her shoulder blades so her chest hit the mattress, leaving her ass up and at his mercy.

Perfect.

It made him wonder why this had taken him so long, why he'd avoided her as he had.

Because you want it too much…

He shook the thought away, then folded the belt over in his hand. The weight and the warm leather of it felt familiar but…terrifying.

He wasn't sure he'd done anything like this before— certainly not recently. He'd gotten used to safer play, to the sort that didn't tempt his darker urges, that didn't remind him of his old self.

But…the desire to give Kat what she needed outweighed his fears.

He took a deep breath before bringing the belt down on her ass through her leggings. Starting off slow was right, warming her up, increasing it until she broke apart beneath him. It was the wait that was delicious, seeing her lose herself one strike at a time, seeing how much she could take.

And her response was as perfect as he knew it would be. She let out a rush of air that turned into a moan, letting Dean set an even pace.

He hit one cheek, then the other. The fact her chest pressed against the bed helped to protect her from any risk of striking too high, of hitting anything important. It allowed him to relax, to test how she responded to each sting, to lose himself in the thud of the leather against her ass and the sexy moans she let out.

She squirmed, as if she couldn't help it, but didn't try to move or get away. If anything, she arched her back more, her thighs pressed tight together.

"You think I've got it figured out?" Dean asked as he landed a slightly harder strike.

She cried out, a sound that went straight to his cock. Still, the girl wasn't done yet, as evident by her quip. "You hit like a girl."

"Like a girl? Can't wait until Toya hears you say that and decides to show you just how a girl can hit."

She opened her mouth as if to respond—no doubt with something snarky—but he took that chance to strike the bottom curve of her ass harder. Whatever she planned on saying was lost to a throaty moan.

Dean dropped the belt for a moment and gripped the waist of her leggings, then pulled them down. She wore no panties beneath, which meant he got a good look at the flushed skin of her ass and, given the arch of her back, her swollen pussy. She was drenched, something he knew without having to touch her.

Not that he'd stop himself, though. He dragged two fingers down her slit, pleased to find her cunt soaking wet and twitching—so beautifully needy.

He rubbed his fingers against her erect clit, aided by her own juices, until she cried out.

"You make such lovely sounds when you're not snarling," he said before plunging two of his fingers into her.

Her pussy swallowed him up, impossibly snug around him, as if she wanted to pull him deeper and never let him go. It made him chuckle, thinking he'd give her so much better soon enough.

However, when he withdrew his fingers, when he stroked over her the heated skin of her ass, her whimper said she hadn't had enough.

And if Dean were honest with himself—which he rarely was—he hadn't had enough, either.

He picked up the belt again, and when he landed the first strike the sound of leather against flesh was a symphony all its own. It reached inside him to those deep, dark places he tried so hard to bury down deep. It spoke to them, both soothed and woke them up.

And Kat, for each hit he landed, only sounded all the more beautiful. Was this why she pushed? Because she wanted this? Because she craved it?

He had no idea, but that didn't stop him from giving it to her.

Hell...the more he touched her, the more he heard her, the deeper into this madness he fell, the more he thought he'd give that girl *everything*.

Wetness tracked down Kat's cheeks but she just didn't give a damn. How could Dean undo her like this? How could he steal her jabs and her barbs and turn her into this?

And why did she enjoy it so much?

Her ass hurt, the skin on fire, but her mind was at peace for the first time since everything had gone wrong.

No, maybe for the first time well before that.

It was as if each strike from his belt and each stroke of his palm calmed her, steadied her.

Her entire body hummed with pleasure, alive and sparking and desperate. The sounds that filled the room were filthy and beautiful, two things she had no idea could work together so well.

And she wanted more. Impossibly more. More pain, more of him, more of this moment.

"I want to keep you on this edge for fucking hours," Dean said, his voice like she'd never heard it before. Normally Dean was well put together, charming, thoughtful. The man who spoke behind her now seemed none of those things. Instead, he sounded ravenous and broken. Still, he went on. "I want to spread your thighs wide and slap your cunt, make you cry until you break and you're begging me to stop. I want to push you right to that edge and tumble off it with you, but you're too fucking tempting."

The belt landed beside her, as if he'd tossed it away, a moment before Dean's large, strong hands gripped her waist and turned her over. Her back hit the mattress, and she was faced with his dark features, with a hard look on his face she'd never seen before.

It was like a different man, like someone she didn't know.

It also let her see him without his shirt for the first time. That surprised her, made her frown. Dean had tattoos on his chest, something she hadn't expected. Dean seemed so put together and clean cut that the idea of him having ink didn't fit at all with the person she'd gotten to know.

She reached up to touch one, to stroke her fingers over something she couldn't read but looked like letters.

Dean caught her wrist, his blue eyes boring into her. "Don't ask," he said, his voice strained.

Kat nodded, more due to the pain in his voice, because it took her back to her own hatred of her marks. She could understand that desire to hide.

Yet…she trusted him. In fact, this felt like the real man, like the one he'd hidden before, like she'd finally peeked beneath the façade he wore. Maybe that was one reason she'd avoided him before without realizing it, because she'd always known that what he showed at the club wasn't who he really was.

And now that she got a look? She wondered how many others had seen it, and this tiny, jealous part of her hoped no one had. She wanted to believe that he had hidden it from everyone else, that she and she alone got to experience it, got to revel in it.

The thought couldn't last long, however, not with how hungry they both were. Dean leaned down, over her, and took her lips in a devouring kiss that stole all her senses. His hard, wide chest rubbed against her erect nipples even through her tank top, teasing them, making her realize that he'd turned her so mindless with so little effort. He'd hardly touched her clit, hadn't touched her breasts at all, and yet she wasn't sure she'd ever been this turned on before.

He braced himself with one hand while his other shifted between their bodies. It took a moment before she realized what he was doing, when he broke the kiss and sat back on his knees, his slacks undone and his hard, tempting cock in his hand. He gestured at her nightstand. "Condoms?"

"Second drawer."

He nodded and leaned up, crowding her as he reached for it.

And Kat, not one to submit easily, took the chance to wrap her own hand around his cock.

He was thick, the skin soft against her palm despite the hardness beneath. His masculine groan made her smile as she stroked him, playing with him simply because she wanted to, because she couldn't help it.

"You know," he said into her ear, his voice dangerously turned on. "You're a fucking handful. Most subs are good girls who ask permission."

"I'd say you're the handful," she countered before nipping at the side of his neck, leaving a small red mark there like a brand on his skin.

His laugh warmed her, the way that even her wild, reckless side didn't drive him off.

The moment she thought that, however, she froze. That was too dangerous, too close to needing someone, which was only a small step from them growing tired of her. Hadn't she learned that well enough?

Dean pulled back enough to look down into her eyes. Did he notice the change in her?

Probably. The man was far too observant.

Instead of addressing it or letting him, Kat fell back on what she always did—snark. "Hurry up. Men your age tend to have trouble keeping it up if you wait too long."

He pressed his lips together, but she got the sense it was less about her barb and more about what he knew she was hiding with it.

"One of these days," he whispered, "you'll be honest with me."

"We'll see," she responded.

He shook his head and sat back, then tore open the foil. He rolled the condom over his length, the sight enough to distract Kat from her previous, troubling thoughts.

Dean grasped her knees and spread them wide, pressing them up so she was entirely exposed. His gaze caught the bottom edge of the wounds Jerry had left, but neither she nor Dean mentioned it.

It was as if that couldn't exist, not in that moment, not between them. Kat refused to let anyone see how much those marks hurt, how much she hated them, so she ignored them.

Dean must have done the same, because he grasped his cock again and pressed the head against her waiting pussy. He paused for a heartbeat, his gaze locked at the place they touched, before he slid into her with agonizing slowness.

Each inch of his thick shaft spread her open. If he'd slammed into her, it would have been over all at once, she'd have adjusted with one go, but this way? This way forced her to endure it all, to feel it all, and it overwhelmed her.

She had no idea just how close to release she was until it crashed into her, until her back arched and she drowned beneath the waves of sensation so strong she struggled to call them pleasure.

Not that it stopped Dean. He kept on, even as her body tightened around him, until his pelvis pressed against her. Only then did he pause, his lips near her ear, his breathing rapid and hard.

"Fuck," he whispered. "Your cunt feels so damned good, Kat, especially when you squeeze down on me like that, when you squirm because it's too much."

And as much as Kat would *never* admit it, that's what she loved, too. She loved that he didn't treat her like she was fragile, like she couldn't handle it. He kept going because he wanted to, because he knew she could take it.

He reached down with the hand not bracing himself, but he didn't grab her thigh. Instead, he leaned enough to grab her sore ass, which set off another wave of pleasure through her. It was as if that reigniting old flames, like blowing air over embers.

She arched against him, crying out, and he took that moment to pull back before plunging hard into her.

He fucked her with a passion she had no idea he had. At the club he was normally funny and cheerful and polite. He appeared to be a perfect gentleman, the sort of soft Dom new subs liked to play with because he seemed safe.

That wasn't the man fucking her right now. This man was wild, teasing every nerve ending in her body as he took her. She'd be sore when they were done — there was no doubt about that — but she couldn't wait to feel the twinges of pain come tomorrow.

Kat gave herself over to it, to him, especially when he growled into her ear, "Hands above your head. Grip the headboard."

Kat's arms moved on their own, it seemed, as if he had a direct line to her body that bypassed her brain. She wrapped her fingers around the metal of her headboard, gripping it and using it to keep her from sliding up despite his punishing thrusts.

Dean set his hand on the front of her throat, the action shorting out her brain further, making her tilt her head to offer him *everything*.

He chuckled, a dark sound that made her pussy clench around him. He didn't tighten his grip, didn't cut off her oxygen, but the threat alone was all she needed. Between the pain in her ass from the spanking, the way he fucked her with all his strength, and the pressure of his hand against her throat, Kat gave up.

She stopped fighting, stopped trying to be anything except in the moment with him.

Dean, as if he realized it, stared down at her with his blue eyes. What was he going to say? The moment stretched on, the two of them locked somewhere between who they wanted to be and who they were.

Instead of saying anything, however, Dean shook his head and leaned down, taking a kiss, and Kat knew the truth.

At the end of the day, they were *both* cowards.

But that was fine with her.

It was always safer to hide the truth.

Chapter Nine

Kat knew before she opened her eyes that Dean had left.

Hell, she was pretty sure she'd known as she'd drifted off the night before in his arms that he wouldn't still be there when she woke. It had been in the way he'd clutched her to his chest, in the look in his eyes before he'd kissed her.

Dean was the sort of man to run, and given Kat was *exactly* the same, she could spot the signs a mile away.

So when she opened her eyes to find the bed empty, it didn't surprise her.

Disappointed sure, but not surprised.

Still, she'd gotten what she needed, right? Sex was all she'd ever wanted from men, or at least all she'd ever expected of them. She'd never been the type to try and get them to stay, to beg them to give her time. In fact, she'd been the one to drive them off more often than not.

So why the hell was it that Dean skipping out left this aching pit in her stomach?

She sighed before rolling over, ready to start her day. A dull ache in her lower stomach reminded her of him, and despite herself, she smiled.

It *had* been a good night, and more than worth a bit of discomfort come the next day.

Kat showered and dressed before venturing into the living room. It wasn't a shock to find Bradley there, sitting on her couch, book in hand.

He'd gone back to his ranch the day before to check in, which was why Dean had been her babysitter for the day. Funny enough, she found herself relieved to see him.

Bradley and she had enough of a past that while things weren't necessarily easy between them, they were familiar.

"Do you always sleep in so late?" he asked.

Kat glanced toward the clock. "It's only ten in the morning. Not all of us feel the need to get up at the ass crack of dawn. Don't put your neurosis on me."

He didn't lift his gaze from his book as he responded. "Long night?"

"Not really any of your business, last time I checked."

He made a soft sound as he turned the page. "You working this morning?"

"I should." Yet the idea of facing that empty page felt too difficult. She still hadn't gotten anything new up on her site.

"Should?" Bradley finally shut his book, a sign that he'd picked up on something he planned to give his full attention to. "Normally dragging you away from your work is like herding cats. You having trouble?"

Kat let out a sigh as she sat down beside him. "I just can't seem to concentrate. It's like…each time I sit down, nothing comes out."

"Whether or not you want to admit it, you went through a trauma. It's gonna take a while to get back on your feet, to get back to normal."

Kat shook her head, unwilling to allow Jerry to have the credit for her current funk. "I think I'm just tired. I just need to focus better, to lock myself in my studio and not come out until I have three new images."

"You can hammer a screw all you want—won't ever work."

"Your country wisdom can't fix everything, you know."

"Anything it can't fix must not be that important." He set his book down on the side table then turned toward Kat. "I'm serious, though. I know you like to keep going, but the fact is, sometimes pushing through isn't the best choice. I remember when you had that client who wanted you to redo an entire campaign, and you stayed up for three days trying to fix it."

Kat suppressed her shudder as she recalled it, back in the days when she did commercial work for businesses. The client had been a man who knew nothing about marketing and even less about art, and despite all the work she'd put into his campaign, he'd done nothing but complain. She'd spent weeks on it for him to trash the entire idea without anything else to offer up. "That guy was a dick," she said.

"He was, but that's not my point. I found you damn near delirious from a lack of sleep, food and way too much coffee."

"If I recall, I was convinced that I needed to invent a new color to make it all work." Kat laughed softly at that, at how hopeless she'd felt about the whole thing.

"Yeah, and you kept saying you weren't really an artist, that you couldn't do it, that you were going to end up on the streets like your mother said you would all because you pursued art."

Kat flinched at the reminder, at the truth behind those words. How many times had her mother scoffed at her? How many times had she made it clear that she fully expected Kat to fail miserably and come crawling back when she crashed and burned as an artist?

Way too many times...

"I showed up, carried your ass to bed and made you stay put for two days as you recovered."

Kat remembered that part of course, the way Bradley had watched over her like she was one of the foals on his ranch. He'd been right there, cooking her meals, making sure she drank water and refusing to let her work until she'd rested enough. The rest of the story was easy enough for Kat to repeat as well. "And at the end of that, I came up with a new idea for the campaign that he loved."

"That's right. You don't give yourself nearly enough credit, Kat. You think that if you just keep pushing harder, you'll get where you need to be, but it blinds you to what's right in front of you." He squeezed her thigh as if driving home the point.

Kat looked right at Bradley, but it made her jerk her gaze away.

He caught her chin and brought her eyes back to his. "Why won't you look at me?"

"What?" She tried to play the question off as she always did. "You're living here. How can I not look at you?"

Still, he didn't release her, didn't let her hide. "You used to look right at me, in the eye, but now? You always look away, or down, or anywhere but my eyes. If you were anyone else, I'd say you were scared, but I know you too well to think that."

Kat took a deep breath and, just to prove him wrong, did as he wanted. She stared right into his dark eyes, into the familiar brown that she'd fallen for so long ago. The moment she did, however, it was as if the past merged with the present and she struggled to find her bearings again.

"Better." His grip gentled and he ran his thumb along her bottom lip. "We know each other too well to play these games."

"We always played games."

"*You* always played games. I was just along for the ride."

Ouch. As much as Kat wanted to argue that, he wasn't wrong. Bradley was honest to a fault, whereas Kat didn't know what she thought, let alone how to talk about it. "So what are you doing back here?"

He didn't answer at first, and the seconds dragged on as Kat waited. Finally, he let out a soft laugh. "Never would have figured I'd fall for a brat, but I guess that can't be helped. Doesn't matter how long passes, seems I can't quite get you out of my system."

Kat's brain worked to find some sharp retort to fire back, to lighten the mood, to make the moment less intense and less serious, but Bradley was a step ahead of her.

He silenced her with a kiss, forcing her to swallow whatever she might have said. The kiss was sweet—almost like a question rather than a demand. His lips teased hers until she forgot whatever she might have tried to say.

When he broke away, he stared at her for a moment before smiling. Whatever he found on her face must have pleased him, because that expression of his said it all.

Kat licked her bottom lip, finding the bitter taste of the French roast coffee he tended to drink lingering there.

Bradley lifted his eyebrow—was he daring her to say something?

Kat had no idea what that *something* might have been, so she rose from the couch. "I should get to work," she said, refusing to look away, to give in after he'd pointed out her avoidance. "Like you said, I got a late start."

Bradley chuckled and picked up his book again. "Sure, Kat. I'll come get you in a couple hours for lunch."

"I might work through lunch," she said.

"You can try, but I'm pretty sure you'll lose that fight." He opened his book and appeared as if he'd stopped paying attention to her entirely.

Still, his words lingered just as his kiss had, and Kat couldn't help the excitement inside her at his words.

Maybe she'd been wrong to write him off so quickly...

* * * *

Those three new images never happened. Despite Kat's best effort, nothing came to her. No cute penguins, no dragons drinking coffee, nothing that she could sell in her shop.

Which meant after half an hour of staring at a blank page, she picked up her brush and started to work on another painting. It was something, right? The pile of finished paintings from the years rested against her wall, forgotten and useless. This one wasn't as dark as the one of the girl in the light, surrounded by shadows. Instead, this showed two faces close together, their lips nearly touching, and the hand of one wrapped around the throat of the other.

However, the mood was different. It wasn't dark, but painted with soft lines and muted colors—something romantic and whimsical.

No matter how much she wanted to work on what paid her bills, she couldn't get her brain to cooperate. Instead, it simply remained locked on this, on things that came to her as she slept.

She recalled her father's cruel laugh when she'd shown him the first piece of art she'd made money from, a painting entered into a contest when she was a freshman in high school. He'd told her there was no future in such things, that she needed to wake up and act like an adult.

Kat rubbed her chest when the ache there reminded her that she hadn't called her parents since the attack.

Not that she thought they'd care much, beyond telling her her own actions had probably led to the whole thing. Instead, it was a passage of time, a reminder that she normally tried to call every other week to help alleviate her of any guilt and yet had let nearly a month pass in silence.

After putting the final stroke to her painting, she set the brush into the water and reached for her phone.

Her mother answered on the fourth ring, just as Kat had started to think she might just get away with leaving a voicemail.

Leave it to her parents to give her hope, then dash it all. It was pretty on-brand for them.

"Hello?" Her mother, Elizabeth, answered with the cultured accent of a woman who spent most of her childhood traveling through Europe.

"Hey, Mom."

"Katherine." The name burned the way it always did, a relic of the woman her parents had wanted her to become.

"It's Kat," she said despite the fact she'd told them that time and time again.

"Kat is the sort of name homeless trash uses. I gave you the name Katherine and that is what I intend to use." Her mother gave no room for argument or discussion on the topic — she never did. There were no discussions to be had with Kat's parents. They gave orders and expected them to be followed.

Which was exactly why Kat had always been the odd man out in a family of overachievers.

"How is everyone?"

"Fine."

Kat nibbled at her bottom lip as she wondered yet again why she even bothered with the call.

Because they'll be gone eventually and you'll feel guilty if you don't reach out.

And, even though Kat never wanted to admit it, she craved some connection with them. No matter how pointless it was, no matter if it would just hurt her in the end, Kat still wanted the people she loved to love her back.

Pathetic.

"Is Dad home?"

"No. He's at a conference in New York this week." And there it was, another barb, another piece of proof of how wonderfully successful their family was—at least until Kat.

Every one of her siblings had become the heads in their fields. Her father ran a large company that oversaw numerous newspapers, her mother an author, her older sister a physicist and her younger brother headed the department of sociology for a prestigious university.

Then there was Kat, the fuck-up who sold cute cartoons on the internet.

She let out a sigh at the knowledge that she would never fit in no matter how hard she tried.

"The reunion is next month. Do you know the date?"

"Yes," her mother said, her tone curt. "The plan is to hold it the last Sunday of the month."

There was no invitation, no time. Again, Kat could have let it go.

Instead, as much as she hated herself for it, she asked in a small voice, "What time?"

"We will sit down to eat at three."

"Can I bring anything?"

"No."

Kat slumped her shoulders at the answer she expected. Her mother wouldn't tell her not to come, but she sure would make it uncomfortable and not just offer the invitation despite Kat always attending the event.

"Okay, well, I should get back to work." The derisive sound her mother gave in response to that hurt, but Kat pressed on. "I'll see you in a couple of weeks at the dinner."

"Goodbye." Her mother hung up the phone without an 'I love you,' or any of the things normal parents said to their children.

Kat dropped her phone on her desk and rubbed her eyes to ease the burning. She *refused* to cry. She wasn't this weak woman. Kat was a hellion, a brat, a woman who danced to her own tune and didn't allow the small minds and opinions of those around her to influence her.

Or, at least that was who she wanted to be. The reality was always more complicated.

A knock on the door made her jump, and Kat rushed to turn the easel around before Bradley could see her painting. She *never* showed this work to anyone. After winning that award, after her parents' reaction, Kat had decided that showing this sort of work to anyone was far too dangerous a move.

"Come in," she said with a shaky voice.

Bradley opened the door, a water bottle and plate of snacks in hand. He'd already dragged her out for lunch, and as much as she hated to admit it, she felt better than she normally did.

Often when working, Kat would forget all about silly things like sleep or breaks or drinking the water she needed to live. However, Bradley watched over her, reminding her every couple of hours to take a break, to move around, to stretch and to drink.

"Thanks," she said, unsure how to react to the sweetness. "I'm done for today anyway."

"Any luck?"

She shook her head. "Nope. I'm going to have to go back to waiting tables if I can't get past this block."

Even as she spoke, she knew it wasn't true. Kat was good with her money and her back catalog of work did more than enough to pay her bills. Still, if she wasn't creating, she wasn't sure what to do with herself.

"You'll manage, Kat. You always do." Bradley held out the water bottle, his tone one of absolute confidence.

It was something she'd craved, something she'd never really had before.

Kat opened her mouth to say something back when the engine of a car caught her attention. It was loud and close…

She'd picked this house because it was at the end of a small cul-de-sac, with no through traffic, and she'd have noticed the roar of that engine before if it had been a neighbor.

Bradley frowned as well, twisting toward it with the look of a man annoyed by his peace being interrupted.

However, the engine wasn't the oddest thing. There was a bang, as if something hit the front door, then the slamming of a car door before the squeal of tires.

"Wait here," Bradley said, setting down the plate and leaving the room, a hard look in his eyes.

Did he really expect Kat to just sit there? Did he know her *at all*?

Kat sure felt like she didn't know Bradley, however, when she walked out of the office to find him reaching into his back near the front door, a series of beeps as if he were entering the code into a safe, then having a pistol in hand as he stood.

He handled the gun as if he were comfortable with it, as if it were nothing new. Then again, he did own a ranch. Maybe he had more practice with weapons than she realized?

He peered out of the front door, and his frown hardened.

Kat's stomach dropped. That wasn't a good expression on his face, and before he could say or do anything, she pulled open the front door, needing to see whatever it was that put that look on his face.

There, on her front step, was a body.

A young woman with blonde hair like hers, naked and covered in wounds and blood and clearly dead, a sickly, ashen pallor over her skin.

It seemed Jerry wanted to make sure his message made it to her this time...

Chapter Ten

Olin drew his hands into tight fists as he walked up to Kat's house, the police cars parked out front something that made his heart speed.

He knew better than most what this many law enforcement could mean, how bad things could get, and even if he *knew* Kat was safe, his body refused to believe it until he saw her.

"Detective Ramiz," a uniformed officer said as he approached.

Olin wanted nothing more than to blow past the man, than to find Kat, to touch her, to reassure himself that nothing had happened to her. Still, he had enough discipline to stop himself and respond with a curt, "Yeah?"

"I'm surprised you came out."

"I'm heading this case, aren't I?"

The man's cheeks paled, and Olin struggled to pull in his temper. It wasn't the officer's fault for his bad mood and it was a dick move to take it out on him.

Olin shook his head and rubbed the bridge of his nose. "Sorry. This case is just important to me and I wanted to come see it myself. Anything new?"

The man shook his head. "Nothing. Still no obvious evidence. Forensics may find something, but that's about our only hope at this point. Blood all seems to belong to the victim—no identification yet. MO is just like the others we've found, so no doubt it they're connected."

"And Kat?"

The man frowned. "Katherine?"

Fuck. That's right… "Yeah, Katherine," Olin quickly amended. "I've dealt with her since her abduction, and she goes by Kat usually."

The officer nodded, seeming to accept that. "She's okay. Her and a friend were here, but the body was left without any direct contact. Seems you were right—it is connected to her. No reason to leave a body here until she was the target."

Maybe Olin should have felt happy that he'd been right, but he sure as fuck didn't. Instead, he was tense, on edge, sorry that Kat had gotten herself put in the middle of this mess. "You almost done collecting evidence?"

"Yeah. Just finishing a few things before we get out of here. We offered protection—"

"But she didn't accept it, right?" Olin let out a rough laugh at that, at just how *Kat* that response was.

The girl wasn't the type to sit back and let others take care of her. Plus, she seemed incredibly devoted to pretending like nothing at all had happened, and accepting police protection would only force her to admit to the problem.

"Let me go talk to her," Olin said. "I doubt I can change her mind about the whole protective detail thing, but maybe I can at least convince her to lie low for a while and hide out with a friend."

The officer nodded. "You want our final report before we head out?"

"No. I'll look at it back at the station when I'm done here. The less we can disrupt her life, the better."

With that, the officer left, and Olin entered the house.

Inside, he wasn't shocked to find Dean and Bradley already there. He knew Bradley had been there when the body had been left, and no doubt the man had called Dean as well. Still, it wasn't either of them that he wanted to see.

He pulled in a much-needed breath when he found Kat, sitting at the kitchen bar, her back to him, her fingers tracing the rim of a coffee cup. No steam escaped the top, making him guess she'd gotten it a while ago but had yet to drink it, letting it go cold instead.

It tugged at his heart in a way that surprised him. So many years in his line of work could harden a man — *had* to harden a man if he was to keep doing the job.

Bradley walked up and kept his voice low. "Any news?"

Olin shook his head. "Nothing yet. They're going to look more into the body, but I doubt it'll be anything different from the others. Jerry covers his tracks well. How is she?"

Bradley glanced over his shoulder, the same worry in his eyes that Olin would guess was in his own. "Girl is blaming herself. She hasn't said a word other than answering the cops' questions."

Boy was that *not* a shock at all. Kat seemed all fun and games, but the woman worried about others to a fault. She was so much more soft-hearted than anyone would guess when first meeting her.

"She can't stay here," Olin said. "It's not safe. I know she thinks Jerry won't make a move, but give him enough time, and he'll get tired of waiting."

"Agreed. She isn't going to come easily, though."

"Leave that to me. If I can break killers in interrogations, I can make her see reason."

Bradley's snort said he didn't agree, but what choice did they have but to try?

Olin passed by the other man and offered a nod to Dean, who leaned against the opposite kitchen counter, watching over Kat.

"Hey there." Olin took a seat beside the silent woman.

She didn't respond, still staring at the cold drink.

"You can't stay here," he said, not bothering to ease into the conversation. What was the point? She knew what he was going to say already.

"I'm not leaving."

"Why not?"

She swallowed hard. "I won't get chased out of *another* home because of him."

That spark was one of the things that drew Olin, but damn if he didn't hate it right then. "It isn't being chased out. It's being smart."

"If he wanted to attack me, he could have done it already. Clearly he's known where I live. Even when I moved and changed my number, he still found me. What's the point in hiding?"

"Just because he found you doesn't mean he did it right away. If you lie low for a while, it'll give us time to find him."

"Time." She huffed softly as if the word were a joke. "What's the point of time? Just so more women can die? To postpone the inevitable?"

Her words cut at Olin. He was the sort of man who was used to fixing things for those he cared about. What use was he if he couldn't even make her feel safe? If he couldn't help her with this?

And despite all his best attempts, he didn't seem able to fix it. He'd followed leads, done what he could, and none of it had helped in the least. Jerry was totally off the map and hadn't left behind any evidence to tie these deaths to him.

It meant no matter if Olin knew who was behind it, he couldn't do a thing to make it better.

Well, other than…

He set his hand on her forearm, and the touch seemed to shake her. She turned to face him, her expression one of fear and despair.

"I survived, right? I mean, I escaped him, I got away, so this is supposed to be over. Why isn't it over?"

Olin rubbed his thumb against her warm skin. "It'll be over, Kat, It just takes some time."

"How much time? How many people have to die while I just wait around and hope it gets resolved? What is the point in running if it hasn't helped so far?"

"Because it's your only choice. Hiding means you can be alive to deal with it another day. Stay put, and he gets you? It's over—for good."

"Maybe that's for the best." Her voice came out a whisper.

Olin froze, somehow holding off on his initial knee-jerk reaction to ask her just what the fuck she meant by *that*. He doubted snapping at her right then would do much of anything good.

Instead, he grappled with his own temper, reminding himself that Kat was going through hell. People reacted in all sorts of ways. "You don't mean that," he said.

"Are we done here?" She rose, as if to walk out, as if the conversation were over.

Olin grabbed her wrist to stop her, unwilling to let their talk end on such a note. "I promise, Kat, we'll figure this out. You aren't alone."

She didn't look at him, instead peering toward the front door, toward where the body had been left. "We're always alone. Don't you get that? At the end of the day, we're all alone."

"Kat…"

She moved her gaze to where he held her still. "Are we done? I want to go lie down."

Olin wanted to tell her no, to demand she discuss it with him until they came to some sort of understanding, until she figured out that she had people who cared about her, that she'd get through this.

Except, he'd done this long enough to know he couldn't force people to believe things, couldn't change their minds until they were ready to accept the truth.

So he let go of her.

Kat didn't storm away, didn't stomp her feet or make a scene. She was eerily silent when she walked out of the kitchen, toward her room. Once she left, Olin placed his forearms on the bar top and sighed.

"She's more stubborn than a mule," Bradley muttered.

"She's scared," Dean said. "People are unpredictable when they're scared."

"Her ignoring good sense is about the most predictable thing she could have done," Bradley said. "I could toss her over my shoulder and force her to leave."

"Pretty sure that's kidnapping." Olin turned in the seat until he could face the other two men. "She'll come around."

"If you think that, it only proves you don't know her that well." Bradley crossed his arms.

Which was probably fair, but Olin wasn't sure what else to do. They couldn't drag her out, no matter how tempting the idea might have been. Of course he wanted her to listen, to go somewhere safe until he could handle this, but wanting didn't mean he could make her.

Kat needed to feel safe, to feel in control. That wasn't possible if they forced her to do anything.

"Let her sleep," Olin said as he rose. "She's exhausted and raw right now, but she isn't stupid. I bet you that tomorrow she'll wake up and see reason."

The looks on Bradley and Dean's faces said neither man agreed, but that didn't matter.

He could only hope he was right, that she'd figure it out, because no matter what he said, he wasn't willing to let her just sit there in danger as long as she wanted.

He refused to have to identify her body next...

* * * *

The groan of Kat's old window was *exactly* what Bradley expected. He nearly grinned when he heard it, when it was so familiar that, despite the risk, he found himself amused. Kat always did this sort of thing, never listened, never did the smart thing. It meant her sneaking out was entirely on-brand for her, and it made him nostalgic.

He slid from the front door, rounding the house quickly, knowing damned well Kat was moving slowly to avoid noise. She probably expected him to be sleeping, to get away before he ever realized.

It seemed she'd been away long enough that she underestimated him now.

Too bad for her.

Bradley fought back the laugh when he reached the outside wall of her room, to find her trying to slide out of the window without making any additional noise. The shrubs that sat below the window would only make that more complicated, which was no doubt the reason for her awkward motions.

And when her foot slipped, Bradley rushed forward without thought, catching her before she crashed into the bushes. She yelped, the sound probably surprise from the fall, or perhaps from *not* hitting the ground.

The moonlight shone brightly, and it meant the gray of her eyes met his, gleaming, highlighting her glare at her failed escape.

"We need to talk," he said, not bothering to hide his annoyance.

He didn't let her down, even when she delivered an elbow to his side. Instead, he carried her inside, putting her feet to the floor only after kicking the front door closed behind him.

"I can walk, you know," she spat as she took a few steps back.

"Yeah, I noticed, since you used that skill to try to take off without a word."

She crossed her arms but didn't respond, pressing her lips together into a tight, stubborn line.

"You were going to give yourself over, weren't you?" Even saying it drove his temper up. What if he hadn't expected it? What if he hadn't been awake and waiting? What if he'd woken the next morning to find her gone, and never saw her again?

Just the thought of what could have happened to her made his blood rush through his ears in a painful throbbing.

He advanced on her, driven forward by his fear and anger. Still, Kat didn't retreat, didn't show an ounce of the self-preservation she should have.

"You know if you went to him, he'd kill you."

"I'm not an idiot," she whispered. "I know better than you do what he'd do." As she spoke, her hand went to her chest, the gesture mindless, as if she hadn't realized she was touching the marks she still carried from him.

Of course she knew what he'd do—she'd already experienced it once.

That splashed over his anger like ice water, forced him to pull back his frustration and rely on the cool head he'd always used. "So if you know, how could you do something so foolish?"

"Because I can't let other people pay the price for me," she whispered.

Bradley opened his mouth to tell her she was an idiot again, that men like Jerry wouldn't stop just because he got what he wanted, but the sight of red on her arm stopped him.

"You cut yourself," he said softly and gestured toward the trail of blood that ran down her arm toward her wrist.

She peered down as if she hadn't noticed it either. "I must have nicked it on the window frame."

He shook his head and went to the closet in the hallway, then pulled out the first aid kit. He gestured at the kitchen stool, then set the kit down and opened it, not bothering to see if she'd listen.

While Kat liked to push boundaries, she was smart enough to know when to stop pushing.

Now was that time.

When he turned back, he found Kat where he'd gestured, waiting for him. Bradley took her arm in his hand, peering at the wound. It wasn't deep, but the red just reminded him of what could have happened if he hadn't caught her.

"What were you thinking?" he asked, not really expecting her to answer but unable to help asking.

She didn't look at him, her gaze down as he wiped the blood from the wound and applied antiseptic. "I tried to lie there and I couldn't get her face out of my head. It was all I saw when I closed my eyes. I don't even know her name, but she died because Jerry wanted me. She suffered like that because of me."

Bradley shook his head as he applied a bandage to the wound. "She died because of Jerry—not you. You didn't force him to do anything. He's doing this because he is twisted, and he wants to inflict pain on people. You can't put that on you."

"Would you feel the same if it were you?"

Bradley froze at the whispered question, and despite his initial desire to give her the answer he wanted to — that of course he'd do the same thing if he were targeted — he forced himself to think about it and answer honestly. "I don't know."

"It's easy to tell someone that they aren't responsible, to tell them not to worry, but it's different when it's *you*. I would tell you exactly what you're telling me if we were talking about you, but I can't just stop thinking about it. I can't ignore it because if I did something different, maybe it wouldn't have happened."

Bradley caught her chin, pulling her gaze to his. "Kat, I understand what you're feeling. I know how easy it is to blame yourself for things, to feel responsible for the whole damned world, but that doesn't mean I'm going to let you run off and get yourself killed."

"But—"

He leaned in, unable to help it when she had that look on her face. It was all innocence, open and not drowning in the years of fights they had between them. *This* was the girl he loved, the one he'd always loved since she'd first bratted at him so long ago. She was tough and sweet and giving and everything he could have wanted. She might annoy him to hell and back, but damn if he didn't love that about her, too. He took her lips in a gentle kiss, one to silence her complaints and soothe his frustration at what could have happened.

And Kat gave in, so fast that it proved how unsettled she really was. Normally she'd have argued more, would have insulted him or mocked him for his reaction. She had to be out of sorts to melt against him as she did.

Which took Bradley back, like every touch of hers did. How was it so easy to fall back into this with her? So easy to forget the bad times, the pain, the fights?

Whatever the reason, he pushed it aside. He slid his hand to the nape of her neck to hold her still as he kissed her, and she responded with the same passion she always had. She curled her fingers into the front of his shirt, clinging to him, desire filling each touch.

He broke away to whisper against her soft, eager lips. "But nothing. *You* matter, Kat. You're important. I know you well enough to figure you out, that you think you're not worth anything, that you think if you can save someone else it's fine if you suffer or get killed, but you're the only one who thinks that's worth it."

She stared at him, those gray eyes of hers locked onto his as if she could work through the confusion in her head.

But he didn't want that. Let her think too hard and she'd come to a wrong conclusion, and give her enough time, she'd believe it as fact. So he delivered a soft bite to her full bottom lip, hard enough that it had to sting. "Pack up your things, Kat. You're moving in with me."

"What?"

He laughed at the nerves in her voice. "Just what I said. You need to lie low, and my place is a good option. It'll take Jerry a while to figure it out, and even if he did, there's cameras and plenty of space. It's the perfect solution."

"I don't think —"

"So don't. Thinking is exactly what gets you into trouble. We'll call Dean and Olin tomorrow and let them know — one or both will probably want to tag along anyway."

She worried her bottom lip, the action reminding him of the soft bite he'd delivered there, made him want to do it again.

However, they had more pressing issues at the moment, so he pulled away before the temptation proved more than he could resist. "Get packed up—or don't. When you're out of clothes, I doubt anyone will complain about you walking around naked."

That flush on her cheeks made his cock ache, made him want to forget the moving idea—at least for a while—and indulge in her instead.

However, Bradley pulled out his phone to let Olin and Dean know about the change.

Kat's safety was the most important thing, and hell...maybe getting her to the ranch was a great idea. She wouldn't be the first unruly mare he'd had to tame, but damn if she wouldn't be the most stubborn.

And the most fun.

* * * *

Kat swallowed hard as she looked around the property. She'd never come to Bradley's ranch before, not even when they'd dated. The very thought had terrified her, made her feel like things were too real, so she'd never tried.

And he hadn't offered, to be fair.

Probably because he'd known she'd refuse.

They'd moved her things in the middle of the night. Bradley had explained that it was far easier to spot a tail in the dark, especially when he'd circled the dirt roads more than a few times since he knew them so well.

After unpacking the car, Kat had fallen asleep without trouble. Even in the unfamiliar bed, with everything happening around her, the exhaustion had caught up and she'd been out by the time her head hit the pillow.

She'd slept in late and woken to an empty house.

Then again, Bradley no doubt had a lot of work to do—*ranches aren't easy to run and he's been spending so much time with me lately...*

So, now that the time was nearly noon, Kat walked around the property. When she'd heard ranch, she'd assumed farm. That probably showed just how *city-girl* she really was. However, she didn't see row after row or corn or whatever else farmers grew.

There was a small greenhouse with some vegetables, but barely enough for just one or two people. Instead, it seemed ranch meant for animals, and there was no shortage of those.

There were pens for goats, some for sheep, lots of cattle and more than a few horses. While Kat would have loved to visit with the horses or cattle, their size made her uneasy. She'd never spent much time around livestock, and the last thing she wanted was to end up hurt because she'd tried to pet something she shouldn't.

Instead, she found herself near the goats. There were older ones, but the babies made her smile. They hopped around, playing like a gaggle of kindergarteners. She crouched down and put her fingers through the slats of the fencing, petting them best she could.

"Careful, they bite."

Kat turned to find Olin there, a smile on his face saying he'd been joking. Still, Kat wasn't the type to let something like that go without joking back. "Well, so do I. It's why we get along so well."

Olin crouched beside her. "They sure are cute."

"All babies are cute. It's a defense mechanism so parents don't throw them out after the third week of no sleep." At that, Kat frowned. "What are you doing here? Don't you have work?"

Olin put his fingers through the slats and one of the black goats with white spots ran over to him. "No. I was taken off the case."

"What?"

"It's fine. It was the right choice."

"But why?"

"I'm too close to the case."

She couldn't seem to make sense of the words. From everything she'd heard Olin was a great cop and a talented detective. What did being too close mean?

Olin must have read the questions on her face because he responded without her having to ask. "They don't want police to work on cases where we have any connection to the suspect...or the victim."

Victim meaning me?

"So you were taken off it because of me?" Yet more guilt poured onto Kat's shoulders as she admitted she was messing up everyone else's life.

A sting in her arm made her frown, and she looked over to find him pulling his hand back. "Did you just flick me?"

"I don't care for that look on your face. Stop worrying so much. It was the right thing to do, and even if they hadn't, I'd have stepped down. Being a cop means being able to look at something objectively, and well... I don't think I can do that when you're involved." His words were soft, and Kat let them roll around in her head.

Did that mean...he liked her?

But Olin was always so careful to keep things superficial. "But, at Sanctuary, you turned me down..."

"Not exactly. I told you I wasn't interested in anything there..."

Oh... "I thought that since you'd been there before, maybe you were into that. Are you a sub?" She didn't think so, but she felt out of other options.

He shook his head. "No. It's just, that's from an old life. It isn't something I have the luxury of enjoying anymore."

Kat tried to make sense of his words, but she couldn't. There were plenty of people in Sanctuary who had important jobs, who had things to lose. In fact, that was why Toya was so careful with members and privacy, to make sure there was a safe place for people to enjoy such things without worry.

However, the way Olin spoke told her he'd experienced the bad side of it, made her not want to push. "Okay," she said softly, not sure what else to say when he made his boundaries clear.

He smiled, as if the conversation weren't awkward at all. "Besides, I needed some time off. My boss has been complaining about me stacking up vacation pay, so I figured, what's a couple weeks here?"

"Here?" The meaning hit her and her eyes went wide. "You're going to stay here?"

"Already cleared it with Bradley. With everything going on, some extra eyes would be helpful. Besides, I don't think I could focus at work anyway. Since I can't work that case, I'd just be worried about you. At least like this there's something I can do." The words held a bit of sadness, as if he accepted that he couldn't work the case but didn't at all care for the idea of doing nothing.

Then there was the other part, that he'd be staying there with her, and Kat couldn't help the way her blood sped at that. Olin had this confidence to him that made her bet he'd made a good Dom back when he'd done that.

And the man was a cop, so he knew his way around handcuffs…

Olin lifted an eyebrow. "What's with that blush?"

"Nothing," Kat rushed out, surprised by her own reaction. She wasn't someone new to the lifestyle, so why was it that Olin could make her blush as if she were some virgin?

"Uh-huh," he said, his lips quirking into a grin that made him impossibly more handsome. "Well, don't stay out here too long—you'll burn. I think Dean's bringing dinner by in a few hours, too."

"Dean?"

"You didn't hear? Yeah, Dean's going to be staying as well. The more the merrier, right? I don't think Jerry'll make a move—hell, it'd be a while before he could even figure out where you are—but I know I'll feel a hell of a lot better knowing there's more people here just in case." With that, he rose and took off toward the house, leaving Kat there to watch him go.

Dealing with the three men one-on-one was hard enough, but to even consider all *three* of them being around constantly?

Kat wasn't sure there was enough cold water in the world to keep herself under control in that case.

Chapter Eleven

Kat let out a sigh when Olin tapped her cheek, a sign that he'd landed a hit.

"You need to focus," he chided her.

"I am focusing. Believe it or not, just focusing isn't enough to become good at this. People don't focus and suddenly become world class fighters."

He snorted softly, then crossed his arms. It reminded Kat that he was dressed down, wearing jeans and a long-sleeve white shirt, and that he looked *really* good like that. It was likely the only reason she'd agreed to this.

This being self-defense training in an open space on the ranch. He'd said he wasn't good at sitting still, and Kat couldn't deny that the thought of being able to protect herself felt especially good with everything going on.

At least, that was what she thought before she actually had to do it. What she'd seen in movies looked so much easier than this.

"It just takes practice," he assured her. "I didn't get this good on day one."

"Well, I have a feeling I won't get that good, even on day eight-hundred-and-twenty-six."

Olin laughed before grabbing two water bottles from the grouping he'd set in the dirt. He threw one to Kat. "You're too hard on yourself, you know that?" After he spoke, he unscrewed the lid to his own water and tipped his head back to gulp. The way his throat bobbed made Kat's heart race.

A sheen covered his skin from the sweat he'd worked up, and it made her mouth even dryer. How was it possible to want someone *this* badly…?

When he met her gaze, she realized he'd caught her staring. She quickly focused on her own water to disarm the tension of the moment — not that it worked.

After she took a drink, she set her water down on the ground beside the others. "Do you really think this will make a difference?"

"Of course. Basic self-defense is something everyone should know. There's no downside."

"Seems like a few fancy moves wouldn't be much use against people who actually know what they're doing."

"That's because you don't get it. Most of those people you're talking about rely on their size and nothing else."

She thought back to when Jerry's henchman had dragged her from Ell's place, to how little her fight had meant to him. She hid the shiver she felt at the memory. "Size is a big factor. I don't care how tough a kitten is — they can't do much against a tiger."

"You clearly have never owned cats, then. I was up in the mountains one time and saw a cat chase a *bear* off."

Kat drew her eyebrows toward each other, trying to picture that. "You're lying."

"I don't lie, Kat. I'm not saying that the cat would have won in an actual fight, but sometimes the confidence is all it really takes."

"I did everything I could when that man grabbed me, and I'm telling you, confidence wouldn't have made a difference."

Olin sighed but kept his distance. "I'm not trying to push you here, I'm sure you don't really want to think about what happened, but I know you're wrong. That man, he was a lackey. I've seen them all my life, put away more than my share, and they're cowards. They're used to looking scary and being big and they rest on that. They're used to people giving in, but the second someone who knows a damn bit of self-defense stands up to them, they get bowled over. I've watched it happen again and again. If a girl like you, someone your size and build, tried what I'm showing you? Trust me, you'd hold your own."

She pushed down her nerves at that, her immediate desire to tell him he was entirely wrong. Doing that would mean admitting to the helplessness she'd felt in that moment, to the way she'd fought despite the terror but hadn't gained any ground at all.

"Show me," she said.

"What?"

"Show me. You're telling me I could have done something, so *show* me what you mean."

He hesitated for a long moment, then sighed. "Maybe that's not a good idea. I don't want to bring up bad memories for you."

"You're bringing up nothing. They're there no matter what—trust me. If you're so sure that you're right, though, show me."

His expression held so much *fuck that* but, in the end, he nodded. "Fine. You tell me if you want to stop, though. We clear?"

That made her smile despite her nerves. He sounded like they were negotiating a scene rather than working on self-defense, and it again reminded her that he'd have made for a great Dom at one time.

He came forward slowly, his gaze hard but surprisingly kind. "How'd it happen?" At her frown, he went on. "I can't show you how to react if I don't know exactly how he grabbed you."

Right. "I woke up, and he was on top of me." Funny enough, *that* wasn't the part that upset her. It hadn't ever been that man who had caused her that sort of anxiety. He'd been *nothing* compared to Jerry.

Without Olin having to say anything, Kat lowered herself to the hard dirt. She wasn't the sort of girl to worry about getting some dust on her.

Olin cursed, the word low but frustrated. "This is a horrible idea."

"If you can't even show me how I could have fought back, you're just admitting that all this self-defense stuff is bullshit."

He crouched beside her but didn't touch her. "Because you don't need me on top of you, not so soon after…"

"Please?" She met his gaze, forcing herself to speak. "I need to know what I could have done. I can't stop flinching at every sound, but maybe if I do this, I'll feel differently."

His whiskey-colored eyes darted away before he dragged his fingers through his hair. "Fine," he snapped, sounding miserable about agreeing. Even so, he shifted down to his knees and straddled her, careful at first to not actually touch her. His body stretched out over hers, warm despite the slight chill in the air from the breeze. "How did he…"

She dragged her tongue over her lips. "He tried to pin my hands, but I scratched his face. I tried to throw him off, but he was too heavy. He wrapped a hand around my throat."

Olin nodded, then wrapped a hand around her wrist, his touch gentle. *Is he trembling?* He pinned that one beside her, then set his other on her throat, grip loose.

It made her heart speed, but amazingly, not from fear. Was it because that guy hadn't been her big-bad-monster, or was it because it was Olin above her?

She wasn't sure, but the things he woke in her sure weren't fear…

"Try to throw me off. Don't worry, you won't hurt me, so give it your all."

Kat nodded and shifted as she had with the other man, trying to unbalance him. She got no farther than she had before. "You're too strong," she whispered.

"It's not all about size or strength. Why did you scratch him?"

"Because it's all I could think of."

"You have blunt little nails, Kat. Despite your name, you don't have claws. You want to know one reason women don't do better in fights? Because they hold back. I don't know why. Maybe it's because they're raised to be humble and meek or maybe it's something else, but I've seen it during every self-defense class I've taken or taught. A woman pulls her hits—she slaps instead of punches or scratches a cheek instead of jamming into an eye. I'm not judging you—just explaining the problem. If you're going to fight, you need to do it like it matters, like your life depends on it, because it just might."

Kat fought the shiver that wanted to run through her, trying to listen to Olin's words despite the way his body pressed more against hers with each second. "So what should I have done?"

"What is your instinct when I do this?" He tightened his hand a fraction, not enough to cut off her air but enough to make her react.

Kat responded without thinking, her hand wrapping around his wrist to pull.

Olin instantly loosened again. "That's right—instinct says to get that hand off your throat. The problem? It's damn hard to get someone to release a grip if you go for their wrist. Instead, you've got to think it through. Sensitive places on a body—eyes, nose, stomach, groin. Solar plexus is good, but you have to know what you're doing there, so it's better to wait for that one."

"But the hand is the issue."

"Yeah, but unless someone is trained extremely well, trust me, you break a nose and they're not going to keep their grip. The nose and eyes are great because they'll both blind a person. Someone in pain who can't see stops being much of a threat."

Kat nodded, then jerked her head forward.

Olin yanked backward enough to miss the strike, which made Kat's cheeks flush. She hadn't even thought about it, but if he hadn't moved, she'd have definitely hurt him.

His laugh said he wasn't angry. "That a girl. If I wasn't expecting that, you'd have just broken my nose. Between the bleeding and my eyes watering, you would have just given yourself a hell of an advantage. Now, women have most of their strength in their legs, so make sure you use that to your advantage."

"You're pinning my legs."

"Yep, I am. So your goals are to distract me — forehead to the nose works for that — then, when I pull back to regroup, your goal is to get your legs into the fight. Remember, no pulling punches here. Let's try again."

When Kat nodded, Olin reset, grabbing her wrist more roughly than the last time before setting his hand on her throat again. Kat swung her head up, and even though Olin dodged, he responded as if she'd landed the hit.

He yanked backward, releasing her to clutch his nose as he sat up. Kat twisted, but with his weight, she couldn't squirm enough to knock him off. His body straddled her just over her stomach.

Legs, right. She thanked goodness for her flexibility as she planted one foot on the ground, then brought the other up to hook around his side and yanked him backward.

The whoosh of his air leaving him screamed that the move had surprised him. He'd probably expected her to keep trying to knock him off, so he'd braced himself not to fall forward or to the side, but he hadn't expected her to pull him *back.*

He toppled, and Kat twisted while he tried to right himself. She was quicker, though. Smaller bodies were a lot easier to move than larger ones, and the speed gave her another boost of confidence. She brought her foot back and tapped his side, a grin on her face before she set the foot on his chest.

Olin didn't look mad as he lay in the dirt beneath her—hell, he looked proud.

And more than a little turned on if the heat in his gaze meant anything.

"Nicely done," he said.

"Maybe I'll find someone to give me a better challenge next time—" Kat's smart-ass remark was cut off with a yelp when he grabbed her foot and yanked.

Kat fell forward, but she didn't hit the ground. She ended up on top of Olin for only a moment before he rolled them again, pinning her beneath him in a way that felt *nothing* like what had happened before.

He stared down at her, the gaze of a man who knew exactly what he wanted. And, given the way his hard cock pressed against her through his jeans, she'd guess it was on board with the plan.

"That was a good job," he said as he slid his fingers into her hair to hold tight, to keep her gaze on his. "I knew you had it in you."

His praise warmed her, made her walk that line between behaving to hear more of it and being a brat.

As usual, the brat won out. "Well, when you make it so easy..."

His grin widened, his chest rising and falling quickly as if he were out of breath. "That mouth of yours is going to get you into trouble."

"From you? I doubt it."

"You think? Because I could easily turn you over right here and spank that ass of yours until you can't come up with a single quip."

She wanted to act unaffected, but the moan she let out at that gave her away. Still… "So do it."

His eyes widened, as if he'd just realized what had come out of his mouth—and that she was on board. "What?"

"Don't make promises you can't keep. If you think you can get me to behave, try it." She wanted the words to sound like a threat, like a challenge, but she was pretty sure they came out a plea.

He blinked slowly then moved his gaze to where his fingers wrapped in her hair. He yanked backward, then moved off her.

"Wait!" Kat called out, sure he was going to turn around and walk away, and she didn't want things to sit like this.

"I *can't*," he said without turning around.

"Why not? You're here, you're taking care of me, you said you were too close to me to work the case, so why not?"

"I'm not like this."

"The way you were just grinding against me says that's not true. You want this, too. Just admit it!"

He let out a growl of frustration then turned back toward her. "Of *course* I want you! Wanting things doesn't make them possible, though."

"Who's the coward, now? What are you hiding behind? What are you so afraid of?"

"I almost lost *everything* the last time I did this!"

That made her frown as she sat up. "What are you talking about?"

Olin rubbed his hands over his face then all but collapsed to a sitting position in front of her, the dust flying up around them. "You know I used to go to Sanctuary. Well, let's just say that my boss found out.

The idea that one of their detectives was tying girls up in a sex club and leaving marks didn't go over well."

"What? That's crazy…"

"Maybe, but it is what it is. I ended up demoted and was on a probation period for almost a year. I damn near lost my job over it. So, no, I can't do that again, I can't risk that again."

"How did they even find out?"

"No idea. My boss isn't the sort to go there, but the world is a lot smaller than we like to think."

"But what if—"

He shook his head. "Even if I just played privately, not at a club, it would just hurt too much. I'd just think about what I want that I can't have, and you'd never be happy with the fact I'd never be able to go to Sanctuary, that I couldn't be a part of your world there."

She opened her mouth to say that wasn't true, but the words wouldn't come. Him just watching that time had been difficult enough—could she really be happy if he just never went? If he never touched her there? If what that became a dirty secret between them?

No… He was right. Kat wouldn't be content with them having to hide in that way.

Olin let out a rough laugh that brought her gaze back to his. "It wasn't as hard to leave as you might think. I didn't have anything serious with anyone, didn't really miss it that much, all things considered. Even in the years since, when I've missed that, when something's been missing in any relationship I've tried, I've never regretted it until now."

"Now?"

He offered her a crooked smile that melted her. "You're the first girl who makes me wonder if the risk could be worth it, who could tempt me to just fuck it and give in."

On the heels of that hope, however, Olin's next words dashed it all.

"But I can't do that. No matter how badly I want you—how much I want *this*—I can't go down that road again."

His quiet *sorry* was the last thing he said before he retreated yet again, leaving her alone like he always did, and Kat sighed.

Maybe there were some problems that just had no solution...

* * * *

Dean sat at the table across from Olin. The sun had started to set, but Kat was still outside. The property had enough cameras for them to easily spot where she was, and no doubt she needed some time alone.

It had been three days there together, and they'd all finally fallen into a routine. Bradley worked the most, up early and working until dinner, but he never failed to arrive back at the house with a sense of contentment.

Dean understood that. It was what his job did for him as well. It gave him a sense of worth, a feeling that he had a place in a hectic and ever moving world.

He'd had to push off some of his own cases to his colleagues, but most of it he'd been able to work remotely with. It let him stay there with Kat and the others for as long as he needed to.

"Anything new?" Dean asked.

Olin shook his head. "Newest body is like the others. Jerry is covering his ass well."

"Why? We already have him dead to rights on abducting Ell and Kat. Why be so careful now?"

"Because the manpower used to track down some gang leader who kidnapped two women but didn't kill them is a lot different from the heat that comes down on a serial killer. If he can keep his nose clean on these charges, he won't get found so fast."

Dean sighed, the answer expected but still frustrating. They *knew* exactly who was behind this, but without knowing where he was, without proof, there wasn't much they could do.

"How's Kat doing?" Dean asked.

"As well as can be expected. The girl is resilient."

"That she is. Damn shame that she needs to be."

Olin nodded as if he agreed. Knowing someone was tough was one thing, but no doubt they'd both rather she didn't have to go through this all.

"About you and her…"

"Stop that right there," Olin said when Dean trailed off. "There is no she and I."

"So you move in with every case you have?" Dean offered a grin. "Or actually, move in with every ex-case you have?"

Olin averted his gaze, as if to hide whatever he was thinking. Fine with Dean—all his time learning to read people made it a fun game for him.

"I know Kat's a lot, but that look in your face says you don't mind it much," Dean said.

"Why are you even asking? Clearly, you're interested, so it seems pretty stupid to be shoving other men onto her."

Dean waved off the question. "I'm not a jealous man. Besides, Kat's enough trouble that she *needs* a few men to keep her in check."

And it wasn't like Dean was the staying type, no matter how much Kat made him wish he were. Just remembering how she'd fit into his arms when they'd fallen asleep made his chest ache, made him want to try that again even if he knew it was a pointless wish.

Dean kept things casual for good reason — no reason to go fucking that up now.

"Well, seeing as we're both staying here with her and Bradley, maybe it's a pointless conversation to have anyway."

"Making decisions for me now?" *Speaking of...*

Bradley walked in through the kitchen door, then stopped by the sink to wash his hands as if he hadn't just interrupted their private conversation.

"Were your ears burning?" Dean asked with a grin.

Bradley dried his hands on the towel hanging off the handle of the oven before turning toward them. "Nah. Kat's reading down by the barn so I figured it was as good a time as any for the three of us to actually have a talk."

Because that wasn't awkward at all... The reality was that while Dean had no idea what his relationship with Kat was — or any of the others — they all had something between them. What did that mean?

"Never figured you for the talking type," Dean said.

"I'm not the 'ignore shit until it comes down to a fist fight' type either." Bradley crossed his arms as he leaned against the kitchen counter, staring at Olin and Dean. "So, what's the plan?"

Dean didn't answer, unsure what to say.

Olin spoke up instead. "What plan? I've already said, I'm not getting involved."

"From what I saw of your little self-defense lesson, you're already involved."

"That was—"

"Self-defense doesn't normally involve grinding against someone," Bradley said without any inflection in his voice.

Dean chuckled at the way Bradley laid it out, the bluntness. It was hard to dislike someone that direct—at least when he was using it against someone else.

Olin cursed softly. "Fine—not like it isn't obvious I like her. I'm just here to protect her, though. That's it."

"You figure you say that enough and it'll be true?" Bradley asked.

"It's got to be true." Olin turned his gaze on Dean. "But since we're deciding to dig into personal lives here, what about you?"

"What about me?" Dean set a hand on his chest as if he had no idea what they were talking about.

Bradley sighed loudly enough for both Dean and Olin to turn their gazes that way. "You two are ridiculous, you know that? And I thought Kat was hard to deal with."

Dean wanted to argue that, but it was true.

Still, he shrugged and answered as honestly as he knew how to. "I like her, but fuck knows that's as far as it goes. I'm not a relationship type of guy. She deserves a lot more than I've got to give."

Even as he spoke, he recalled the way she'd clung to him that night, the way her lips had tasted, the sound of her little moans. It wouldn't be terrible to wake up beside her and—

He cut off his thoughts before they went any farther.

"I've told her I'm not interested in anything long term or serious. If she's cool with that, then I've got no problem indulging in any fun. I'm also not someone who minds sharing. What about you?" Dean asked Bradley.

"Kat and I have a lot of history. Never figured I'd have her here, and sure as fuck never figured I'd have the two of you here, but so long as we are?" He shrugged then tucked his thumbs into the belt loops of his jeans. "I've wrangled some wily horses before, and one thing I learned is that it's a hell of a lot easier to do it with a few extra bodies."

Dean couldn't stop his laugh at the explanation, at the way Bradley connected it to horses when they were talking about the three of them sleeping with the same woman. He'd bet if Bradley tried that analogy with Kat, she'd be the one to geld *him*.

"So, that settles it?" Dean asked, glancing between the other men.

It seemed none of them knew exactly what they wanted, or where any of it would go, but at least they'd come to some sort of understanding.

That understanding being that they didn't mind sharing the feisty brat that they'd all fallen for. Hell, maybe between the three of their sorry asses, they might just make one decent man...

Chapter Twelve

Kat stared at the large horse who moved through the fenced-off area. It had been a couple days since arriving at Bradley's ranch but she hadn't gathered the courage to actually interact with the larger animals.

This horse had drawn her, though, and she'd sketched it out there as she watched it gallop around. It bucked, flinging its back legs out, having itself a great time.

"Figures you'd like this one." Bradley's rough voice surprised her, since he'd mostly avoided her.

Kat twisted to look over her shoulder, finding him standing there, his arms crossed. He looked so much more at home there on the farm than he had anywhere else. It was as if he finally fit in, that rough masculinity he carried so easily matching his surroundings and a sense of confidence. "It looks like it's having fun."

Bradley leaned against the fence, then crooked his fingers at Kat. "She, not it."

Kat rose from the ground, leaving her closed sketch book behind as she went to stand beside Bradley. "She, huh?"

"Yep. Most difficult horse I've ever owned. Has a mind of her own and likes to do her own thing."

Kat chuckled at that. "Seems she and I have a few things in common. Makes me wonder why you keep her around."

Bradley lifted his eyebrow but kept his gaze on the horse. "Easy never meant much to me. She's feisty, sure, but that doesn't make her worthless."

"You're the only one who thinks that."

He clicked his tongue, and the horse trotted closer, though not all at once, as if she wasn't willing to give in too fast. "I learned a long time ago that obedient doesn't always make for the best animals. Had a dog before who listened to every word I said. People kept saying he was the perfect pet, so obedient, so submissive."

"Sounds like what everyone wants." Kat ignored the pain in her chest at that, at the reality. How many Doms had decided she was too much work? How often in her life had people turned away from her because she wasn't meek and quiet?

"Maybe, but then a pack of feral dogs attacked — this pack that had been running the desert a while. They went after the goats, and that dog, it was supposed to sound the alarm and protect the livestock." Bradley shook his head. "Turns out beasts who are too timid don't make for the best guards. Lost more than a couple goats that night."

Kat frowned as she tried to make sense of his meaning.

Bradley let out a rare chuckle after giving her a side-eye. "Don't get it, huh? If I wanted easy, I'd never have lasted a single day with you. I kept that mare because I know that the best of anything isn't always easy, isn't always comfortable, but maybe that's what makes 'em worth it."

The horse came over the rest of the way, pushing her face against Bradley's open palm.

His expression held fondness as he petted the large horse, a smile making his face seem softer than usual.

"But what about when you get sick of that? When you decide that someone who isn't always testing you is better?"

He wrapped his other arm around Kat, pulling her to his side so she could reach through the fence to pet the horse as well. Despite a snort, as if a token protest, the mare accepted her touch with ease. "Every damn day makes me laugh. I don't think I ever realized just how boring life can be until you have someone interesting in it, you know?"

She stole a glance at Bradley's face, but found that instead of staring at the horse, he was staring right at her... It made her chest tight, made her head spin.

He leaned in, brushing his lips against hers with a surprisingly gentle kiss, as though he were trying to explain something with the touch. Whatever it was, Kat didn't get it. Maybe because she refused to, because understanding was too dangerous, so she just accepted the kiss and returned it, unsure.

The horse trotted away, as though they'd grown boring and she planned to go find better things to do. It left Kat there with Bradley, the moment surprisingly sweet.

He pulled away too fast, long before Kat had her fill of his lips or his touch or his taste. He grinned at whatever he saw on her face, and that only made Kat thankful for the setting sun—it should help to hide the blush she was *sure* was on her cheeks.

"I'll see you inside," he said. "You and Brat can hang out a while longer if you want."

"Brat?"

Bradley chuckled as he walked away, speaking without turning back toward her. "Named her after another difficult female I know. Like I said, fitting you two started to get along."

Kat watched him go, the horse's name ringing in her ears. Brat…like Kat? Bradley had named the horse after her?

Something warm sprang up inside her, but it only frightened Kat. Bradley had said such sweet things, but sweet words never lasted all that long. The truth was that Bradley would get sick of her eventually—she'd learned that everyone did, that they all had their limits, that no one could tolerate her for long.

So that warmth inside her, that voice whispering that maybe there was some happily ever after for her felt like nothing more than a cruel joke.

And Kat wasn't sure she could handle getting to the punchline of it.

* * * *

Dean frowned as he walked through the house, checking on everyone. It was a holdover from his youth, a habit formed from living in places where he never knew if he was safe.

Hell, it had taken him years to be able to sleep more than an hour or so at a time.

Still, he found each time he woke, he couldn't fall back asleep until he checked the doors and windows, until he knew the house was secure.

Which meant he found himself doing so around three in the morning.

He didn't even curse himself for the behavior anymore. What was the point? It was just a part of him, just a ritual he had to do to feel comfortable.

And…of course…he couldn't deny the need might have grown a bit since sleeping not so far from Kat. Before his big point had always been to ensure his own safety, but now? Now he felt the need to check on that frustrating woman, to know she was safe and sleeping well.

Except, when he peeked into her open door, he found her bed empty. A moment of panic hit him, the thoughts of what could have happened to her, of where she could have gone swirling in his head.

Before the panic could take him entirely, however, the sound of water from her private bathroom eased him.

Though… a shower at this time wasn't normal behavior either. He stood there for a moment, wondering if he should just let her be. Maybe he should turn around and take his ass back to bed. She was fine, and if she wanted to shower in the middle of the night, what business of his was that?

Except, his feet wouldn't move. A quick glare at them didn't help—it seemed at least a part of him refused to leave without ensuring she was okay.

He cursed himself as he went into the room and knocked softly on the door.

No answer.

He tried once more, louder, before figuring she couldn't hear him above the water. He twisted the handle and opened the door, met with a blast of steam that said she'd turned the water far too hot.

The clear glass of the shower had fogged up, turning Kat into a silhouette, but he could still make out the generalities. She stood there, one hand against the tile of the shower, the other covering her face. Her shoulders didn't shake, didn't show signs of tears, but the exhaustion that hung on her was obvious.

Poor girl... Dean considered all the times she'd said she was fine, that there were no problems, that nothing had happened. He didn't believe her, of course, but he couldn't deny some amount of respect for holding up that front for as long as she had.

There was no doubt she was suffering, trying so hard to keep it to herself that she would run herself ragged just for the chance to keep up pretenses.

And Dean had grown tired of it. He was sick of seeing her fall apart, of seeing her let herself get weaker, more run down, all for what?

He slid his pajama bottoms off, the action leaving him nude, then opened the door to the shower.

The squeaking of the hinges alerted Kat, because she twisted so fast she was lucky not to slip. Still, those wide eyes narrowed when she spotted him.

Annoyance is better than panic, right?

"What are you doing here?" she asked, a quiver to her voice telling her she wasn't quite holding it all together.

"Look, some of us care about the environment. Taking long showers alone makes Mother Earth cry." He offered her a smile like some consolation prize, the joke stupid but better than the truth.

She glared at him but didn't argue. At least, she didn't until he dropped his gaze down her front, the first time he saw what Jerry had actually done to her.

And the pain in his own chest hit him hard enough he had to fight to keep his face blank. She had one long cut that went from the center of her breasts down, over her stomach, and to her pubic bone. He'd seen the bottom of it before, but not the entirety, not the truth of it. There were a few other cuts, none as long or deep as the largest.

Kat dropped her gaze, shame coloring those gray eyes of hers and breaking his heart. She went to turn, to hide, but Dean refused to let her.

He caught her arm, keeping her facing him. "Don't hide."

She opened her mouth as though she were going to argue with him, but Dean didn't want to let her gather her wits, to create distance between them, not right then when he felt so raw, so he silenced her with a gentle kiss.

Kat melted, as if his kiss could do something the hot water hadn't.

"Couldn't sleep?" he asked.

She shook her head.

"Well, showers are for cleaning, baths are for relaxing. Come on, let's run one."

She nibbled at her bottom lip, the action so innocent that he could have groaned. "Together?"

Dean chuckled, amused that she could be so damned shy after everything they'd done. It was one of those times when he felt like he was getting a rare glimpse, something few others saw, and something he'd treasure. "Remember what I said? The environment?"

She chuckled as he stepped out of the shower and ran water in the large clawfoot tub. "So you're just an activist, huh?"

"That's right. I'm a very passionate man, you know?"

"About the environment?"

Dean offered her a devastating grin, one he knew was full of desire. "About a lot of things."

Kat didn't know why she felt so nervous. Dean had seen all of her already, had been *inside* her, so what was with the anxiety running through her?

She'd walked around damned near naked at Sanctuary, so it wasn't like there was much modesty left inside her.

The reasons didn't change the reality, though, and Kat couldn't deny her anxiety as she sank into the large bathtub, Dean already in and behind her. She expected to keep her distance, to sit at the other side, but Dean had other plans. He grasped her hips as she sat and pulled her toward him, so her back rested against his chest, so she was pressed tight to him.

The water and bubbles soothed her tired muscles, the ones sore from her self-defense training and her general lack of self-care. She wasn't sure she'd ever actually bathed with a man before, but she had to admit...

It was sort of nice.

Dean had a way about him that eased her, that took her defenses down.

"Nightmare?" Dean asked softly, the lights lowered in the room, giving the place a frighteningly romantic feel.

She nodded before she could think better of it, her tongue loosened from the heat of the water and Dean's strong body. "Thought a shower might…I don't know, wash it away?"

He wrapped his arms around her from behind, the action surprisingly welcome. "Nightmares happen. It's a part of life."

"A shitty part of life."

His huff of a laugh blew warm air over her neck. "Maybe. I think it's just the brain's way of coming to terms with something, of figuring it out."

"You don't strike me as a nightmares sort of man. Not sure you get to have an opinion."

His arms tensed around her for a moment, and it took a while for him to respond. When he did, his voice was uncharacteristically quiet. "You'd be surprised. I've had my share of nightmares. How do you think I knew a bath was better than a shower to soothe them?"

She wanted to turn, to look at his face as he spoke, but she also knew there wasn't a chance at that. There was this quiet tension between them, as if they both had things they didn't want to say but maybe needed to? It was a tightrope to balance across, and Kat had to admit, she didn't want to have to stare into Dean's face when admitting to her own secrets.

So she didn't turn, and instead wrapped her hands around his and squeezed softly, encouraging him to go at his own pace.

"You know, no one else could ever get me to open my stupid mouth like this. What is it about you?" He must not have wanted an answer to that, because he kept speaking. "You know a bit about Ell's past, right?"

"She grew up in foster care."

"That's right. Well, so did I. It wasn't what you'd call a good childhood."

His words sent a shiver through her, the simplicity of them, the truth of them. She'd heard a bit from Ell, about the uncertainty, the fear she'd had as she'd been sent from one bad home to another. While she'd known Dean had been friends with Ell from childhood, she'd somehow not realized what exactly that meant, hadn't thought about how that might mean Dean had suffered similarly.

"Your tattoos..." She paused, recalling the way his sharp tone had told her to leave the topic alone the last time she'd seen him shirtless.

"Ell survived by keeping her head down for the most part. Me? Guess I wasn't ever as smart. I figured I preferred to be the person with the power instead of being stepped on. Ended up in a few groups Olin would have loved to dismantle."

Kat tried to picture Dean—the perfect image of sophistication—being some sort of wannabe gangster who was running around in a gang and causing trouble. "I can't picture that," Kat admitted.

"I was a different person then. When people are trying to survive, they'll do things they never thought they were capable of."

"What happened?"

"I figured out eventually that I didn't want to be that person."

"Eventually?" Clearly, there was a story behind that word, something he didn't want to admit to. People didn't just change for no reason.

He stroked one hand over her arm, the touch absent-minded as if he needed the contact. "I got a call from Ell. She was having problems with the son of a foster parent, a boy who refused to take no for an answer and kept harassing her. I was in the middle of a...job." He forced that word from his throat as if it were poison. "I dropped everything to go help her, but when I showed up? I had blood on my hands. Actual fucking blood there, and I scared off the boy, made it clear what would happen if he ever so much as looked at her wrong again."

"So you saved her?"

"I guess. The thing is, I stood there, and I realized that I wasn't any better than that boy. Ell didn't know it, hadn't seen it, didn't have any idea the sorts of things I did when I wasn't around her, but I just kept thinking if she did...she'd look at me with that same fear." His fingers trembled as she stroked across the bare, wet skin of her arm. "I never wanted that, so I got out of that life. I got serious at school, passed my classes, focused on my future, put myself through law school so I could be someone different. These tattoos, I hate them. They're a reminder of who I was." His voice dropped so low, Kat struggled to hear the next part over her breathing and the movement of the water in the tub. "Of who I really am."

That broke her heart, the self-hatred in those words, the fear. Kat shifted, turning so she could see his face even in the dim room. He let her, and she straddled his waist then set her hands on his cheeks. "You're not who you think you are."

"No? Can you really say that when you have no idea what I've done?"

"Yeah, I can. I know who you are now, and who a person is, deep down, that doesn't change." She took one of her hands and dragged her fingers over one of the tattoos on his chest as she spoke. "These are just a part of your past, part of what you had to do so you could get here."

She jumped when his fingers moved over the mark on her chest.

"You want to maybe tell yourself the same thing?"

His point was clear — and a good one — but harder to accept. Still, Kat didn't argue it right away, didn't want to lose the quiet moment with Dean, one where he seemed so unguarded. Instead, she leaned in to kiss him, his fingers still dancing over the tattoos he seemed to so hate.

Still, he spoke softly between the kisses. "I don't know how you feel about these exactly, but I can guess you hate them. I get it, but, Kat, they're proof you lived, that you survived, that you're still breathing and going and that he didn't win."

"I didn't win yet, either," Kat said.

Dean broke the kiss to stare into her eyes, the moment almost painfully honest between them. "My money's on you, every damned time."

Between the nightmare and her exhaustion, Kat let Dean's words soak into her. She didn't think she could accept them, didn't think she believed them, but for tonight? For tonight she didn't mind pretending at all.

Chapter Thirteen

Kat bit her lip softly as she stared in the mirror. The truth was, she was *bored.* No matter how much she tried to fill her days, she couldn't stop this horrible sensation of one minute bleeding into the next until the day was just over.

The men tried to entertain her, made sure she had books and everything else she could want available, but nothing worked.

And Kat figured out why easily enough.

It wasn't normal boredom. It was *that* sort of ache, the one deep inside her when she wanted to push boundaries, when she wanted to play.

Bradley was so busy with the ranch and Dean worked constantly and Olin seemed to give her space that she didn't actually need nor want. Basically?

She wanted attention and was not getting it.

Which was the point of her little plan.

She grinned, feeling a bit like her old self, before she headed into the kitchen for some fun. She had started dinner in a slow cooker that morning.

Kat didn't mind cooking, and given the fact she hadn't had much to do, she'd taken over a lot of it after Dean had ordered food each night the first week or so. A hearty beef soup currently simmered in the slow cooker, filling the house with a delicious scent.

The men filed into the kitchen around six at night, though Bradley showed up slightly earlier to jump in the shower before sitting down at the table. The action made her laugh and wonder if his mother's voice played in his head.

"Smells great," Olin said as he took a seat at the large, country style table.

"Your cooking beats takeout, that's for sure," Dean agreed.

"Need any help?" Bradley asked as he peered toward the kitchen.

"Nope," Kat said cheerfully. "I've got it!"

Bradley narrowed his eyes, as if he could tell just by that response that she was up to something. Then again, he knew her pretty well...

His suspicion only made her all the more excited, however. What fun was bratting when no one expected or knew how to deal with it? One of her favorite parts was when someone watched her like that, when they were just *waiting* to see what she'd pull next.

Which they were about to find out.

Kat balanced three bowls in her arms, the work easy after having waitressed to put herself through school. She set them in front of each of the men with the flourishes of some butler in a movie. "Oh, silverware!" she said as though she'd forgotten it entirely.

She returned to the kitchen, grabbed the items, then set them down in front of each man.

"A fork?" Bradley asked, his dark eyebrow raised.

Dean snorted but picked up the fork and used it to spear a piece of meat.

Olin said nothing, just watching Kat as if he wasn't sure where it would go.

"Silly me," Kat said with a grin, as though it was an absurd mistake. She went back into the kitchen to grab the next item.

"Kat…" Bradley said, his tone full of warning.

A warning Kat would *not* be listening to, of course.

Instead, she handed out the tiny baby spoons she'd found in Bradley's pantry — probably a holdover from having his nieces and nephews visit. Kat hadn't wondered too hard — she counted it as great luck.

Smiling as if she were being the most helpful person in the world, Kat sat at the table at her spot.

Dean's lips were quirked into a grin still, though Olin and Bradley looked *far* less amused by the whole thing. Which was just perfect for her. In fact, she found she enjoyed the way they reacted differently.

Sometimes behaving as she did got exhausting when the Dom either seemed angry all the time or when she couldn't get a rise out of another. With the three men there, they all reacted differently.

Dean appeared pleased by it all, Olin seemed confused but oddly charmed and Bradley just seemed ready to put her in her place.

Which she really wanted them to do.

"You never change," Bradley muttered before using the fork as Dean had. It seemed he wasn't willing to play just yet.

Which was fine by Kat. She didn't mind pushing boundaries. Hell, if Bradley had reacted too soon, she'd have missed out on more of her planned fun.

"Problems?" Kat asked, giving Bradley her brightest smile. "Is the spoon too difficult? That's why I figured a baby spoon would work well for you—for practice!"

Dean snickered, earning a glare from Bradley.

"Don't encourage her. She'll just get worse," Bradley snapped.

"You can't deny that dinner gets boring. She's just looking for some fun." The way Dean spoke made Kat's smile falter for a moment, the way he seemed to see beneath her behavior to a cause that was more than just 'being difficult.'

Bradley pointed his fork at the other man. "Look, I've known her a long time. If you laugh, she'll just take it as a challenge to do something worse the next time."

"So what did you do before?"

"Either ignored it or tried to spank it out of her."

"And how did that work out?" Dean lifted his dark eyebrow, amusement dancing in his eyes.

Bradley didn't answer, dropping his gaze to his bowl. The meaning was clear. Ignoring her or trying to correct the behavior hadn't ever worked that well.

Still, Kat didn't want them fighting with each other. She'd much rather all that annoyance directed at her.

She rose from her seat. "I totally forgot about the rolls!" As she headed for the kitchen, she *accidentally* dropped her spoon. When she bent down, she ensured to do it slowly, reaching for the spoon and taking her sweet time to do it.

A breeze against her bare skin and the groan of one of the men behind her made her heart race, but she straightened up and headed for the kitchen. As soon as she went into it, she tried to breathe slowly, to stop her racing pulse.

Why did this excite her so much?

Because she was desperate for these games again, because she had no idea how to ask for anything which meant she had to do this to hope to get what she wanted.

And by this, she meant annoying the hell out of the three men at the table and making sure to bend over when wearing a short skirt with no panties, the idea from the filthy things Dean had whispered to her before.

And yet, amazingly, none of them had moved. It excited her, made her want to see how far she could push this before one—or hopefully all three of them— gave in. She grabbed the platter with rolls on it and brought it out, met with Bradley's dark, predatory gaze that nearly made her trip.

Head in the game, Kat. She smiled as she set the rolls down on the center of the table, then took her seat again.

"This isn't going to go well for you," Bradley said.

"What isn't? Is the food not good?" She tried for innocent but knew damned well she'd never managed that worth a damn.

Bradley pointed his fork at her. "You should think *very* carefully exactly how far you want to push this. You're approaching a line you can't walk back from."

Kat swallowed hard and met his gaze. He was trying to warn her off, trying to tell her that maybe it was a fire that would burn her, but she didn't give a damn. She ran her tongue along her bottom lip. "Make me," she whispered.

"What?" His tone made her glad she was sitting again, because she doubted her knees would hold her.

"I said make me. There are three of you, right? Maybe the odds are finally in your favor."

A glance around the table made her hesitate for just a moment, made her wonder what the hell she was thinking. All that confidence she'd had before melted away under the intensity of the three men's looks.

She was playing with predators and Kat knew she wanted nothing more than to watch them snap.

And judging from the way a smirk crossed Bradley's lips, she was about to get bit...

Why do I like this so much?

Bradley couldn't shake the feeling he shouldn't be so damned happy about Kat's defiance. He should hate it, should want her to listen, to be a good girl. If he'd have said what he wanted when he was younger, he'd have sworn he wanted an obedient submissive, one whose main joy was in serving her Dom and being protected by them.

So what was it about Kat that made that all go out the window? Her whispered "*make me*" spread across his skin like a fire, heating him up and making him want to rise to that occasion.

The more she fought, the more she misbehaved, the more desperate he was to make her listen, to see that moment she truly gave in and melted beneath his demands.

It had drawn him in before, had made him fall for her. There was a strength inside her, one he'd wanted from the first time he'd met her in Sanctuary, back when her mischievous smile had drawn him in.

Jayce Carter

Right now was no different, as Kat sat at the table, wearing a shirt that was tighter and thinner than was even close to appropriate and a short skirt that he damned well knew had nothing on under it. The girl might drive him crazy, but she sure as hell knew *exactly* how to wind him up, too.

He rose from the table and collected the bowls of food without a word, taking the items into the kitchen. It took him a minute, and he allowed Kat to stew, to worry, to wonder what would happen. No doubt each second that passed increased the tension inside her.

Good. With a woman like Kat, he needed to use every trick he had access to.

When he returned, Dean nodded, a sure sign the other man was on board. Then again, it was hard to turn down or walk away from Kat.

Olin, however, said nothing. He sat there still, staring at her, seemingly undecided if he wanted to join in or not.

How he'd resisted at Sanctuary, Bradley still had no damned idea. Olin had a lot more self-discipline than Bradley did, that was for sure.

After the entire table was clear, Bradley walked over to Kat. He grasped her chin and tugged her to her feet. It brought those gray eyes closer to his, and the flush on her cheeks went straight to his cock. He wanted to see those defiant eyes of hers go soft, wanted to taste the moment she gave in, the moment she offered up her everything to him.

"You really are trouble," he said, the amount of affection in his own words surprising.

She swallowed in an audible gulp. "Or maybe you're just not strong enough to deal with me."

"You really think that? Because we *both* know that I'm more than enough to deal with you, no matter how much you push me." Bradly kept his fingers on Kat's chin, kept her gaze locked to his, not giving her a moment of reprieve.

Dean rose and came over, sliding in behind Kat. She jerked when his fingers touched her, when he brushed against her thighs at the short hemline of her skirt.

"Be still," Bradley said, his tone sharp. "You wanted to wear something like this for a reaction, right? Well, you're going to get a reaction all right."

Dean's chuckle was dark and dangerous as he dipped his fingers beneath her skirt. "Is this what you were hoping for? You could have just asked if all you wanted was attention." Dean slid his tongue along Kat's earlobe before nipping at the lobe.

Kat let out a softest of moans, but a spark in her eyes said she wasn't ready to give in just yet. "I only ask when I'm pretty sure the person is capable of what I need. Asking you all to help me get off would be like asking a dog for help with my taxes."

Bradley snorted at the barb. No doubt other Doms might have gotten mad about it, might have gotten their egos bruised by Kat's harsh words, but he knew better. This was a test—it was Kat pushing because she couldn't not push.

And Bradley had no problem showing her exactly what he was capable of. He set a hand on her shoulder and pushed until she slid to her knees and *boy* had he missed the sight of those gray eyes of her staring up at him. It startled him so much that he paused for a moment, unsure how to continue, what else to say.

When Dean knelt behind her, however, it reminded him to pay attention.

Bradley undid the belt on his jeans, then opened the button and pulled down the zipper. He would have told her to do it, but she'd have just taken that as another way to argue, another thing to fight over. Kat was difficult tonight, and he didn't plan on giving her any more power than she thought she had.

He grasped his cock from his boxers and pulled it out, the chill of the air amazing on his heated skin.

It wasn't Bradley who slid a hand behind her head and pulled her in, though. Instead, Dean did that, grasping her hair in his fist and leaning in to whisper to her ear. "Be a good girl now and suck his cock, huh? I think you've caused this particular issue, so isn't it your job to deal with it?"

She opened her mouth, those red lips of hers parting to toss out a jab no doubt, but Dean took the chance to push her forward.

The heavenly warmth of her mouth enveloped him, even better when she made a sound of surprise muffled around his cock.

Still, despite her lack of warning, Kat was no slouch. She tightened her lips around his length and used her tongue to lavish attention, the sensation enough for him to shudder and groan.

"Look at that—she can behave." Dean laughed softly before reaching beneath her skirt again. She jerked, and even though Bradley couldn't see what exactly Dean was doing, he could guess. "Good girls get treats," Dean said, his voice low and smooth. "Next time you want attention, try being good from the start, hmm? Because if you'd have gone and dropped to your pretty knees and begged sweetly to suck his cock, I bet he'd have said yes. Play stupid games, get stupid prizes."

Dean's words had an immediate effect on Bradley, even. He groaned as the images mixed with the sweetness of Kat's mouth. He couldn't exactly picture Kat doing the things Dean said, so it wasn't that idea exactly that got him.

Instead, it was the knowledge that if Kat tried it, she'd have an ulterior motive. That excited him, the feeling of battle, the fact that Kat stood toe-to-toe with him. She wasn't some delicate submissive who did as she was told — no, Kat needed a man who would stand up to her, who could prove he could handle her.

And Bradley sure as hell wanted that job.

Dean moved behind Kat, reaching for his slacks to unbutton them. He scooted away just long enough to slide them off, to remove his boxers, then reach into his pocket. He opened a condom and put it on, the motion quick and practiced as if he couldn't stand the idea of waiting another moment before sinking into Kat's heat.

Which Bradley understood. Something about Kat's passion, her defiance and her strength could turn any man impatient.

She made a filthy sound around Bradley's cock when Dean returned, when he shifted Kat so she was on her knees then plunged into her cunt with a rough thrust. She caught herself by setting her hands on Bradley's hips, and why exactly did that excite him even more?

He'd never minded watching others, but he'd never been all that interested in it, either. At Sanctuary, he'd been the type to either participate or ignore most things — watching hadn't seemed worth it. So why was it that the sight of Kat being fucked by Dean turned Bradley on so much?

It should have been the opposite, shouldn't it? He should have some possessive anger at it, should want to punch the other man for enjoying Kat's pussy, should feel like growling out *mine* while knocking him away.

Yet, none of those feelings sprang up inside Bradley. If anything, he wanted to see more. He wanted to watch Kat come undone on Dean's cock, wanted to see Kat cry out as the other man fucked her, as he took her in every way imaginable.

It confused Bradley, but he shoved that worry aside. What did it matter right then?

He slid his fingers in Kat's hair and used the grip to control her movements, to force her to take as much of his cock as he wanted. Stealing even that little amount of control from her pleased him, made his cock twitch like some warning about him not lasting long.

But then again, who could blame him? Kat was plenty talented with her mouth, and she'd managed to wind him up with her little games as well. How could life be this much fun with this woman?

He pressed her in, rewarded when she gagged slightly, when wetness tracked down her cheek. She'd always had such pretty tears, the sort that made her eyes shine impossibly brighter.

Guess she takes all my control away, too.

He would have rather sat while she pleasured him, but the power he felt standing over her was worth the discomfort. There was something great about looking down at her, about seeing how small she looked trapped between them. It soothed that primal part of him that still wanted to take over his mate, wanted to own her, a holdover from back before humans thought themselves civilized. He felt like one of the animals on his ranch, something driven only by need and instinct.

And Kat was no different. She swirled her tongue around the head of his cock, her fingers digging into his hips, taking him deeper each time Dean slammed his dick into her and knocked her forward.

Bradley watched it all, not wanting to miss a damned second of it, not wanting to lose any of the moment. He'd learned the hard way that things don't last as long as he wanted them to, and he'd already lost her once. If she left again, he wanted to at least remember this.

"You sure are close," Dean said. "You like being used like this, don't you? You pushed us so we'd do this. Bet you wanted to get held down, get your thighs spread and fucked by all of us, huh?" His voice was rough, like he was near his end. Well, at least the end of round one.

Bradley had a feeling they'd end up indulging a few times before the night ended.

Kat nodded, even with Bradley's cock in her mouth. It was sexy in a way it shouldn't have been, and he struggled to hold off just a little longer.

Which was pretty much a losing battle.

He tightened his fingers in her hair until her scalp had to sting and her eyes opened, until they lifted to him. *Yes.* He liked those eyes on him, liked the way she looked at him as if he were her whole damned world in that moment.

He pulled back and out of her mouth, his grip keeping her from following her despite her trying. "Don't think so, Brat. You didn't just want to get fucked — you wanted to come, and you wanted to taste us, right? Good girls get what they want — bad girls get whatever we say."

She pouted, her bottom lip sticking out in an impossibly adorable way. Hell, he almost considered doing as she wanted before shaking his head to wake himself up.

"Mouth closed," he ordered.

Kat obeyed, despite that bottom lip still sticking out.

He wrapped the hand not in her hair around his cock and stroked himself. It wasn't as good as her mouth, but her saliva helped him glide smoothly and the sight of her waiting there, staring at him, was damn sexy. It was funny…he'd never given a damn about women all dressed up.

He couldn't care less about a sexy dress and well-done makeup. Instead, he liked *this*. He wanted to see a girl messy, to see her with tears on her cheeks and a flush to her skin. He wanted smudged lipstick and running mascara — the signs of a woman lost to pleasure.

Dean didn't stop or slow, fucking her hard, as if he couldn't help it. Each time he slammed home, she rocked forward despite the way she held Bradley's hips, and Bradley *loved* it.

It didn't take long before he felt his own release crashing through him.

"Close your eyes," he managed to order before coming, before painting her pretty face with his seed.

He milked each drop out, letting it fall to her cheeks, her nose, her chin. He avoided her lips and her eyes, but when a bit dripped down to her chest, he groaned.

As soon as he'd finished, Dean pulled from her. He moved fast, pulled the condom off and shifting around to stand where Bradley had been. The reason was clear when he stroked himself over her, letting his cum spill onto her breasts and throat.

She collapsed forward, so a little bit even finished onto her shoulder.

And Bradley couldn't believe just how deep that sight got to him.

He didn't think he could ever let her go again...

Kat gasped and shuddered, her body a mess of conflicting emotions. The warmth from their cum sat on her skin, but she hadn't gotten off. It meant her body still hummed with want.

But...that was part of what she loved. She liked pushing Doms, liked when they snapped, when they did as they wanted. She even loved the frustration inside her, the desire for more, the denial.

A hand on her arm pulled her to her feet, and she opened her eyes expecting to find Dean or Bradley there.

Instead, it was Olin. Before she could say anything, he took her lips in an aggressive kiss. It melted her, made her whine with impotent desire. It was as if he'd been holding back this whole time, and the passion there shocked her.

Despite thinking Olin *did* want her, he'd always been closed off, always careful.

It was why it shocked her when he moved her backward, when he set her onto the table. She hadn't realized he was naked, but when he pressed his cock, condom already on, into her, it made it clear.

Olin wasn't as long as Dean, but he was thicker. She savored the burn as her body adjusted, but Olin didn't give her any time. He leaned over her, then took her hands and pinned the to the table above her head. The wood of the table chilled her back, perfect against her heated skin.

"I was supposed to resist you," Olin muttered between the kisses he stole. "But it seems my control is far from perfect."

She'd expected him to be sweet and careful, but Olin didn't treat her that way. He didn't act as if she needed it, and perhaps that pleased her the most. Instead, Olin took her with hard, deep thrusts, filling her entirely before pulling back until he almost left her, then plunging in again. The rhythm was quick, and Kat wrapped her legs around him to keep from sliding away. She twisted her hands, that instinctual need to struggle from a restraint, but Olin couldn't be moved.

It was one of those times when she was reminded that despite his calm and easy going exterior, he was a cop, he was strong and he was a Dom. Being reminded of those things excited her.

He bit down on her bottom lip, the sting going right through her as if he'd touched her clit directly. The stickiness of Dean's and Bradley's cum rubbed between them, but Olin didn't seem to care a bit. Hell, given it had been on her face, she had trouble believing he hadn't tasted some as he'd kissed her.

It meant Olin was kinkier than she'd realized, and didn't that thrill her? He pinned her wrists with one hand, his other grasping her thigh as he had his way with her. The feelings Dean and Bradley had started inside her grew from her surprise, from finally feeling Olin, finally having him give in.

He broke the kiss, then licked her cheek. "You look good covered in cum, Kat. I never had a chance, did I? You've been wanting this, wanting me, so I expect you to come hard on my cock. Do you understand me?"

Kat nodded, but he pinched her thigh, making her gasp out the verbal response he probably wanted. "Yes, Sir."

He groaned and licked clean another spot on her cheek. "Good girl. I've been wanting this so badly, I won't last long, so you'd better hurry up. If I come before you, you'll lose out on the orgasm I *know* you want."

That added a delicious pressure to her, and actually pushed her toward the release she was desperate for. Each place Olin touched her drove her mad—the grip of his hand on her wrist, the way he held her thigh, his strong body stretched out over her.

Kat came with a cry that Olin swallowed as he kissed her. He groaned against her lips, and the jerk of his cock made Kat twist beneath him, the sensation too much on her exhausted body. It took a long moment when he rocked his hips forward in tiny motions before he withdrew, releasing her hip to grasp his condom.

Kat let her thighs lie open, too tired to even think about covering up, to give a damn about modesty. This had been *everything* she'd wanted. She was content, ready to curl up with the men and close her eyes.

Except, it seemed she was the only one who felt that way.

When something touched her sensitive pussy, she gasped and tried to snap her thighs shut. In front of her stood Dean, his lips pulled into a smirk as he stroked along her slit. "Oh, you think you're done? You wanted to play this game with us, so we're playing." His smile sent shivers through her body. "And we're going to play just as long as we want."

The promise sank into Kat, and she doubted Dean had any idea just how much it meant to her, how tempting it was. For a girl who was used to people leaving her, Dean's words made her pretend that he meant it, that they'd stay finally, that she wouldn't be alone anymore.

She knew it wasn't true, but right then? She let herself pretend.

Chapter Fourteen

Kat washed dishes as she stood in the kitchen, swaying to the music that poured through her headphones. Bradley and Olin were outside and Dean was locked in his room working, which left Kat bored.

She'd already spent time painting that morning, working on the large piece she'd started days before. By noon, however, her hands had started to ache from holding the paintbrush so she'd called it quits.

No one expected her to clean up, and each of the men chipped in, but Kat didn't mind taking care of the kitchen. It felt nice to lose herself in the music and the familiar motions.

At least, that was until her phone started to ring. She sighed and paused the music, then turned off her headphones.

"Hello?" she answered, putting her phone to her ear.

"Come out, come out, wherever you are."

Kat froze, as if the voice on the line were in the house with her, like he could snatch her through the phone. It was instinctual, and no matter how much she hated it, she couldn't keep herself from doing it. Even though she told herself she shouldn't be afraid of him, something about his voice took her back to the helplessness she felt in that hotel room.

"Stunned to silence? Really, Katherine, you should have more respect for me than that. Before you get your hopes up, the phone I'm using to call you from won't be used again, so there is no reason to try to trace it. You can change numbers as many times as you'd like—I'll make the effort to find you, always."

"Why go through the effort?"

"Because you took off. I didn't expect that, honestly. You seemed so tough before, so I really thought you'd stay put until you gave in." His tone wasn't pleased, as if her surprising him annoyed him.

"You thought I'd just stay put and wait for you to do something?" Her voice shook, but she shoved the words out. There was a strength inside her that she was afraid she had lost, one that had grown since the last time he'd spoken to her. Was that a sign she was doing better?

She couldn't quite believe that, not with how she felt inside, but she clung to the hope.

"I already told you that you'd come to me on your own. I'm a man of my word, Katherine. I told you I'd wait for you, so I will. Those pretty screams of yours are worth waiting for."

Those words took the floor from beneath her, made her knees weak. Before she could say anything else, before she collapsed, a strong arm came around her and tugged her against a firm chest. A hand plucked the phone from her, but her brain rushed too fast for her to identify who it was.

Until Dean's familiar, smooth voice spoke into the phone. "Jerry, I presume?"

Kat could just make out Jerry's side of the conversation as well. "And who exactly are you?"

"Doesn't matter. What exactly do you think is going to happen if you keep harassing her?"

"She'll eventually do as I say. She'll realize there isn't another option, and she'll obediently return to me."

"Over my dead-fucking-body she will." Dean's voice made Kat want to pull away, to retreat. It held so much anger, so much violence that it sounded nothing like the man she'd gotten to know.

"Oh, are you getting attached?" Jerry chuckled. "That's not the best idea. See, I rarely give up on something once I set my sights on it. How do you think I've amassed the business I have? It hasn't been by being afraid, by being unsure. I've done it because I saw what I wanted and I stopped at nothing to get it. Let's not mince words here—I want Katherine. I will stop at nothing to get her. Whatever you think you have with her, whoever you are, I don't care. It won't stop me, it won't even slow me down. She will realize that she has no other options, and she will come to me."

Kat forced herself to look up and into Dean's face, his gaze locked on a far wall. When he spoke, his voice was even darker than before, a side of him she'd never expected, never wanted to see.

"You want to be clear? Let me return with the same—you won't touch her. I don't give a fuck who you think you are or what you think you want, you'll never lay another goddamned finger on her."

"And you think you'll stop me? Really?"

"Yeah, I will. You think you'd be the first life I've ended? You think I'd lose any sleep over adding you to that list? It's been a long damned time since anyone put me in a position where I even thought about that again, but you've fucked up, now. So keep pushing this, keep screwing with her, and I'll happily wash your blood of me like I have so many others."

Kat's chest froze at the icy words, the ones that lacked any of the humor she'd come to expect from him. Dean was always friendly, always smiling, rarely serious. To hear him speak like that chilled her to her core, made her question everything she'd thought she knew.

Dean hit the End button before dropping her phone on the counter, and Kat stared up at him with eyes she knew were wide from shock.

He looked down at her, his gaze still hard and foreign to her. She expected him to pull away, to smile, to apologize and tell her that had all been an act. Instead, he caught her chin between two of his fingers so her eyes remained locked on his. "I wasn't kidding, Kat. I may not have a lot to offer, but I promise you, I'll do whatever it takes to keep you safe from him, and I don't care what it costs me."

The words, no doubt meant to reassure her, only made her tremble.

This man might be more of a monster than the one chasing her...

* * * *

Olin spotted the wayward brat watering the herb garden out back, and he was again startled by just how much he enjoyed watching her. She reminded him of fish at an aquarium, how the antics as they swam back and forth calmed him.

She was bright and often oblivious of the large predators just around her. She moved from one place to another, never still, never realizing the dangers of the world.

He remembered the phone call from Jerry and pressed his lips together. *She's well aware of the dangers now...*

He hated that she'd had to learn that, that she'd had to deal with that. He'd have much rather sheltered her from the uglier parts of life, from her having to endure what she had, from having her sense of safety shattered. Unfortunately, if his job had taught him nothing else, it sure had made him learn that no one could be saved from everything. Life got its claws into everyone sooner or later.

He'd had the station look into her records, to try and chase down the number that had called her, but as Jerry had claimed, they'd had no luck. It seemed he'd used it the once, then discarded it. It left them with nothing, as usual.

Kat filled a large watering can at the hose, but when she went to lift it, she struggled. The sight brought a smile to Olin's lips, so he jogged over. "Here, let me."

He lifted the watering can, surprised to find it heavier than he expected. It wasn't plastic like so many but made out of metal. Still, he lifted it with ease. "Lead the way."

"Thanks," Kat said before offering him a brilliant smile, the sweet one he adored. Sure, he liked her feisty side too, her bratty side, but there was something about when she gave him that unfiltered smile, something about the unexpected sweetness that robbed him of his wits.

He followed her back to the herb garden, the one she'd set up a few days before. While Bradley grew some vegetables, he hadn't had herbs. It seemed they all spoiled Kat, because it had only taken one wistful comment the night before and Bradley had built a raised bed just outside the back door early the next morning, then had one of the farmhands pick up a selection of herbs to plant.

And Kat's face had glowed, even though Bradley hadn't said more than a word or two about it.

When they reached the garden, Kat pointed at the plants she wanted him to water and told him when to stop. Once the watering can had lightened, he handed it over to her to finish.

Still, she kept her distance, leaving a few feet between them as if unsure of her welcome.

Which he couldn't exactly blame her for.

"Can we talk?" he asked, his voice low.

"It seems we are." Kat's response lacked heart, as if she wanted to brat but just lacked the energy.

Which was his fault for acting as he had the other night.

"I'm sorry," he muttered. When she didn't respond, he silently cursed her for being difficult even as he admitted he owed her more. After a long breath, he went on. "I'm sorry about the other night."

"You mean the one where you had sex with me, then avoided me since? That one?"

"You could make this a little easier, you know."

She lifted the watering can high to pour a stream onto a small plant of Thai basil on the third shelf of planters. "I've always lived by the idea that you should never make the same mistake twice. Make new, exciting mistakes instead." She set the can down when she finished, then turned and sat on the edge of the planter. "So if I don't understand the mistake I made and you don't understand the one you made, how are we not going to repeat it?"

He pressed his lips together, then sighed softly. "You know, you're smarter than people give you credit for."

"Or you're just not as smart as you think. I don't want an apology, Olin. I want to understand."

His name on her lips made his heart race, even though he knew that was an entirely foolish reaction. He turned and sat beside her, letting himself stare out at the distance instead of at her. "I already told you that I almost lost everything before, that this lifestyle really screwed me over. I swore I'd never look back, that I'd never let it do that to me again."

"So why are you here? You keep telling me how you don't want any part of that, how you can't do that, but you also stay here. I don't think you know what you want, and that isn't fair to me."

He leaned his elbows on his knees. "I've asked myself why I'm here every damned night as well."

Kat rose in a huff. "Well, in that case, why don't you just leave?" She went to storm off, her emotions no doubt running high.

Olin caught her wrist before she could get more than a foot away, then tugged her until she sat on his lap. He forced himself to look into her eyes, to not hide, no matter how scary that felt. Hell, he'd rather face off against a gun-wielding lunatic than bare himself to her like this.

Still, he made himself. "Why am I here? Because I can't stop thinking about you, Kat. No matter what I tell myself, no matter how much I lecture myself about how dangerous this is, I just can't seem to stop."

"That's your problem. You can't jerk me around because you're unsure."

Which was true. "I know," he said, trying to keep his voice gentle. "I know it's not fair. It's just...I tell myself one thing, then I see you and it's like everything I thought goes out the window. I thought I could just be your friend, I thought I could just be vanilla, I thought we could keep this casual, but you undo all my plans, Kat. You smile at me—or you glare—and it's like nothing I said before matters."

She melted slightly at that, her shoulders drooping as if some of the tension slid away. "So what does that mean?"

"It means I don't know where this could go, not after we leave here. I still have my job to think about, still need to consider the logistics of how much I can give, but for now?" He stroked his finger across her soft cheek, warm from the sun. "For now I want to stop resisting, stop telling myself I can't have you."

"So you're offering me a 'maybe, but I don't know for how long'?" When she put it like that, he had to admit, it sounded like a bad deal to her.

"I can't lie to you, Kat. I won't sit here and tell you this'll be forever, that things will suddenly become easier, and we'll have no problems. I don't know if I'll ever be able to go to Sanctuary, if that's something I'll be able to give you. I'll understand if you tell me that isn't enough for you, that you don't want that, and I'll respect it. I'll leave you alone while we're here, won't push you. I just know that I'm tired of writing things off before I even get a chance to try, and I sure as hell don't want to lose you before we've even seen what it could be. It's up to you, though."

Olin had no idea just how nervous he'd be after saying something so honest. It was as if he'd shown her some deep wound of his and was now waiting to see if she'd poke at it or not.

Kat stared at him, her eyebrows furrowed. Finally, her lips pulled up at the corners. "I guess we never know how long something lasts, right? Thanks for being upfront. I don't know if, after we leave here, what you're offering will be enough, but I don't want to give up yet, either."

"So we'll give it a try here? Stop fighting it?"

Her smile turned from sweet to mischievous in a heartbeat, and Olin knew right there he was lost. He didn't think there was anything he wouldn't do for her, anything he'd deny her, not when she gave him a look like that. "I mean, if you think you're up for it. Younger men than you have failed to keep up with me."

Olin pulled her in for a kiss, before tasting her lips as he'd wanted to do for so damned long. He was tired of resisting, tired of telling himself he couldn't have what he really wanted.

And even if it cost him everything, even if it ruined him all over again, Olin wasn't sure he'd ever be able to let her go.

Chapter Fifteen

Kat stomped her foot as she rolled her shoulder that ached from when Olin had put her on her back again. Weeks of self-defense training and for what?

No matter how hard she worked, it never seemed to matter. She improved, but that improvement didn't give her the upper hand.

It felt like learning to swim in hopes of racing a dolphin. Sure, she could get faster, but she'd never be fast enough for the goal. She might get tougher, but she doubted she could overcome the sort of men she'd seen around Jerry.

Or Jerry himself.

Which left her frustrated and pacing after telling Olin she was done for the day.

The crunch of hay behind her made her spin toward the sound, but instead of Olin there — she wouldn't doubt if he'd come back to check on her — it was Dean.

She'd seen little of him after Jerry's call. He hadn't said he was avoiding her, instead claiming work had swamped him.

She could spot a lie with ease, especially that one.

"Sorry," he said, dropping his gaze as if he didn't want to look right at her. "I didn't realize you were in here."

"Barn's big enough for two," Kat snapped before taking a seat on a bale of hay. "Don't let me stop you from finding a new spot to hide."

He lifted a dark eyebrow but didn't rise to the occasion and take the bait. Instead, he crossed his arms and stared at her. "Aren't you in a bad mood?"

Kat should keep it to herself—Dean wasn't exactly acting like someone who gave a damn about her. Still, she couldn't stop herself from letting the words pour out.

Bradley would have rolled his eyes and told her to get over it. Olin would only tell her to keep working and she'd get it. Neither answer felt helpful at the moment, so who the hell knew? Maybe Dean had some sage advice for her.

"I've been working on self-defense with Olin and it's no use. No matter what he tells me, I'm just not big enough or strong enough or fast enough. If he can put me down so easily *here*, then just think about what anyone else who actually wanted to hurt me could do."

Dean's lips pressed together into a thin line, his face serious as if he were deep in thought. Finally, he let out a soft snort. "The problem is that you're getting taught by Olin."

"What does that mean?"

"Olin is a cop. He learned to fight as part of his job. Don't get me wrong, he's capable, I'm sure, but it's not the same thing."

She frowned, his words making no sense no matter how she twisted them.

Thankfully, Dean went on. "Any law enforcement is taught to detain a suspect, to bring them down, to fight fair and with honor or whatever other nonsense they teach them."

"Isn't that a good thing?"

"You give me two people—one is fighting by the books and fighting fair while the other fights dirty. Do you really think anyone gives a damn about their tactics when only one of them ends up on their feet? Fighting fair is all well and good, but it can't overcome the dirty tricks."

"I doubt Olin will teach me anything like that."

"You've got that right."

Kat paused at the words, at the reminder of what he'd said to Jerry the other day, the words that had frightened her so much. Clearly Dean had a past a lot darker than she'd have guessed for the impeccably dressed lawyer she come to know. "Will you teach me?"

He froze, as if the question surprised him. "What?"

"I'm not picking this up fast enough. I thought it would make me feel better, make me feel like I was safe, but the more I practice, the more out of my depths I feel. It just feels like a reminder that I can't protect myself. You seem to know something, so please…will you show me?"

He didn't move at first, his gaze on the ground. "You were scared of me the other day."

"I was surprised."

He lifted his gaze that time, his blue eyes calling her a liar. "You were both."

"Fine, I was both. Can you blame me?"

"No, I can't, which is why I avoided you after that. I don't think this whole idea of yours if going to make it any better, though."

"Please," she asked again. "I just want to feel safe again."

Another long exhalation before Dean nodded and undid the cuffs on his long-sleeve shirt. "Fine—but don't blame me when you decide it was a bad idea."

* * * *

It was a bad idea.

An hour later, Kat winced at the pain in her hip from when she'd stepped wrong and ended up tumbling onto the hay-covered barn floor. Sweat and dirt covered her, her muscles all ached, but at the same time...

She felt better.

"Remember, it's about those weak spots. Take those out and your opponent is screwed. Not many full-sized men react well when their goods are treated like a hacky sack."

Kat tried to implement the moves Olin had taught her, but Dean easily countered each one. It was like he knew what she was going to do before she did.

"Stop playing by the rulebook," Dean growled into her ear when he pinned her to his chest after she'd failed to land another hit. His voice, low and angry, did plenty to spark to life feelings that had little to do with the fight. "Everyone has a copy of that book, so if you listen only to it, your enemy is already a step ahead."

She yanked at his hold, her heart racing and having nothing to do with the fight or with fear. How was it that sparring like this could turn her on so much? Maybe it was the way Dean manhandled her, the way it forced her to acknowledge him as a man, the strength and agility in his body and the thoughts of how else it could be put to use...

Whatever it was, Kat struggled to hold in a pitiful moan, hoping Dean didn't catch onto that.

Still. Her lessons moved in her head, made her think instead of just reacting. His points had been clear the whole time—do the unexpected, get in under an enemy's guard, get closer to them without them realizing it, and strike hard with whatever she could.

Play dirty.

So Kat let out a sigh.

Dean paused, turning her and loosening his grip. "You okay?"

"I am now," Kat said, hiding her grin before leaping at him.

The surprise must have worked, because he lost his balance, stumbling backward to keep from falling. Kat twisted, then managed to jump enough onto his back to wrap her arm around his throat. She didn't do it enough to obstruct his breathing, but her thighs tightened around him to hold on, to keep him from being able to throw her off. The action caused him to trip, and they both tumbled to the ground.

Still, Kat didn't let go, didn't relinquish the hold she had on him. Even when the air was knocked from her, even when her side ached from the fall, she held fast.

At least, she did until he tapped her arm. At that, Kat let go, relaxing back on the ground with a breathless laugh. "I won," she muttered with a grin.

Dean rolled, but his gaze wasn't anywhere near a happy one. He didn't look proud — he looked *pissed*.

It made her scoot backward, unable to help the reaction, especially given how unusual the look was on Dean's face.

He jerked his gaze from her and to the wall, as if to collect himself.

Kat scrambled to her feet, though she winced when it made her back hurt.

That must have woken him, because Dean narrowed his eyes on her. After a moment, he nodded toward the house. "Let's go."

Kat gulped but followed, unsure how she could be so anxious and yet so turned on at the same time...

* * * *

Dean sighed as he moved the wet rag over Kat's ribs. She'd taken a hard fall and scraped herself. Thankfully, nothing seemed broken, so it was just a matter of the skin and probably some bruises.

Not that that helped his attitude at all. He'd kept his mouth shut, not wanting to snap at the girl, especially because he knew he had no good reason to do so.

A tremble moved through Kat's shoulder, forcing him to take a deep breath and calm himself down.

Which was frustrating since Dean hadn't needed to do much to control himself in a long time. He didn't normally have to worry about losing his temper, about anger. He was level-headed just about always.

Except now, when he really needed it.

"I'm not mad," he said softly, trying to gentle his voice.

"You're a terrible liar," she responded.

He let out a soft laugh at the way she saw right through him. "Fine, I was mad, but I know it isn't fair so I'm trying not to be. Better?"

"You were the one who was willing to teach me. I can't believe you're mad that I won once..." Her voice sounded as if she were pouting over it, and damn it, Dean couldn't resist that.

He pulled her shirt down when he noted the scrapes were clean and not even bleeding. She'd be fine. "I'm not mad that you won."

"Then why?"

"I was mad that you got yourself hurt, that you were reckless."

"You were the one who told me I had to look for any opening."

He pressed his lips together, hating that she was right. "Yeah, well, it's easy to give that advice when we're thinking about the worst that could happen. It's a different matter entirely when you pull that shit during practice and end up hurt. In case you didn't notice, I'm a lot bigger and a lot heavier than you are. You could have broken a rib if I'd come down wrong on you."

She twisted to peer at him, her expression hesitant. "You're upset because I could have gotten hurt?"

"Of course I am. I know you need to learn this, but that doesn't mean I have to like it. It just reminded me of what could happen, I guess." He took a deep breath, then let it out slowly. "And I think I'm already in a weird head space after that phone call..."

"You avoided me after that call," she said softly. "You didn't seem to want to talk about it."

"What's there to talk about?"

"Well, maybe the fact that you said you'd killed before?"

Dean flinched at the words that she so easily said, as if they were nothing. He'd never wanted her to know that, never wanted to think back on what he'd been through that he'd tried to put behind him. However, the expression on her face said she wouldn't let it go.

"Right. That."

"If you don't want to tell me, you don't have to. I just want to understand you better."

If she'd have demanded, he'd have shut up. If Kat had thrown a fit and cried and screamed, he'd have dug his heels in and told her to go to hell. Why was it that when she was sweet like that, he had no defense against her?

Dean sat on the end of the bed beside her. "I already told you that I've done some horrible things, crossed lines no one should to get by when I was younger. I decided that I wasn't going to be that person anymore, but I guess..." He sighed softly. "I guess it doesn't much matter how far someone goes, how much they try to change, they are who they are. I'm not going to apologize for what I said—I wasn't kidding, I'll do whatever it takes to keep you safe. If I need to become that person again, I'll do it, but I never wanted you to see it. Never wanted anyone to see it, honestly, but especially not you." Each word brought back another memory he'd tried so hard to lock away, forced him to face his past and face the things he'd done.

No matter how far he ran, how well he dressed, he was still that same thug he'd been before, wasn't he?

He went to rise, to walk out, because there was no way Kat would want him to stay, not after that.

Kat grabbed his arm, though, kept him there.

"Kat…" he said softly, refusing to let himself give in to hope. "I'm not a good bet, okay? You deserve a lot more than me. I can put on these nice clothes, and I went to school so I can talk fancy, but none of that changes what I really am deep down."

She didn't let him go, though. She didn't listen — did she ever? Instead, she shifted so she straddled him, so her thighs pressed against his hips, and she sat in his lap. She placed her palms on his cheeks, staring into his eyes in a way that made him feel *far* too seen. "I'm not afraid of you."

"Yeah, well, maybe you should be. There's something dark inside me, Kat, something that let me do those things. It's still there — that call proved it."

"There's something dark inside of everyone. You're right about one thing, though — people don't change, not really. We learn, we adjust, but we're the same people deep down."

The words hurt, as if she'd cut him with them. Even though she said it with that voice, while she held his cheeks and stared into his eyes, they still were exactly what he'd always thought and feared.

People don't change. He was the same man, deep down, as the one who had done things that chilled him now.

He tried to turn his face away, but Kat wouldn't relent. She brushed her lips to his. "People don't change, so I know that the person you were back then is the same one who is sitting here now. I'm not afraid of you now — I know you've got a good heart — so I know that whatever you did before, you weren't the monster you seem to think you were."

Dean blinked slowly, her words unexpected. He'd thought she'd write him off, that she'd think this was a horrible idea, that she'd realize how dangerous he could be.

Instead…she'd completely accepted him…

He had no idea what to do with that, with the way she hadn't condemned him.

"That's why you hold back, isn't it? Why you don't play with the same women more than once or twice, why you're always going from one to another, why you're careful to keep things very casual."

He nodded, the answer pulled from him by the softness of her voice and sweetness of her lips. "I feel like if I go too far, if I give in, that other part of me wins. I can't risk that. What if I'm really as bad as I think I am? What if I really hurt someone?" He paused, then sighed. "What if I hurt *you*?"

Kat's lips curled into a sarcastic smile. "You worry too much, you know that?"

"You don't worry enough. That evens us out."

"Who would have pegged you as the responsible one? I figured that was more Bradley's forte."

Even with her joke, Dean couldn't bring himself to laugh. "If I ever really hurt you…"

"You won't."

"But this thing inside me—"

She silenced him with a kiss, one more aggressive than the last, as if to try to get him to focus and get out of his own head. When she pulled away, her breath warmed his lips. "You're just you. I'm not afraid of you, Dean, not any part of you."

He stared at her, her eyes so damned honest that they were nearly as scary as whatever was inside him. Still, he forced himself to speak. "You never had the good sense to be afraid."

"You should take that as a win, then, and stop worrying."

He wanted to argue it farther, but it became clear Kat wasn't interested in hearing it. No matter what he wanted to say, how much he wanted to warn her, Kat didn't seem to believe him.

It meant that even as he gave in, even as he pushed aside his worries, they didn't go away entirely.

He slid a hand behind her neck and pulled Kat in, ending their conversation with a kiss and headed for more.

He'd do whatever it took to keep her safe...and that included from himself.

Chapter Sixteen

"Thought the livestock dogs were supposed to keep wild animals off the property." Bradley offered the words with no smile as he walked up on Kat, who had a large canvas on an easel facing away from him.

She turned her gaze to his, her gray eyes vacant for a moment. It took a few blinks before she seemed to realize who he was, before her mind switched over from her artwork to his presence. The way she could lose herself in her work had always impressed and frightened him. She poured so much of herself into it that there were plenty of times she'd fail to eat or drink.

Still, the passion always made him smile. Seeing her work like that, seeing her find herself again after Jerry, it was worth any number of times he had to go give her food or water.

"Was that a joke?" she asked.

"If that's the only thing you can come up with to say back, clearly you're more distracted than I thought."

The corner of her pink lips curled into a smile. "You should just take advantage of the moment—it's the only time you can outwit me."

He let out a chuckle as he came closer, peering around to peek at what she was working on.

As soon as he did, she tried to object, but it was too late. Bradley was stunned for a moment, staring at the large canvas that had a partially done painting of his horse, Brat, on it. The colors were blocked in, but she was still adding the details of shadowing on the fur and the beautiful night sky covered in stars.

"It's nothing," she tried to say, grabbing the edges of the canvas as if to run away.

He caught her arm to still her. "It's still wet, right? Don't move it until it dries or you could ruin the work you've done."

She gulped, a slight tremble in her arm where he held her. "It's embarrassing. No one sees these."

"It's beautiful, Kat. Why hide this?"

"I don't hide—"

He narrowed his eyes, not above using that *I'm your Dom and I expect an honest answer* look.

She blew out a slow breath, but the drooping of her shoulders signaled his win. "I do paintings like this for me—that's it. The cartoon work sells."

"But you clearly like this. You're passionate about it. It's really fucking good. Why hide them so much?"

She stared at her feet instead of the painting, as if even the sight hurt.

Which meant there was another method. Bradley had long ago learned that if one route didn't lead to success, it was time to try another.

He nodded back at her chair. "Don't stop on my account."

Kat glared but his hand on her back to guide her over worked, and Kat sat down and picked up her paintbrush to work again.

Bradley grabbed another chair from beside the stables and took a seat beside her.

After a few strokes, Kat's voice came out small. "I put myself through college, you know?"

"Waitressing—yeah, I know."

"The thing is, my parents, they were more than wealthy enough to pay for me to go."

He frowned. "Did they just believe in kids paying their own way?"

"No. It was more like...they felt putting me through art school was a waste of money. They thought if they helped me, it would only encourage me to make bad choices like that."

An ache in his chest at her words—so full of pain—made him rub the spot. Kat was a bright light in a dull and dark world. The idea that her parents couldn't recognize that broke his heart. It also explained a lot.

"You never talked about your parents."

"What was there to say? I'm the screw-up kid. I'm the one who never does the right thing, who is always a problem for them." She didn't say that as if fishing, as if waiting for him to tell her how wonderful she was. Instead, she offered it with the same sort of simplicity as if she'd said she had gray eyes or blonde hair.

She *believed* that bullshit.

"You're not a screw-up."

She lifted an eyebrow but didn't take her gaze from the painting.

"I'm serious. You're a handful, yeah, but you're not some hopeless screw-up. If people can't see that, it's on them. Ain't your job to make everyone happy."

"I couldn't make you happy," she whispered.

That drew him back, made him stare at her as he tried to sort out just what the hell she meant by that.

"What?" he asked when he couldn't make heads or tails of it.

"I couldn't make you happy. You were sick of my behavior, too."

"As I recall, *I* didn't leave *you*. So whatever you're trying to pull here, you can't rewrite history."

"I left because you're too good of a guy—you weren't going to on your own. I don't think I could handle seeing you getting sick of me. Sometimes it's easier to just let things fall apart instead of trying to hold it together when it won't work. It's like trying to hold on to an angry cat—it'll just end up hurting you in the end."

Bradley frowned as he stared at her, at the shining of her eyes that said she held back tears.

Fuck. Was this really why it had all ended? Because Kat had been so sure he'd get rid of her and had wanted to strike first?

Well, that sounded a hell of a lot like her, didn't it? Quick to run, to hide what she really thought, to make dumb ass assumptions instead of just talking to him.

"Well, I'm sorry."

Kat blew out a slow, long breath, her shoulders slumping. "It's okay. I know I'm a lot. It's not your fault you don't want to deal with—"

He silenced her by flicking her temple, an action that made her set her paintbrush down and turn a murderous glare on him.

"I'm not sorry that I was getting sick of you, because I wasn't. I'm sorry I wasn't paying enough attention to realize the stupid shit you had rattling around in your head. I should have seen it, should have set you straight instead of letting you run off thinking what you were thinking. That's on me, Kat, and I'm sorry."

She froze as she stared at him, as if she wasn't sure what to say.

Then again, *neither* of them had been that great at expressing themselves. Kat was forever hiding what she really thought or felt beneath countless layers of pranks and insults and jokes, and Bradley just straight up buried his feelings like any red-blooded American rancher would.

She slid her tongue over her bottom lip, leaving a sheen behind that made Bradley's mind go in an entirely different direction.

"Maybe we were both wrong," she said softly. "Sometimes it just seems easier to leave before getting left, you know?"

"Is that why you push people so hard? So you have an excuse about why they're gone?"

"Maybe." She pressed her lips together and stared back at the painting. "I love to do these. Sometimes I can't sleep because I have some picture in my head. I have a storage unit full of paintings that I've never shown anyone."

"Why not?"

"Because these are *real*. They're me. If people laugh at my cartoons, who cares? They're cute and they're silly—they're what everyone sees me as. The fun, airheaded troublemaker. My paintings though, those are real, they're the me I don't let people see. If others saw them and hated them…"

Bradley nodded, the reasoning clear. If people rejected the cute stuff, Kat could shrug that off. They weren't important to her. These paintings were, though, and having people reject that was like rejecting her.

So the cartoons were just another way to hide who she was, to keep herself safe by not showing her truth to anyone. Her antics, it all made so much more sense.

Why hadn't he ever bothered to really ask her before? Or maybe he had and neither of them had been at a place where they could talk about it honestly. Maybe they'd both needed that time to grow.

"All I can tell you, Kat, is that you're talented. You can't let the world dictate how you're going to act all the time, can't let them have that power over you. It'll crush you."

"Maybe," she said. "But at least I'd be crushed as whatever people see me as and not as *me*."

Bradley shook his head at the stubborn woman, then set a hand on her cheek, rubbing his thumb against her soft skin. "You're tougher than you give yourself credit for. The girl I fell in love with would put up one hell of a fight before letting anyone get anything over on her."

"Fell in love with? Past tense?"

His cheek ached when he smiled, a reminder that he hadn't had anything to smile about without her in his life. "Nah, not past tense. You're not the sort of girl who's easy to forget, no matter how many times I wished you were over the years."

She opened her mouth, no doubt to say something else snarky, but Bradley didn't want to hear it. He quieted her with a consuming kiss, one he ended by biting softly at her full, tempting bottom lip.

And didn't those wide eyes of hers just look lovely? It wasn't always easy to surprise Kat, to get one over on her, but when Bradley managed it, it made it all the sweeter.

"I should get the painting inside," she said, clearly flustered.

Which made Bradley chuckle before pulling into his lap. "It's still drying, remember? Guess I'll get to enjoy you for a while, at least until it's all dry."

"Acrylics dry fast," Kat whispered against his lips. "So I guess you're not planning on lasting too long? That sounds about right."

Those words, which might have annoyed a lesser man, which might have made him feel insecure, only drew an honest-to-god laugh from Bradley as he was forced to realize just how empty his life had been since he'd shut himself away on that ranch.

"Let's just see who lasts longer."

The wariness in her eyes melted him, made him realize just how damned much he still loved this girl. That hadn't ever changed, had it? He'd been in love with her since the start, and the years he'd spent telling himself that wasn't true didn't matter.

He loved her and he wasn't ever going to make the mistake of letting her go again.

* * * *

Kat winced as she stretched in her room, trying to go through the yoga poses she knew to loosen the aching muscles that covered her.

As it turned out, self-defense was hell on the body. She'd exercised plenty of times in her life, when she'd been sure she'd turn into some buff badass femme fatale. Instead, she'd done a few weeks before realizing — that shit was hard.

Yet, she couldn't deny how she felt stronger, how she had more confidence as she'd walked around the ranch the more she practiced. It was a strength she'd never experienced before.

Kat hadn't been afraid of the world before Jerry, had thought most people were good at their cores. She'd known that she wasn't strong, that if anyone did attack her she didn't have much of a hope, but she'd accepted it.

This was different. She'd come face-to-face with the reality of the world, with the darkness in it, with the evil of some people, but that fear had started to loosen with each lesson. It was like learning the world was big, but learning to read a map so she could get home even if she got lost.

Olin and Dean traded off on training her, and a mix of the two styles had really helped. Olin's discipline was amazing, the way he taught her to anticipate and counter. Dean's viciousness took it to another level, however, teaching her the things to survive that Olin shied away from.

All of that, however, led to her shoulder feeling tight and miserable. A long bath had helped, but all too quickly, it ached again.

A knock on her door had her calling for the person to enter.

Olin walked in, a bottle of oil in his hand and a towel over his shoulder.

"Little forward, isn't it? You shouldn't just let yourself into a girl's room with lube. Flowers before anal."

Olin snorted, the response melting Kat. He never took what she said too seriously, never seemed shocked by her words. He held the bottle up. "Massage oil. You've been favoring your left arm all night. I'm going to guess it's hurting?"

The fact he'd noticed made her pause. Kat usually did everything for herself, was used to taking care of herself. The fact that Olin had seen her pain and wanted to help made her feel all sorts of ways she wasn't ready to deal with yet. "It's fine," she said instead, not sure what else to say.

He spread the towel over the bed. "No, it's not. You're working hard, and you're going to be sore. There's no good reason for you to suffer needlessly. Come on, shirt off, face down."

Kat pressed her lips together.

At her failure to obey, he lifted his eyebrow. "You're a strange girl. I didn't walk in here and tell you to strip for sex—just for a massage."

"It'd be easier if you told me to strip for sex. Isn't that an option?"

He set the oil on the nightstand, then patted the towel again. "If you're a good girl, maybe afterward. You know how this works, though. I give you what you need, not always what you want."

"I thought you were out of that lifestyle."

"And you're the only thing in the world that could draw me back in. Now, the massage will work better if you just listen, but I'm not above strapping you down for it, either."

That got her going. She sat with her back to him for a moment, then removed her shirt and bra. Despite the men having all seen her marks already, she found she didn't care for exposing them. There was always this moment of fear that happened, one when she was afraid to look at the men, when terror washed over her that they'd see her differently.

Olin sighed but said nothing as she twisted to lie down on her front.

He shifted beside her, then squirted some of the oil on his hand. It was surprisingly warm when he touched her back, when his strong hand slid across her skin.

And the moan she let out at the very first touch was downright humiliating. She'd been brought to orgasm by those hands—hell, she'd been fucked in front of a room of people at Sanctuary—yet this entirely innocent massage could force *that* sound from her lips?

It was witchcraft. Had to be.

Olin laughed at the sound but went on. He stroked over her lower back, easing the knots she hadn't even realized were there. "I'm proud of you. You've worked hard at learning."

"You were right when you said I should learn."

"Yeah?"

She nodded, her face turned away from him, her cheek against the blanket on her bed. "I feel safer, I guess."

"Good. That was part of the point." He dug the heels of his palms into the sore places on her back. When she whined softly, he focused in on that area, as if he knew it was where she needed the most attention.

It reminded her of how twisted her view of love and sex was, though, because that edge of pain heated her up in entirely different ways as well. The noises she made, they were only partly in protest.

And no doubt Olin knew it, the observant bastard.

"Any word?" she asked, forcing herself to ask the question she wanted to know just as much as she didn't want to know.

Olin didn't pretend to not know what she was talking about. "No. I'm still getting reports from others at the station even though I'm not officially on the case."

"Any more bodies?"

He didn't answer, his hands pausing for a breath. Though, his lack of an answer told her plenty, didn't it?

"How many?"

He sighed softly. "Two more. Same as the others."

Kat couldn't ignore the pain in her chest at that, the reminder that those women had died because of her.

"It's not because of you," Olin said as if he could read her mind.

"We've had this talk before — you aren't going to convince me otherwise."

"Was it Sunny's fault that her dog got hurt? Do you blame Ell for getting you involved with Jerry?"

The question made Kat push up from the bed and give Olin a hard glare. "Absolutely not, and if you dare say something like that to them — "

Olin's lips pulled into a *gotchya* grin. "See? You can see the truth when it comes to other people, so you just need to work harder to see it when it comes to yourself. You can't blame yourself for other people's actions. I mean, if I'd been a better detective, I might have stopped Jerry before he could do any of this. If Bradley and you hadn't broken up, you wouldn't have been in that position at all. If Dean had kept a better eye on Ell, Jerry couldn't have abducted either of you. You can't take this all on your own shoulders, Kat. Either Jerry is responsible for his own actions or we *all* share in the blame."

Kat tipped her lips down, trying so hard to find a way to refute his words. She wanted to lay the blame on her own shoulders because she was used to that, was comfortable with it. Being at fault meant she could do something to change it.

Having to admit it was all Jerry's fault, however, made her uneasy, made her feel unsafe.

Olin set a hand on her shoulder and pushed her back down, moving to work on her sore shoulder. The action blanked her mind, took her away from Jerry and the women who had been killed and everything else.

It shrank the world to her and Olin's touches, to the way he pressed into the tense areas of the muscle, to the sharp pain followed by the gentle easing.

Before she knew it, she was putty, just malleable contentment under his talented, strong hands. Her sounds had moved from ones that held pain to all pleasure, just wanton moans that *begged* for more.

He rubbed over her hips, dragging his fingers so softly that goosebumps pebbled over her skin. Each place he skirted burned, made her want more. Without even thinking about it, she inched her feet outward in invitation. She wore only her night shorts, which were so short that he likely caught a glimpse of her cunt, especially since she'd opted against underwear.

His laugh was deep and made her flush. "Well, I said if you were good..." He dipped his fingers into the leg hole of her shorts and slid them down her pussy. "You are drenched, Kat." He pulled his fingers away, earning a cry from her as she twisted to look at him.

Her glare fell away when she watched him slide those fingers into his mouth, as he licked them clean with an almost feral quality to his honey-colored gaze. It made her wonder how she could have thought of him as cold before. It seemed crazy, now.

"Well, at least one part of you is sweet," he said with a laugh before reaching for the button of his pants. "But don't worry—I plan on forcing out lots more of those sounds you make."

"But I'm still sore…" She complained only because she wanted to, because she liked making him work for it, not giving everything up even though he'd just seen exactly how turned on she was. "My muscles hurt."

"I don't mind." The smile he offered was downright sadistic. "The more of those little whimpers you let out, the better, the harder I'll go. Think you can take it?"

The challenge drew a shiver through Kat, but she knew there was only one answer. "Think you can?"

His answering laugh made her remember that despite the careful way he spoke, how cautious he was with her, he wasn't the nice one…

Chapter Seventeen

Kat sighed as she stood in front of the large front door to her family home. Funny that despite only living about an hour away, she felt like a stranger each time she showed up.

Well, that and the fact she lacked the code for the gate or locks for the front door...

Bradley, Dean and Olin had come with her — much to her dismay. It wasn't that she didn't understand their reasoning or accept it.

Jerry was still out there, and she was still in danger. The fact that she needed to attend a family gathering didn't change that there was still a risk.

In fact, she was a bit shocked that the men had even agreed to it. Not that they had at first.

At first, they'd told her hell no. Bradley had outright refused at the idea of risking her by seeing her family — after their talk before, he'd gotten a glimpse at their dysfunctional relationship. Dean had been less direct, using the way he twisted facts to make it clear he didn't care for the idea while not dashing her hopes all at once. Olin hadn't said no, but had discussed instead the risks.

In the end, however, they'd relented. No one knew how long the issue with Jerry would last, and with the three of them going, there wasn't nearly so much of a risk.

Well, from Jerry, at least. Kat had a feeling there was a big risk when it came to the men seeing just how wide the chasm between her and the rest of her family was.

It started with the house, with the immaculate gardens, the large, imposing fencing. Everything in its place, everything doing exactly what it was supposed to. Which was exactly why Kat had never fit in...

A weight settled on her lower back and Kat jumped, unable to help it.

"Easy," Bradley said from beside her, his touch like a reminder that she wasn't alone.

"Funny that this is scarier than facing off against Jerry, huh? I'll take a psycho with a knife over my family any day."

"I wouldn't," Olin muttered, the look in his eyes saying he didn't care for her joke.

"You say that because you don't know my family." She took one more deep breath before adding on something else. "Please, don't fight with them."

"We're not planning on embarrassing you," Dean said, a frown on his features as if insulted by the very thought.

"I don't mean it like that. My family, they're...a lot. You three like to be protective, and while I appreciate that, I'm asking you to just let anything they say go. I'm used to it, and it'll cause me way more problems if you try to argue with them."

All three men pressed their lips together as if they weren't fans of her idea, though that was why she'd waited until she was on the doorstep to say a word. She got it, she did.

Kat was sure if anyone said anything about Bradley in front of her, she'd give that person a piece of her mind. The same went for Dean or Olin. She couldn't even picture sitting quietly as someone talked shit about them.

However, it was what she needed, and the sharp nods from each man said they understood. They'd come to keep her safe, so they had to be understanding about the rules.

Kat rang the button on the intercom, and a familiar voice answered. "Hello?"

"Hi, Tessa, it's me, Kat."

There was silence at first, which made Kat want to roll her eyes. She'd called in from the gate already—it wasn't as if they had no idea she'd arrived. Still, it was part of the games they all liked to play.

"I'll be right there." The intercom clicked off, and Kat sighed.

"Family?" Olin asked.

"Almost. Tessa has run the household as long as I've been alive. She's like a second mom." And she disapproved of Kat every bit as much as her actual mother did.

After a few more minutes, the door opened, and Tessa's familiar scowl made Kat feel like she was home. Wasn't that weird? That someone looking at her so negatively could actually make her homesick? If she walked in and everyone was nice to her, *that* would have made her suspicious.

"I wasn't aware you would be bringing... *friends.*" The censure in that statement was loud and clear.

"There's an issue going on, so I needed to bring them." Kat kept it nice and vague, but Tessa's expression didn't soften.

"Very well. Come along." When they stepped inside, Tessa looked to a man standing to the side. "Set another three places at the table, please, and let Mr. and Mrs. Grant know that Katherine has arrived with guests." The man scurried off, the same hurry in his step that Tessa could put into any person.

Being led through the house made Kat uncomfortable as it always did. She remembered going to friends' houses over the years for holidays, to the way they just walked into their family homes, to how welcome she felt, to how they acted as if they still lived there even if they didn't. It was a far cry from the way she was escorted through the halls as if she needed supervision.

She wasn't going to steal the candle holders, for fuck's sake. They were way too large to hide.

The thought made her laugh, a momentary break from the discomfort. Dean gave her a side-eye then chuckled, as if her laughter had made him feel slightly better.

The dining room was set up as it always was — impressive and all for show. The huge table filled the room, and large windows overlooked the backyard and gardens there. It wasn't like Bradley's property, where everything had a reason and practical function. Instead, this house had land and plants just to have them, not because they were useful in the least.

In fact, she doubted her parents ever ventured outside to enjoy the gardens they paid so much to maintain.

"Please, sit. Your parents will be down shortly." With that, Tessa left, and took at least some of the heaviness of the room with her.

"Nice place," Dean said as he took a seat, his words full of meaning.

"Yeah," Kat agreed as she sat to the left of the head of the table, the spot she was expected to sit. Olin and Bradley sat farther down, which made her happy. The farther her men sat from her parents, the better.

Not because she was ashamed of them, but she didn't want to give her parents any more ability to focus on them.

"Didn't realize you grew up like this," Dean pressed.

"Yep. Lucky me, huh?"

Dean shook his head. "Money isn't everything. Judging by that tight look on your face, I'm guessing it wasn't all it's chalked up to be here."

Boy, wasn't that right? She recalled how many of her friends had been jealous upon seeing her dropped off in a town car with a driver, upon seeing where she lived. They had no idea the pressure that sort of life created, though.

Kat would have happily grown up dirt poor so long as it was a happy house, a place where she felt loved and accepted. Instead, she'd had all the money she could want but nothing else.

Instead of answering, Kat sighed and shifted in her seat. Thankfully, the door opened before she had to display any more of her painful past.

At least, she was thankful until she lifted her gaze and spotted her parents walking in. It seemed no matter how old she got, no matter how many years passed, it always came back to this.

Kat felt like a child desperately wanting nothing more than her parents' approval, and judging from the scowl on her father's face, she'd guess she wasn't getting that today.

Olin said nothing as he watched Kat's parents walk into the large, formal dining room. He had to admit, the mother resembled Kat.

Or, at least, the features did. They had the same color hair, the same pale skin and freckles. The thing that made them different was the way they carried themselves.

Though Kat was sweet—always smiling and laughing and causing trouble—this woman was hard around the edges. She had no lines in her face, as if she never made an actual expression.

"Katherine," the woman said, her tone giving away that the get together wasn't exactly a happy one. "You should have told us you were bringing others."

"Sorry," Kat said. "I didn't know they were coming until this morning. I sort of sprang it on them."

"This morning?" The sharpness in her tone said she didn't care for whatever assumption she'd come up with.

No doubt it was questioning why their daughter would be with three men early in the morning.

Olin could have spoken up, but he let Kat handle it for now.

"Since my daughter refuses to follow basic etiquette, I suppose I'll do so. My name is Barlow Grant, and this is my wife, Elizabeth." Kat's father, Barlow, offered the introduction—and a not-at-all-subtle reprimand—as he sat at the head of his table. Elizabeth sat beside him, across the table from Kat.

"Right, sorry," Kat said, her tone surprising Olin. She was always feisty, always full of herself. How was it that she could look like a beaten puppy with just a few words from her parents? "This is Bradley Smith, Olin Ramiz and Dean Havers."

Barlow stared at Dean, probably because he was dressed the most professional, his gaze hard. "And how is it you know Katherine?"

Dean pulled on an obviously fake smile. "We're friends."

"She doesn't normally bring friends by, especially not to important family meetings like this." The sharp words told Dean that the man was smart. He might be an asshole, but he wasn't someone to take lightly.

Olin spoke up next, his tone just as sharp. "I'm a detective, and Kat has been part of a case we're working on. Due to threats against her, it isn't safe for her to go places alone currently."

"Katherine," Elizabeth said, her tone exhausted. "What have you done, now? If you expect us to clean up your mess again—"

"Mom," Kat said, voice soft but breaking into the tirade. "It's not like that. I didn't do anything."

"How am I supposed to believe that? I know you, and you show up here with three men like this? What were you thinking? What would the neighbors think?"

"We had today planned. I wasn't going to just cancel."

The look on her mother's face said she should have.

It made Olin have to close his hands into fists to stay quiet. Funny, because he didn't normally feel this protective over others, this quick to anger to defend them.

"Well, what's done is done. Have you considered getting a real job?" Her father asked the question as he took a bite from the plate someone had brought and set before him. He hadn't even looked up at the person, hadn't acknowledged them at all.

Kat, on the other hand, said thank you to the server before responding to her father's question with a tired tone. "I have a real job."

"Hamilton's son, Greg, just opened up a second location to his medical practice."

"He puts implants into vapid women, Dad. Let's not act like he's curing cancer."

Her father sat straighter, and Olin *almost* pitied him. Or, he would have if the man wasn't such a colossal asshole. Olin knew exactly how it felt to be at the other end of Kat's biting tongue and her wits, dulled against her parents as it was.

"Sorry," Kat rushed out, the apology surprising him as much as anything else had. Kat never apologized for the things she said, never even seemed bothered by them, so what was with that? "I'm sure Greg's parents are very proud of him."

"Of course. It would be nice if we had something positive to say about you."

"She's a talented artist," Dean said, breaking into the conversation and getting a simultaneous look from Kat and her parents. "She works hard and supports herself from her work. Before I'd even met her, I'd seen her artwork around."

Elizabeth made a derisive sound and took a slow drink from her glass of water before answering. "Yes, I've seen those little cartoons before. Do you really expect me to sing her praises at gatherings while showing off a crudely drawn racoon with the words 'trash panda' beneath it?"

Fuck. She wasn't even talking to Olin and he could feel layers of his own skin coming off at her caustic words. It made Olin take a second hard look at Kat, wondering just how the hell she had managed to grow into the sweet woman she was when she'd been raised by people like this? People without a speck of warmth within them.

It seemed like a miracle.

However, where Kat would have taken anyone else to task for the rude comment, she just crumbled further in front of her father.

"About the reunion," Kat said, her voice quiet in what was clearly a change of topic as she looked at her father. "I still haven't gotten the official invitation. I can take work off, but I just need to know the exact times so I know when to come."

"You aren't getting an invitation."

A heaviness started in Olin's stomach, like the herald to a disaster.

"Oh? That's fine, I don't need a regular invitation. Sending one to your daughter who lives so close would be silly —"

"You misunderstand," Barlow cut in. "You aren't getting one because you are not invited to this reunion."

"What?"

"Just as I said. I've spoken with your mother and we feel it would be best to do this event without you. There will be a lot of important guests attending."

"Guests?" Kat's voice trembled. "This is a family reunion, Dad. It's about *family* and whether you like it or not, that means me."

"Family isn't just about blood. It is about people who support one another, who all move toward the same goal. You have never wanted to move with us, have caused us so many problems, that we don't feel this is the right place for you."

Olin struggled to keep himself in check as he listened to Kat's father talk about her that way. He talked about cutting her off from her family as if she were some diseased limb he had to sever for the good of the whole body.

And Kat?

Her eyes shone, telling Olin she held back tears. "But won't everyone ask where I am? Won't *that* cause you problems?"

"Not really," her mother said. "Honestly, no one asks about you, Kat. After this many years with nothing positive to say, it is an awkward situation that most people are polite enough to leave well enough alone."

"You can't do this!" Kat slammed her hands on the table and stood, leaning forward.

Her father didn't jump. Instead, he set his fork down as if it were the most natural thing in the world. "This is part of the reason, Katherine. Your hysterics, your refusal to dress appropriately, your constant rebellious streak. If you behaved properly, like a good daughter should, you would be invited. Consider this a wakeup call, perhaps. If you choose to shape-up, then next year you might find yourself invited."

Kat swallowed hard, but as she went to sit, to just accept the things her parents said, Olin had had enough. He stood and set his napkin down on the table. "Come on, Kat."

Her father nailed him with a hard look, as if daring Olin to intervene in a family problem that was so far above his station. But Olin had faced down the barrel of gangsters before—some rich man who thought too much of himself wasn't about to shake him.

Kat turned to look at Olin, and he gave her the softest smile he could. "Let's go. There's no reason to sit here and listen to them."

"But—"

Bradley stood as well, having said all of nothing during his time there. Then again, Bradley didn't tend to be a talker. Maybe that was why it surprised Olin when the man finally did. "Always heard that you should never listen to people who don't know shit. Had a hand come out to work the ranch one time, and they kept telling me my stallions were too headstrong. Turned out the idiot had only worked with geldings, and old ones at that. If I'd have listened to him, I'd have passed on some of my best horses. Point being?" Bradley turned a cold look on her parents as he said the last part. "People say a lot of stupid shit, but that doesn't make any of it your problem." He held out a hand and waited.

Kat set her hand into his palm without hesitation, and he tugged her toward the door without another look at her parents.

"She came here with three men and thinks we're supposed to just overlook everything? She's too brash, too quick to do things that could ruin us," Barlow said.

Olin kept in what he wanted to say, that they could go fuck themselves, and looked toward Dean instead. "Ready?"

Dean stood, his gaze sharper than Olin normally saw it. Dean could be charming and funny, but Olin had always seen him decimate people in a courtroom and bring even the most secure to tears. In fact, Olin was rather glad not to be on the receiving end of all that anger.

"You know, after meeting you, I'm even more impressed with that woman. For her to have grown up with assholes like you and for her to still have turned out the way she did? Well, I'd say it was a miracle if I didn't know better. There was nothing miraculous about it—she's just tougher than either of you, and she's a lot better off without you." Dean turned his back on the sputtering couple as if they meant nothing before walking out of the room.

Which was for the best, really. What would yelling at the two do? If two people could be that cold toward their own daughter, nothing any of the men said would change a thing. Her parents saw what they wanted, believed what they wanted, and there wasn't a damn thing Olin could do about that.

Well, other than make sure he loved Kat enough that she knew her parents were idiots, that she didn't take it to heart.

And he was pretty sure he could love her so much that she *knew* she didn't need those idiot's approval.

* * * *

Kat wiped her eyes, hating the headache she still had from crying. It seemed entirely unfair that she not only got to spend most of the evening crying, that her face was a puffy mess because of it, but then to also be in pain?

It felt like an insult being tacked onto the whole thing.

At least the men had left her be. Maybe they'd realized she needed a break, that she needed to regroup. She'd never have brought them if she thought for even a moment that the meal would go like that.

Sure, she'd expected her parents to berate her — that was simply the language they communicated in. Nowhere on her list of things to expect, however, had been them not inviting her to the annual family reunion. She'd gone every time they'd held it for her entire life. Originally it had been hosted by her grandparents, back when she was little, before her parents took it over when she'd been a teenager.

A knock on the door had her pressing her cool fingertips to her eyelids to try to ease the swollen look of them as she called out for whoever it was to come in.

Olin had already brought her food, so that wasn't it. Most likely, they'd simply reached their limit of allowing her to hide and cry by herself.

Sometimes being with Doms was great — made her feel safe and cared for — and sometimes it annoyed the fuck out of her.

Like right then, when she wanted to bury herself in an igloo of blankets and pretend the whole world had disappeared but no doubt her men felt if something was wrong, she should talk to them.

Stupid Doms…

More than one set of heavy footsteps echoed off the wooden floor, so Kat wasn't surprised when she finally moved her fingers to find Olin, Dean and Bradley all in her room. "What?" she asked, not bothering to soften her tone at all.

"You can't hide all night," Bradley said. "I'm getting sick of hearing you cry in here all by yourself."

"Well, I'll try to do it more quietly," Kat snapped.

Bradley, who normally took the bait when pressed, only came over to sit beside her and put his arm around her.

And there went the tears again...

Something about the weight of his strong arm, about the way he tugged her against his side broke her down. It was a sense of belonging she'd never felt at her home, something she'd craved her entire life, and yet here he was offering it without hesitation.

Did he even *know* how much it meant to her? Probably. Despite Bradley not saying much, he seemed to know everything.

"It's okay," he said softly.

Olin sat on her other side and rubbed her back in soothing circles despite the way she sobbed. His voice was soft and warm, like honey gliding over the raw places inside her. "I'm sorry you went through that."

She sniffled, trying to hold in the tears, especially as her father's words about her hysterics came back to her. *Don't show anyone who you really are. They won't like it.*

The words she'd heard so many times as a kid circled her brain, leaving gouges in it as they passed. She'd worked her whole life at trying to act up just to prove something, anything. "I acted up a lot just so they'd get mad," she said.

Dean pulled over a chair to sit in it, placing him right in front of her. "Why?"

"Because if I was doing that, they were at least paying attention to me. And every time I tried to do what I thought they wanted, it never worked. No matter what I did, I was never good enough. So I figured, why try? Why try to fit into that little box they'd created for me if I never succeeded? If they hated me, at least it was because of this image of myself I created, so they rejected that and not *me*."

Dean sighed, then took her chin between his fingers, his touch gentle. "You'll drive yourself into the ground trying to be what people want, trying to live up to their expectations. It's a game you can't win, Kat, especially if those expectations are impossible. You know why?"

"Because I suck," she said, knowing she was whining and just not caring.

He shook his head. "No. Because your parents want you to be small. They want you to be simple, like them. You aren't small, though, and that's why no matter what you do, how much you twist yourself up into nothing, it'll never work. You'll never be what they want, and that's okay. You want to know the funny part? You don't *have* to be what they want. They gave birth to you, but you don't owe them jack shit. You took care of yourself, put yourself through school, did it all without them, so if they don't like it? Well, fuck them. You'd never let anyone else put you down like this."

Kat sighed as she listened to the same words she'd said to herself enough times. Hearing something and believing it were two very different things. She knew this all, knew that her parent's expectations were unreasonable, but that never stopped her from wanting it. "I just want to feel like I belong," she said softly. "I've spent my whole life being the one who was too much, being the person who causes problems, who everyone has some funny story about when I fucked things up. If even my own parents can't respect me, can't see me as something good, can't even love me, what hope do I have?"

Dean didn't answer at first, his blue eyes unwavering as he stared at her. Finally, he curled his lips into a smirk that held an edge of cruelty. "Oh, Kat, you shouldn't have said that." Before she could ask, Dean came forward and took her lips in a kiss. Despite what a mess her face must have been, despite the tears and the puffy eyes and the overly emotional baring of her soul, Dean kissed her as if he were starving for her touch. He broke the contact only long enough to whisper, "Guess you're about to learn that what those fuckwits think of you doesn't mean a damned thing. You are wanted, respected and loved by *us*, and if it takes three Doms to get that point through to you…" He pulled back and grinned. "Well, doesn't matter how slow a learner you are — this lesson can take all damned night."

Chapter Eighteen

Dean couldn't believe how sweet Kat's lips were. There was an edge of saltiness to them—no doubt a result of her tears—but that only made him harder.

He'd wanted to fuck her in the car on the way home, to be honest. Maybe it was twisted, but he wanted to leave some sort of brand on her, wanted to claim her to wipe away those worries that had haunted her eyes.

The woman was far too terrified of failure, of letting anyone close enough to her to hurt her. What he'd thought was a reaction to Jerry had turned out to be more of a reaction to her entire past, to her piece-of-shit parents.

He wanted to ruin them, to use every contact and dirty trick he'd learned as a lawyer to take everything from them.

However, that was for another day. For the moment, he could content himself with trying to show Kat exactly what she meant to him, to show her she had a place with them even if her parents didn't recognize her worth.

And Kat tended to be someone who needed very hands-on lessons.

Which Dean didn't mind one bit.

She moaned into the kiss, the way she was always so damned responsive making him want her all the more. Kat might be difficult, she might be a handful, but that didn't change that she warmed up so quickly. Turning her from a snarling stray into a contented kitten was a thing of beauty.

Dean broke the kiss, not wanting to but knowing they needed space to disrobe and get ready.

And, no matter how selfish Dean could be, especially when it came to Kat, what she needed was to realize all three of them loved her, and that meant he couldn't monopolize her time.

He reached for the buttons of his shirt and undid them as Bradley leaned in to steal the next kiss.

Olin slid his hand over her waist, up her rib cage, then cupped her breast through her pajama top. Kat had an amazing figure, and she often insisted on wearing so little that it was impossible to ignore.

And Dean found a perverse thrill in seeing Olin's hands slide over her, in watching as she enjoyed the attention and fell beneath the spell of the other two. While Dean was a man not afraid to get his own hands dirty, he hadn't realized he had such a voyeuristic kink.

Though he was perverted enough not to be bothered by it.

Kat cried out against Bradley's lips when Olin closed his fingers around one of her nipples even through the fabric of her shirt. He released her quickly, then brushed his thumb over the hard bud.

Dean shrugged his shirt off and hung it over the back of the chair, then left for a moment to collect what they needed. He doubted Kat even noticed his absence — consumed as she was by the other two — but she sure noticed when he set the items down on the nightstand.

Condoms and lube.

She furrowed her brows. "That's it? I'd have figured you'd bring more."

Dean laughed before undoing his belt, then the fastener on his slacks. "Not tonight, Brat. Tonight is more hands-on. I plan to show you I don't *need* toys or cuffs to keep you in check."

A flush on her cheeks said she got his meaning perfectly, and her freezing let Olin grasp the bottom of her shirt and pull it up and over her head.

Which bared her to Dean, and he again found himself struck by just how damned pretty she was. The fact he'd gotten to fall for her, that she let him close to her at all, it felt like yet another miracle from Kat.

But he wasn't about to waste it by questioning it.

And, for the first time, Kat didn't freak out. She didn't try to hide the mostly healed marks on her, didn't try to wrap her arms around her waist so Dean and the others didn't see them. A slight unease, a tension that ran through her shoulders, said she was uncomfortable but unwilling to actually hide.

Brave girl.

Olin must have noticed as well, because he leaned in and pressed a kiss to the top of her mark. That made the tremble stronger, but he didn't stop. He followed the long mark down her front, between her breasts, over her stomach, taking his sweet time as he lavished attention to the entire thing.

"What a good girl," Dean said as he removed his pants and boxers, wanting to feel every inch of her body.

She whimpered at his words, even more so when Olin shifted himself off the end of the bed so he knelt between her legs. He grasped the waist of those shorts she wore and tugged them off.

It left her naked and exposed—exactly how Dean liked her.

Not that Olin gave Dean any time to stare. Instead, he set his hands on the inside of her knees and spread her legs obscenely wide before leaning in to swipe his tongue up her glistening pussy.

And Kat responded by arching her back and grasping the back of his head.

Dean clicked his tongue and moved up to grasp her hands. He lifted them, pinning them to the mattress above her. "We're showing you, aren't we? So you'll be a good girl and just take every last thing we have to give you. If you can't be good, well, I don't mind forcing you." He tightened his grip on her wrists as if driving home the point that even if Kat could have possibly overpowered one of them, she had zero luck against the three.

And that made her eyes light up, reminding Dean that no matter his doubts or his worries, she was *perfect* for him.

Yet, Kat, never one to be outdone, got a mischievous glint in her eyes. "You'd know about that, wouldn't you? With your level of charm, force is probably the only chance you get."

Dean huffed out a laugh. "Not ready to sheath your claws? That's fine, Brat, but let's put your mouth to use so you don't get yourself into trouble. As much as I'd love to end the night by spanking your ass until you're crying, I think you'd prefer something a bit more fun for you."

He didn't wait for her to respond, instead swinging his leg over her so he straddled her chest. He leaned forward, his cock dangling just in front of her perfect, sweet lips.

Kat's wrists fit inside a single hand of his, so he held her with just the one while he reached between them and grasped his shaft with the other. He slid the head of his cock against her lips, which she'd pressed tightly together.

Stubborn woman. Yet it didn't annoy him. Hell, playing these games with her was fucking fun, something he'd had too little of in his life recently.

Bradley made an amused sound in his throat, one that drew Dean's attention. Bradley reached out and cupped one of Kat's exposed breasts with a teasing stroke. "You see, Kat, this is why we never worked. I figured it was because we were both too stubborn, but the reality? It takes more than one Dom to deal with your difficult ass. You're in trouble now that we've figured that out." He drew his hand back and closed his fingers around Kat's nipple, pinching hard and without warning.

Which was exactly what they needed to throw her off balance. Kat parted her lips to cry out, the sound making Dean's dick impossibly harder as he plunged it into the warmth of her mouth.

He glanced down at her, at the way her soft lips wrapped around his shaft, at the way the resolve in her gray eyes bounced between wanting to fight them and the absolute bliss of submission.

And he knew damned well he was falling more deeply in love with this impossible woman.

Kat couldn't believe how quickly these men could undo her.

She was far from a virgin, yet each place they touched made her feel like she was discovering all this for the first time. She teased Dean's cock with her tongue and her lips, savoring the salty pre-cum that spilled from it and the way his position — over her and trapping her — made her feel entirely taken over.

Olin lapped at her pussy as if he were dehydrated and she were the only source of water in the world. His relentless hands kept her thighs pinned open, leaving her at his mercy as he licked her no matter how sensitive she was, no matter how she tried to squirm.

Bradley had released her nipple, the sadistic bastard, but he was *far* from finished. He teased her breasts, keeping her guessing, alternating between soft touches and hard tweaks. She couldn't even *see* what he was going to do, couldn't prepare herself for anything.

And yet, together, that all made her painfully aware of just how much she loved all three. They were different, each man with varied pasts and personalities, all broken in their own way, yet somehow they all fit her perfectly.

Bradley's no-nonsense sensibilities, Olin's sweet nature and Dean's darkness all worked together to form something more from them all.

Her thoughts were rattled when Olin released one of her legs only to plunge at least two thick fingers into her cunt. The sound she made was quiet, muffled by Dean's cock, and it didn't stop Olin at all. He fucked her with those fingers as if possessed, as if he needed nothing more than to have her in some way, to be inside of her as he brought her toward release.

Kat yanked at Dean's hold on her wrists, wanting to touch, to hold. Nothing could break it, though. The arrogant asshole even *laughed* at her attempt. "You look good when you struggle. Maybe later we'll tie you up and just tease you, just watch as you pull and squirm and try so hard to get out."

Her heart raced at the thought, at the helpless feeling she'd have and at just how much she *wanted* that. She wanted the feeling of their eyes on her, to be the thing they wanted that badly, to see them resist just so they could witness her straining against bonds they knew wouldn't break.

How could just the idea Dean put forward excite her that much?

Something overwhelming and almost painful touched her clit, and it took a moment for Kat to realize Olin had nipped her. She wanted to argue, to tell him to keep his fucking teeth away from her, when instead, a moan slipped out around Dean's cock.

Olin's chuckle was surprisingly dark for the normally sweet man. "You were about to complain, weren't you? Well, your cunt isn't complaining as it squeezes around my fingers. Want to try it again?"

She tried to shake her head, but even if she could, it wouldn't matter. Like Olin had implied, her mouth might say whatever it wanted, but her body never lied.

Olin repeated the motion, harder this time, and that sensation rushed over her. It was a mixture of ecstasy and agony, something stronger than either when twisted up together, and it dragged her under the tsunami of her orgasm.

Kat lost track of the entire world as she came, as she arched and squirmed as Olin didn't let up, as Bradley tormented her sensitive nipples, as Dean sank so deep into her mouth that she worried she'd gag.

But each of those things just heightened the intensity, and Kat sank beneath the feeling, surrendering to it, to them, to the men she couldn't fight against anymore.

Bradley teased Kat's hard nipples, fascinated as ever with the fact they had darkened so much. Normally they were a soft pink, but between his rough touches and her excitement, they'd moved to an almost plum color.

And he really enjoyed plums...

Kat shivered, her body exhausted and overworked, no doubt. Not that they were anywhere close to done. Even if Kat would have happily fallen asleep, Bradley wasn't about to let her.

When they all moved, Kat remained still, in the half-awake state as if groggy from the sensations still running through her. Olin delivered one more lick to her cunt, and it made Kat gasp and shake harder.

Beautiful.

Still, she didn't fight when they shifted. A quick look back and forth seemed to solidify the plans with Olin and Dean.

Olin moved to the top of the bed and grabbed a condom. He tossed another to Dean before putting on his own. It took little work to move Kat, to get her to spread her knees around Olin's hips. "Such a good girl," Olin whispered, his voice almost impossible for Bradley to make out. "You're absolutely perfect, you know that? I don't care what anyone else says, don't even care what you say, you're amazing and if you ever think differently…"

Olin made the rest of his point by grasping Kat's hips in his large hands and forcing her down onto his waiting cock.

Kat's lips parted, and she let out a moan so sinful Bradley worried if he'd even hold off long enough to enjoy any part of her. How was it that she could get him so close to release with just a moan?

Dean slid his own condom on, then moved behind Kat, setting his knees on the outside of Olin's. He took the lube from the nightstand and added extra to his condom. He didn't try to prepare her, didn't tease her by sinking one thick finger into her ass then moving up to two.

It seemed Dean wanted more than that.

"I'm going to fuck your ass," he said, his voice not as quiet at Olin's, as if he didn't give a damn if anyone else heard. "I'm not going to get you ready, but this won't be the first time you've had your ass fucked, so you can take that for me like a good little slut, can't you?"

Another one of those delicious shivers ran through Kat as she nodded. "Yes, Sir."

Why was her saying *Sir* so hot? Probably because she'd lost all ability to think, to argue, to do anything but submit to them. They'd pushed her far enough that all that existed of her was this moment and the things she craved.

Dean pressed the tip of his cock against her ass, then held tight to her hips, not plunging in, but teasing her. "You know, I used to be afraid of the things I wanted. I used to be so fucking careful because I thought there was this darkness inside me that was some horrible monster. You made me realize it's just a part of me, that it isn't bad. You're the first and only woman to see that part of me and not run away." He leaned in to press a kiss to her sweat-soaked back. "And I guess that means I'm not that sorry that you're the one who gets to deal with that part of me, the one that wants to hear you cry out when I fuck your ass like this."

He sank into her, and just as he'd said, she *did* cry out. It was the sort of sound Bradley would *never* forget, one burned into his memory no matter how the years would pass.

Yet, she didn't struggle, didn't even have the expression of a woman who doubted if she could handle it. No, not Kat. Kat didn't back down from anything, which seemed to include being fucked by the three of them.

That reminder took Bradley over, so he knelt on the bed beside Olin. Kat's eyes remained closed, as if she were savoring every sensation that ran through her body, as if she could focus on nothing else. It made Bradley pause, gave him a moment to stare at her lost to passion as she was.

She was stunning. He'd thought it so many times before, but that didn't stop it from hitting him like this every once in a while. Her lips were parted just a bit with soft, teasing moans escaping them. Her arms had wrapped around Olin's shoulders, clinging to him, and her back arched as Dean slid into her ass with long and slow thrusts. She was like something ethereal there, something that didn't belong in the dirt and grime of their world.

Olin broke him free of his thoughts, however, when he caught Kat's chin and turned her face toward Bradley. *Right.* It shook him, let him reach out and run his fingers through her hair. The memory of how her family had treated her lingered in Bradley's mind, but he planned to make it perfectly clear to her how he felt—how they *all* felt.

Maybe this had all started because of the threat from Jerry—maybe that had driven them forward when they would have otherwise continued in their rut, but that didn't matter. What Bradley had found he didn't plan on letting go again.

Kat parted her lips when he grasped his cock and brushed it against her. The offer was sweet, and he couldn't deny himself any longer. He pressed forward, sinking his dick into the heat of her talented mouth while Olin grasped her chin.

Not that Kat needed direction or force. On the contrary, she eagerly sucked him, taking him deep as if she couldn't help it, as if she couldn't get enough.

And Bradley, who was hardly some slouch when it came to sex, was damned sure he'd end up spilling well before he wanted to all because of the brat before him, the only creature who could possibly manage to tame in instead of the other way around…

Chapter Nineteen

Kat couldn't stop smiling as she walked the property line. Despite it being her normal routine, something about that morning felt different.

Memories of the night before flashed in her head, brought back how she'd spent it tangled up with the three men. Sure, they'd had sex before, but something about last night had been special.

Maybe it was because, for the first time, she hadn't held back. She hadn't hidden, hadn't pretended to be anything but what she was. After them witnessing her family rejecting her, after them seeing firsthand just how little her actual blood family cared for her, she'd been raw.

Yet...they hadn't turned away. They hadn't seen that and thought, 'you know, these people are right. Kat *is* too much.' Instead, even after she'd cried, even after her face was a mess and her mind was jumbled, they'd simply loved her.

She was sore today, but that was to be expected. While the sex had been sweet, in its own way, the men were nothing if not demanding. She wasn't sure when exactly she'd gotten to sleep, only recalled the way Bradley had stroked his hand over her side, how Olin had pressed his lips to her shoulder, how Dean had told her they cherished her as she'd drifted off.

Kat had never really believed in love, at least not for herself, but she couldn't bring herself doubt it now. She loved them, each of them, more than she thought possible. She loved Bradley and their history and the way she felt safe with him no matter what. She loved Olin, his sense of justice and the way he never failed to know how to make her smile. She loved Dean, how intense he was, how he never shied away from her own darker sides.

But…love wasn't everything. She knew that as well as anyone. Love didn't mean things would work, didn't guarantee some happily ever after.

For the first time ever, though, Kat wanted to try. She didn't want to let them go, even if it ended up breaking her heart. She'd never been willing to risk herself before, to open herself up, but the thought of letting go without trying sounded far more painful than the thought of them leaving her later.

Which was a terrifying thought.

The breeze held a chill as it ran through the large ranch, but Kat just pulled her light wrap tighter around herself. Bradley was no doubt somewhere, taking care of some animal, while she'd left the other two working at the house.

Some time alone was probably for the best, and Kat had to admit, she cherished these walks. Her favorite of the livestock dogs, Max, trailed behind her as he always did, as if she were one of the baby goats he needed to look after. It made her smile, made her think about how complete her life felt here.

She walked along the far back fence line and tipped her head back to enjoy the way the sun warmed her face. These walks always calmed her, and so long as she stayed within range of the cameras that spanned the property, her overprotective Doms tended to allow it.

The soft crunch of dirt made her frown. A small dirt road ran the back length of the property, despite Bradley owning that as well. He'd only fenced part of the ranch, however, so the livestock dogs knew where to patrol.

No one should drive there, but it wasn't the first time it had happened. Folks from out of town often assumed no fence meant free use to the public, and Kat had watched Bradley scoot off others who had tried to camp on his property.

She pulled her shoulders back as the car stopped, ready to defend his land the way Max would. The thought had her smiling, the further proof of just how much she loved this place, how much at home she felt there, that she had no issue with telling people off just to keep it safe.

The back car door opened, and Kat readied herself. No doubt they were someone from LA, especially driving a car like that, and she expected them to dress as most of the tourists did — like they thought they were in some fancy western movie, with fringe and cowboy hats.

Except, Kat's breath froze when it wasn't some out of towner, some lost tourist who had no idea what they were doing.

Instead, Kat came face-to-face with Jerry.

* * * *

Dean leaned back in his chair, balancing it on two legs. To most people looking at him, they'd think he wasn't working. How often had his bosses, back at the start of his career, thought he was slacking off?

It wasn't the case, though. Instead, he was entirely focused on the problem at hand, trying to figure out the best defense for his client. It was a girl who had stabbed her boyfriend. There was loads of proof—no real denying it had happened.

However, if it had just been a malicious attack, he'd have never taken the case. The black eye the girl had worn, the way she'd flinched when the officer had escorted her by the arm, it had all said what really happened loud and clear.

Convincing a jury that a stabbing was justified was a hard sell, though. Too often people liked to blame women. They asked why she didn't leave sooner, as what she did to stop it, but when the woman actually did something, she got punished.

Dean sighed and let the chair drop, the strike of it against the floor loud even above the music that filled the room.

He needed to dig deeper into the abuse, show the jury that if the woman had done nothing, she'd have been killed. To start with, the hospital records after the last time she'd run away should help…

Dean yawned, his mouth stretching wide. He hadn't gotten nearly enough sleep the night before, but he wasn't sorry about it. There wasn't a better way to spend an entire night than wrapped up with Kat, then enjoying each sound she made, each expression that stretched across her lovely features. She was a delight, and he'd happily suffer the exhaustion today.

Thinking about her made him grin, the way it always did. She never shied away from him, had never condemned him. He'd been so sure that she'd take one look at the real him, at the things he'd done in his past, and she'd walk away.

Then again, Kat was braver than she was smart.

He chuckled and left his room, needing some coffee to try to spur his brain into action. He paused at Bradley's office, a normal part of his routine, so he could check the cameras to spot Kat. She was usually taking a walk around now, though she might have set up to paint already. Seeing her sink deeper into her art, into the paintings that clearly made her happy, thrilled him.

Dean enjoyed catching a glimpse of her to reassure himself that she was fine or to let him know where to go to track her down.

He went into the office, the monitor for the security system already on. Countless camera views lined the screen, and Dean took the mouse to click through them, searching. He spotted Bradley out at the stables and Olin reading a book in the hammock near the house.

No sign of the brat, though.

He narrowed his eyes, scanning through one set after another.

When he finally landed on the right one, he took a deep breath. Something about seeing her always did that to him, allowed him to release tension he hadn't even realized he held onto. She was like an instant anti-anxiety medication.

Though that relief didn't last long, not when the top edge of the camera caught the tires of a black car on the back road just outside the fence line. Someone was there?

The car door opened, and black shoes appeared. Still, Dean couldn't tell who it was, and with Kat facing the other way, he couldn't guess from her expression. Still, he couldn't shake an unease.

The figure walked closer, and the moment their face came into view, Dean had his phone in his hand, his feet already moving as he bolted from the house.

A fear unlike anything he'd ever known before took him over, and nothing mattered but getting to Kat.

* * * *

"What are you doing here?" Kat hated that her voice cracked at the question. Even after all her work, all the growing she'd done, he still frightened her.

Jerry smiled, though it had tense edges. "Don't ask stupid questions, Katherine. They're beneath you."

The way he said her name stung as it always had, reminding her too much of her parents, mixing with the way he'd said it when he'd dragged that knife down her front.

It made her stomach churn, made her worry she'd throw up her breakfast if she couldn't calm herself down.

Max growled, lifting his lips, the hair on his back standing up straight. However, when a man in the front passenger seat got out, a gun in his hand, Kat gripped Max's collar and told him to calm.

The dog did, though there was no doubting he was still on edge.

"You said you'd let me decide," Kat said, knowing how stupid those words were. He was a murder — what did promises mean to him?

"And I am. A good businessman knows when to apply direct pressure. You're tougher than I thought, more stubborn than I realized. I guess that's why I like you, though, why I can't stop thinking about you. So I came to persuade you."

Kat shook her head. "I'm not going to give in to you."

She recalled how she'd nearly done exactly what he wanted before, when that body had been left on her front porch. The thing was...she hadn't thought she had anything worth living for back then.

She'd thought she was just a burden on those around her, just waiting until they left her. Now, though?

Now it was different... Now she wanted the life she'd seen with the men she loved, the ones who loved her, flaws and all.

Jerry let out a laugh that chilled her before he turned around and reached into the car. A cry left the lips of someone inside — clearly a woman — a moment before he stood straight again, yanking someone from the car.

The woman was naked with blood on her, but she was standing and alive. Her hair was white, though Kat could *smell* the chemicals from the dye used. It made her want to vomit all the more.

"I'm not above negotiating," Jerry said, his expression one of a man sure he'd already won. "So here is the deal. You come with me, and I leave her here. Maybe just seeing the aftermath isn't real enough for you. Maybe you somehow think that it would happen if I had you or not, so here is my chance to show you the truth, so you can look her in the eyes and tell her you won't save her."

The woman cowered, not even bothering to try to hide her nakedness. It showed just how broken down she was from Jerry's abuse.

Still, Kat tried to stay calm, to think things through. "If I come with you, you'll just kill me and be right back at it. It won't stop anything." She spat out the words Olin had said, even if she wasn't sure she believed them.

"I only play with these toys because they're cheap knock-offs. I break them because I don't give a damn about them—they're replaceable. You are not. I assure you, I would not break you in the same way."

No...he'd break her in another way. He might not kill her, at least not right away, but he'd torment her. He'd destroy her piece by piece until there was nothing left of the woman she was, until she was a hollow doll for him to toy with as he pleased.

And yet, knowing that didn't stop her feet from moving. She told the dog to go home, having to order it three times to get it going. She didn't need the dog to get hurt—she had enough blood on her hands already.

"You'll let her go?"

Jerry nodded. "I promise, and I haven't lied to you yet. I'll leave her here with those idiot men you're staying with, the ones who thought they could keep you from me. Maybe they'll take her as a cheap substitute—I really don't care. Neither she nor they interest me at all."

The girl whimpered before locking eyes with Kat. She shook her head, as if to tell Kat not to trade herself.

Which solidified Kat's plan all the more. She reached the barbed wire fence that ran with two lines as more of a visual deterrent and slid easily between them.

"Let her go," Kat said.

"Not until you're over here," Jerry argued.

"No. I want to know that she can get away because I don't trust you. I'm close enough that I couldn't run and get far, not with the fence, so I want to see that she's safe."

Jerry let out a sigh, as if Kat were annoying him, but nodded and released the woman.

The woman nearly collapsed without him holding her up, but she barreled toward Kat, grabbing onto Kat's arm. "You can't—he's a monster."

Kat forced a smile before sliding off the large wrap she wore and pulling it around the woman's naked shoulders. It wasn't much, but anything was better than nothing. "It's okay. See that way?" Kat pointed into the distance. "There's a house there and you'll find three men who will take care of you, okay? As soon as you get through the fence, I want you to run straight there, okay?"

The woman's eyes were wide, the blue of them almost lifeless. The desires warred inside those eyes, the want to stay, to help, to not leave Kat, but also the yearning for freedom and safety.

Kat squeezed the woman's hand once more, trying to break her loose of her thoughts. "It's okay. Go."

The woman finally nodded and went, following Kat's example through the fence before taking off at a run.

Kat's gaze followed the woman before looking down at her arm where the woman had grabbed. *Blood.*

Not the last that would be on Kat, no doubt.

"You know, I came here expecting you to give in, to do as I wanted, but I find I'm still a bit surprised. Do you have any idea how rare it is for me to be surprised? Perhaps that's what made me fall for you, the fact that I struggle to ever predict you."

The praise, which from Dean or Olin or Bradley would have made her heart race, did nothing to Kat.

"We should get going," the man who had been in the passenger side of the car said. "The men who live here will come when they find that woman."

Jerry waved the concern off and crooked his finger. "Come along, Katherine. I said from the start that you would come to me, that you would give in and submit. So, submit."

Kat gulped down the sickness that threatened to rise in her throat as she put one foot in front of the other, doing exactly what Jerry had said she would. It reminded her of all the times her parents had said she'd fail, that she'd never succeed, that she wasn't good enough or strong enough or smart enough to make it on her own.

A tremble started inside her as she forced herself forward. When she reached just in front of Jerry, he still didn't grab her.

"Look at me," he demanded.

Kat did it, no matter how little she wanted to, and met his gaze. It was empty, as if there were no real person inside the monster, and the shaking inside her intensified.

At least, until the sound of hooves hitting the ground caught her attention.

Jerry took that moment to grab her and haul her against him, a hand on her throat to keep her still, and Kat saw the last thing she wanted to see.

Brat, the horse, at an all-out gallop, with Bradley on her back.

And a whole new sort of terror filled her.

Bradley couldn't stop the relief he felt at seeing Kat still there. Dean's voice in his ear remained, the terror filled explanation that Jerry was there, that Kat was alone.

Olin and Dean were on their way as well, but Bradley had been the closest. Not that he knew what the hell to do. He didn't carry any of his guns on the ranch normally, since getting thrown from a horse with a pistol on his hip wasn't much fun. Unless he had reason to need one, he preferred to keep them in the gun safe. Maybe he should have started carrying again given Kat was there, but he'd been overconfident in the safety of the ranch.

That didn't matter, though. All that had mattered was getting there, was doing something — anything — so Kat didn't slip away again. After finding this happiness, he wasn't about to let it go.

"Well, this is awkward," Jerry said, his hand wrapped around Kat's throat despite Jerry not appearing to have a weapon. Instead, the man to his side had a pistol out and aimed at Bradley. "If you're here for goodbyes, please get them over with quickly. Katherine and I need to get reacquainted."

Bradley swung himself off the horse then slapped its hindquarters to get it to go. He didn't need it taking a bullet or panicking in the event that the muscle over there fired his gun. A panicking horse would just make the situation worse.

It took off, letting Bradley focus on the scene in front of him instead. He peered at Kat. "You okay?"

She nodded, but her gaze dropped as if she couldn't bear to look at him. Why? Shame? Maybe it was too hard since she assumed she was going to never see him again.

Fuck that. If Kat thought she was going *anywhere,* she was sadly mistaken. "It'll be okay, Kat."

"It won't," Jerry said, his voice full of arrogance. "You see, *Katherine,* I fell for you because of how much trouble you are and how much fun breaking that will be. You are the sort of woman who brings chaos to everything around her. You caused the death of all those women, and the one you just '*saved*'? She's going to carry those scars all her life and they're your fault. If your buddy here does anything stupid, his death'll be on your hands, too. Haven't you figured that out, yet? Look at how much every person around you has suffered all because of you."

The words were cruel, but it wasn't hard to see each one taking apart any confidence Kat had inside her.

The sound of the golf cart made Bradley breathe in deeply. Sure enough, a moment later, it pulled to a stop beside Bradley and Olin and Dean got out.

"The woman..." Kat said, the foolish brat always too worried about everyone else.

"She's fine," Olin assured her. "She's safe at the house waiting for an ambulance."

"Detective Ramiz," Jerry said with a grin. "When I heard you were involved in this, I'd assumed at first it was just because of me. Then I heard you took time off just to watch over Katherine. It seems you were ensnared by her just like me, but are you really willing to die over it?"

Olin didn't back down in the least, his chin held high, a gun in his hand though not raised. "Yeah, I am.

Killing women is one thing, but killing a police officer on camera like this? I don't think you want that sort of attention."

Jerry lifted his gaze as if he'd just spotted the cameras that sat on large poles around the property. Still, he shrugged. "After everything that's happened, I knew I couldn't stay here. I already have a lovely place waiting for us in a non-extradition country. So whatever I do here won't matter a bit."

Bradley closed his hands into fists, hating how useless he felt in that moment. Another man was threatening the woman he loved and there was *nothing* he could do about it.

Dean spoke up for the first time, ignoring Jerry and focusing on Kat. "What are you doing, Brat?" His voice was soft and almost sweet despite this undercurrent of darkness, the sort of sound Dean usually tried to keep secret. "I thought you understood that turning yourself over for any reason wasn't allowed."

"I couldn't let him hurt that woman," Kat answered.

"Foolish girl," Dean muttered, though the harsh words came out affectionate. "That's enough selfless crap, don't you think? You made me a promise, remember?"

She frowned, as if she wasn't sure what he meant.

Not that Jerry gave a damn. "A promise? Pointless. Katherine isn't in the position to promise anything. She's mine. She has always been mine and she will be mine until the day I choke the last breath from her body. I don't care what you've done to her or with her, because she has been and will always be *mine.*"

Bradley didn't let the words deter him, especially as he realized Dean's play. Instead, he followed Bradley's lead. "Dean's right, Kat. I've watched you outsmart every scary Dom at Sanctuary, seen you outlast the more stubborn people in the world. You're tougher than you think."

She blinked slowly, as if the words had started to sink in.

Olin spoke next, his voice relaxed. Then again, out of any of them, Olin had been in the most high-risk situations, no doubt. "I'm not done with you, Kat. This can't be the end of it. I want to hear you insult me for years more to come, and I want to smile as you pull stupid pranks and I want to watch you walk circles around anyone who thinks they can control you. You want that too, don't you? What that asshole says, none of that matters. He's a coward, just trying to convince you what other people have tried to convince you of for *years*. That you're not good enough, that you're too much, that it's inevitable you fail. They're liars, though, and they're just trying to make you small enough for their little brains to sort out. Don't fall into their trap."

Bradley held his breath as he watched, desperate to see the spark in Kat's eyes, the moment she realized what they meant.

Because if they couldn't get through to her, if she didn't figure it out, Bradley would lose her, and that wasn't something he could allow.

Kat struggled to make sense of the words of the men, the way they spoke to her and ignored Jerry.

Her head was a mess of guilt and fear, a feeling that she'd failed everyone around her. The words of her parents came back to her, like they always did, like wounds that would never heal and that Jerry only made that much larger. She'd failed, over and over again, and so many others had paid the price for her.

"Look at me," Dean said, his voice compelling her to meet his blue eyes, as if he controlled her alone with that voice. When she did, he smiled, though it held no warmth. "You swore you wouldn't give up, didn't you?"

His words reached through her confusion, through all the negative things that had swarmed her. She had said she wouldn't give up, hadn't she? It suddenly felt like the most important promise she'd ever made.

Because...she wanted to come back to Dean. She wanted to see Bradley let out one of those snorts when she did something he found funny even if he didn't want to admit it. She needed to feel Olin's kisses over her bare skin and needed to watch as that switch in Dean flipped, when he stopped holding back and she glimpsed the real him.

But none of that would happen if she gave in, if she listened to Jerry.

"Isn't that sweet?" Jerry said, the mocking words still holding no fear. The man had no idea just how much trouble he was in.

"You really are stupid," Olin said. "You think you've got some toy that you're holding there, but you've got the meanest stray. You ever try to hold on to a cat who's pissed? It's a failing proposition, every damned time."

Kat forced herself to think, to remember everything she'd learned. Olin had a gun, but he couldn't take a shot, not right away especially. They needed an opening and they needed Kat to not be covering Jerry.

One deep breath helped to settle her, to unknit her muscles. She locked eyes with Dean for a split second, and a tiny nod let him know she was ready.

Kat forced her body to go limp, the action unsettling Jerry's hold on her. He knocked forward. At the same time, Olin lifted his gun, but the other guard must have expected that, must have been watching since Olin was the only one armed.

A bullet rang out, but Kat couldn't see, couldn't tell what was happening as Jerry toppled forward, over her. Sharp rocks dug into her knees and she was sure she was bleeding.

None of that mattered, though. She could deal with injuries later, could patch herself up. She didn't even allow herself to think about the gunshot that had rang out, to worry about who might have gotten hurt. Instead, she twisted, slamming her elbow into his face.

Dean's words came back to her, made her remember she wasn't fighting someone who was fair, someone who would follow the rules, so if she wanted to win, she had to be willing to get just as dirty.

Kat closed her fist around a handful of sand and threw it at his eyes, rewarded with an angry shout from Jerry. She shifted backward, scooting through the dirt, until she could lift her foot and drive her heel into his face as he tried to rub the dirt clear.

Another shot ran out, and terror filled Kat, fear at who might be hurt. Still, she couldn't give in—she'd sworn she wouldn't.

Kat got to her feet, ready to run, but slammed right into someone. Fear only held her for a moment before she realized who exactly she'd run into.

Dean.

Except he wasn't the Dean she knew, the one she was used to. This was the darkness he'd said before, the parts of his past honed by a desire to survive above all else. He held Olin's pistol in his hand, and Kat peered around to find Bradley on the ground, Olin holding his hands against a spot on Bradley's side.

Bradley was shot...

Kat couldn't come to terms with that, couldn't make sense of it, and Dean only looked down at her for a moment. He set a hand on her cheek, brushing against her skin as if it were precious.

Even still, the hard look in his blue eyes didn't fade, especially when he moved his gaze over to Jerry who had managed to turn over, his eyes red from the dirt and blood pouring from his nose.

The car they'd come in took off, dirt flying up. It seemed the driver had realized the turn in events and wanted nothing to do with the fallout.

Jerry turned his gaze toward the car as if he couldn't believe it, but when he looked back, it wasn't the expression of a beaten man. No, Jerry still seemed to think he could get out of this. "This isn't over," he said.

"Yes, it is," Kat spat, for once feeling powerful and in control. "You did everything you could to get me under your thumb and it still failed. You'll go away forever."

"No, I won't. Men like me, we don't get taken down by little girls like you. Maybe I go away for a year or two, or maybe my powerful friends help me out and I'm back for you sooner than you think. Are you ready to spend every day of the rest of your life thinking about me? Looking over your shoulder for me? Because that's what you have to look forward to." He let out a vicious laugh.

Dean let go of Kat's cheek, dropping his hand away to stare down at Jerry. "That isn't going to happen."

Jerry laughed. "Yeah, it is. You're a lawyer and your buddy there is a lawman. Neither of you will do shit to an unarmed man."

"I wasn't always a lawyer," Dean said, his voice flat. "There was a time when I did horrendous things all to protect myself. I told you that, but you didn't believe me."

"You don't have to kill me, though."

"No, I don't, but I've realized something. I stopped that bull because survival wasn't everything, because keeping myself safe wasn't worth living with my actions. Survival matters, and I've done things that haunt me for it, but the things I'll do to protect the woman I love? You haven't seen what I'm really capable of, the lengths I'll go."

"You're lying—" Jerry didn't get the rest of whatever he was going to say out before Dean lifted the gun and squeezed the trigger, sending a single bullet through Jerry's forehead.

And just like that...

It was over.

Chapter Twenty

Kat sat in the chair outside Bradley's hospital room, leaning forward as she hyped herself up to go in and visit him.

She'd already heard that he was okay, that, while he had been shot, he'd recover. The bullet had gone into his shoulder when he'd shoved Olin out of the way, the action probably saving them both. Dean had taken Olin's gun at that point, and Kat knew exactly what happened from there.

The sight of Dean with that cold look on his face haunted Kat, the flatness of his eyes, the way the touch of his hand on her cheek had been so at odds with how he'd so easily pulled the trigger. She'd done that.

Bradley could have been killed, Dean had to do something she knew would wear on him and Olin was no doubt being questioned fully, which meant his job could be at risk due to his connection with her and Sanctuary, and it was *all* because of her.

Each of them had risked so much and for what?

The only blessing was that the cameras hadn't caught all the exchange. The other man had survived his wound, and it seemed he'd been only too happy to throw Jerry under the bus and offer up all the information he had on their group to lessen his own sentence. It meant the official story was that Jerry had been shot in self-defense.

That story would save Dean from going to jail, but it didn't stop the pain Kat knew he must be in.

The door opened, and a nurse came into the hallway. She paused, as if surprised to find Kat there. "Are you waiting to visit?"

Kat stood, smoothing down her clothes, wishing something could calm her nerves. "Yeah, I am. I was waiting until he was ready."

The nurse nodded toward the door. "Well, he's comfortable for now, so it's a good time." The nurse paused before walking past Kat, as if she spotted something in Kat's face that she recognized. She set a hand on Kat's forearm and squeezed. "He'll be okay, honey."

Kat nodded, even though she didn't believe it. The nurse didn't understand. She was talking about the moment, about that bullet, but she didn't understand that it had all been Kat's fault. "Right," Kat said, because there was no reason to burden all that mess on the nurse.

The nurse offered a kind smile. "You'll feel better once you see him — I promise. Go on in."

Kat forced herself to do as she said, though when she entered the hospital room she didn't look right at Bradley. It was too hard, so she kept her gaze on the floor. The beeping of machines was *so* damned loud and it just reminded her of how close she'd been to losing him for good.

"Hey." Bradley's voice was rough, though not laced in pain. Then again, no doubt they'd given him the good drugs since he'd have to stay in the hospital for the night.

Kat didn't lift her gaze, even as she stood beside the bed, and it seemed that wasn't good enough for Bradley. He caught her wrist and held it tight. "Look at me."

Kat shook her head.

He sighed, then tugged until Kat leaned on the bed.

"Wait," she said and tried to yank back. "I might jostle your arm!"

Bradley laughed as if she were being absurd. "Well, you should have looked at me. Since you wouldn't, this is the next best thing. Stop fighting or you'll end up hurting me."

Kat finally looked at him just to glare. "You're so manipulative."

He let out a laugh, one that didn't sound entirely like him. It was probably the meds. "I learned it from you. Now, stop worrying—I'm fine."

"You were *shot*. I don't think that counts as fine."

He looked over at her, a grin across his lips, his cheeks pinker than usual. "All's well that ends well, right? I'll take a bullet for you anytime."

"Well, technically, you took a bullet for *me*." Olin chuckled as he came in, Dean on his heels. "I mean, I appreciate it, but I'm not into men."

"Seeing as I castrate most of the males in my life, it's probably not the best match for you, either," Bradley said, his good arm over around Kat.

Olin laughed softly as he came closer, with he and Dean standing beside the hospital bed. "Doctor says you'll live."

"So it seems."

"How long are you in here for?" Dean asked.

"At least until tomorrow. They want to start me on physical therapy." Bradley groaned as he said it, as though physical therapy was the worst thing he could think of.

"You need some help on the ranch?" Olin asked. "I took off a full month already, so I've got time."

The men spoke back and forth about nothing, but the tension inside Kat kept growing. They acted as if nothing had happened, as if they hadn't all been in danger hours before, as if they could leave the hospital and everything would go back to how it had been.

Kat stayed quiet as long as she could before it just bubbled up, and she cracked from the pressure of what had happened, of what was in her head. "This is over."

The men all went silent, the tension in the room thick.

It made her keep going, let her spill out all the thoughts locked inside her. "You almost *died*, Bradley! All because of me, you could have died." The more she spoke, the more came out. "And Olin, you could end up losing your job. You were already taken off a case because of me, and what happens if they figure out you went to Sanctuary? What if your boss realizes I go there and they blame you?"

Kat moved her gaze to Dean, who had his arms crossed as if waiting for his turn. "And *you*... You've worked so hard to move on, but you ended up going back to exactly what you hated before to save me."

No one answered right away, and the more the silence pressed in on Kat, the more she wanted to escape. She wanted to slide from the bed and leave them be, to stop ruining their lives.

Still, Kat whispered the rest of what was on her mind. "This isn't me thinking I'm not good enough anymore. I fought Jerry because I wanted to live, because you helped me realize I was worth it, but this is different. I can't ask you all to risk so much just for me. It isn't fair. I..." She paused, but knew she couldn't keep this inside. Even if it didn't matter, even if she left them and never saw them again, she needed to have told them. "I love you too much to let you pay the price like that."

After a long, tense minute, Dean spoke up. "You done?"

Kat nodded and went to leave, ready to let them get back to their real lives, to leave them be.

Except, Bradley tightened his arm around her, keeping her in the bed and against his side. "Not so fast, Brat."

"But Dean said..."

"I asked if you were done because I wanted to give you the chance to say all the stupid shit you want before we make ourselves clear." Dean leaned in and caught her chin, forcing her gaze to his. "I knew exactly what I was doing when I pulled that trigger. I wasn't in shock, wasn't confused. Jerry might not have had a gun, but he was still a threat. What I did when I was younger, I did it because I thought survival was all that mattered. Later, I questioned myself, wondered if it was worth it to do that, but when I was standing there? *You* are worth doing that for. You're worth whatever I have to do to keep you safe, to keep you by my side."

"I remember you when you said that you woke up from nightmares…"

Dean offered a smile, one that Kat cherished, one that reminded her of the man she'd fallen for. "And I might just have some more, so don't you think you should be there when I wake up?"

Kat sighed, wanting to argue, to tell him he was wrong, but unable to.

And Olin seemed to take the break in the conversation to speak up. "You need to stop worrying about things that aren't your problem. Fact is that I already got a talking to about Sanctuary during my debrief, and you know what? I spoke to my lawyer a few days ago because I realized just how much you matter to me. Turns out my personal life like that isn't up for discussion with my job. The second I mentioned my lawyer, my boss shut up fast."

"But why didn't you do that before?"

"Because I didn't know anyone worth doing that for. Sanctuary versus my job was an easy choice, but as it turns out, you're a lot more important. You're worth the fight and you're worth the risk."

"But what if—"

"No more what-ifs. You need to listen to me, to trust that I know what's most important to me, and now? That's *you*."

Kat swallowed hard, unable to wipe away what she was thinking.

Bradley tightened his grip around her, but didn't speak until she looked at him. Once she did, he offered her a drugged, lopsided grin. "I got shot. I don't think you should be trying to leave me after I got shot."

Kat froze, his words unexpected and not at all like him. She'd thought he'd give her some sort of pep talk, some declaration of love. The longer she stared at him, the more absurd it sounded.

Another moment later, Kat burst into laughter. She leaned in and brushed her lips against Bradley's. "You are surprisingly adorable when you're high."

"Just returning the favor. You were pretty cute when you called me high." He blinked slowly, then returned the kiss, which made her heart race even if it was messy and uncoordinated.

Kat turned so she could move her gaze between the men. "Are you sure? I mean, you've seen my baggage, you know I'm not that easy to live with. Are you really sure this is what you want?"

"No doubts for me," Olin said.

"Again, I *took a bullet for you,* so if that doesn't answer it, you can fuck off," Bradley tacked on.

Dean grinned, though it warmed Kat as much as it made her nervous. "I'm sure. You're the only girl who could keep my attention, and I know I'll never get bored with a brat like you around."

Kat gave up. She let go of her doubt, of her fears, of the worries in her head that had held her back for so long. It felt like a weight she'd shrugged off finally.

Even surrounded by three Doms, Kat had never actually felt free before, as if they'd released her, and she knew she'd spend the rest of her life annoying the three of them.

Epilogue

Three months later...

Kat shifted as she tried to keep her anxiety in check. What had she been thinking? After years of spending her time in her nice safe little corner of the world, she just *had* to venture out?

She let out a sigh before running her fingers through her hair to move it out of her face.

"Is this where you're hiding?" Olin's voice made her smile, somehow easing her nerves just by speaking. His strong arms wrapped around her from behind, tugging her back against his solid chest. He pressed his lips to her shoulder. "I'm pretty sure you're supposed to be out there."

"Why? Other artists get to never show their face. Can't I be one of *those* artists?"

"Sorry, no. There are people to see you."

She turned in his arms so she could see his face, and immediately, Kat fell even more for Olin. He smiled down at her, his honey-colored eyes so familiar. How many times has she stared into those eyes? How many times had she enjoyed the touch of his soft lips and his whispered demands?

"Your cheeks are red," Olin said, leaning down so he whispered into her ear. "Are you thinking something filthy? You are a handful, aren't you?" His breath warmed her, made a shiver run through her body.

"Why don't I *show* you?"

"The door doesn't lock."

"So? If you hold me up against the door, I'm pretty sure no one will come in."

His smile widened, and for a moment, Kat thought she'd won. However, when she turned toward the door, he smacked her ass *hard*.

Kat yelped in surprise, then rubbed the sore spot.

"Sorry, Brat, but you can't trick me. I'll enjoy you later when we're alone. For now, no more hiding."

"What if no one likes them?" she finally asked, admitting her true fears. "What if I went through all this and no one wants my real work? What if no one buys any? If they laugh at me because I was an idiot who thought I could do this?"

Olin cupped her cheeks and brought his forehead to hers. "You worry too much. Come on."

Kat sighed but nodded. It was true—she couldn't just not go out. This was her first art exhibit, the first time she'd ever put herself out there and showed off her paintings. Dean had helped her get in touch with an agent who had worked out all the details, but even with that, Kat felt like the new kid at school.

She was terrified she'd show up only to find no one actually wanted to sit with her.

Olin released her, then interlocked his fingers with hers and squeezed softly. It gave her the courage to do what she knew she needed to do and leave the safety of her little hidey-hole.

"You find her?" Bradley asked when they exited, his eyebrow lifted.

"What can I say? Cops are trained to be amazing at hide and seek."

Bradley let out a soft chuckle, the sound melting Kat. Bradley could seem so closed off, so serious, which was why the way he'd softened only for Kat drew her in. "So what's my job, then? Taming?"

"Well, you're used to dealing with unruly and dangerous animals." Dean walked up, and his comment said he'd been listening. Then again, Dean was *always* one step ahead, too smart for his own good—and often for Kat's good.

Kat gave him a playful glare. "Then what's your job?"

He caught her chin and tipped her head up before stealing a kiss that soothed all her worries. Something about the way he never seemed to worry, about how damned confident he was, it made Kat feel as if they could handle anything. And there was also the fact she knew he'd do anything to keep her safe...

When he broke the kiss, he gave her the sort of smile that made her wish they were back in that room alone. "*Obviously* I deal with punishment. Nothing better than turning your pretty ass red."

The words made her cheeks flush and her heart race, but she didn't have time to try to talk them into anything. Instead, her agent walked over and broke into the private moment. "Kat! I was looking for you!"

"Sorry," Kat said despite not feeling sorry at all. She braced herself for bad news when she lifted her chin. "So, what did you want?"

"Well…" The pause after that took forever, but finally, the agent went on. "You've sold out."

"But we haven't actually started yet," Kat said, unable to understand the words. People were coming to the exhibit to look at her art, and her agent had explained that it was common for only a few to sell the first time. They were creating buzz, mostly, getting her name out there.

"When we did the sneak peeks over the last week for media, we started getting calls from collectors who wanted to buy pieces before the exhibit so they didn't lose them. They're *all* sold, Kat, every one of them." Her agent grinned even though Kat had trouble keeping up. "Smile, Kat, you're a success."

And right there… Kat thought she might just collapse.

* * * *

Dean took a drink of the champagne that a server had handed off to him. He wasn't drunk, and he wouldn't drink enough to get there. Still, it was hard not to celebrate as he watched Kat float around the room from person to person with that smile.

She'd doubted herself for so long, been so sure she wasn't any good, that no one could really want her, that watching her finally realize people respected her was the best damned thing.

It only made him fall harder for the impossible, stubborn and infuriating woman.

And I've already fallen pretty damned hard.

"You look happy." Ell smiled as she walked up, her smile easing Dean as it always did. She was his oldest friend, more of a sister than anyone else in his life. She smiled more than she had before, telling him that domestic bliss agreed with her.

"I am," Dean said, not bothering to make a joke. Ell would see through it anyway. "Never figured I'd get here, but damn it, I am."

"Girl talk?" Kat came up and wrapped her arm around Dean's waist, snuggling in. It was one of the things he loved about Kat, that she never worried about who was watching, that she never tried to hide how she felt when it came to him.

He wasn't someone's dirty little secret, and Kat would stand up to anyone who treated him like that.

"Always," Dean said. "You jealous?"

"Hardly. I know Ell's Doms, after all, and Clint would murder you if you touched her."

Dean snorted at the joke, especially the fondness in Kat's voice.

"Congrats," Ell said, breaking into the back and forth. "You did amazing, Kat! I had no idea just how talented you are."

"Thanks." Kat leaned more against Dean, her gaze moving over the room as if she couldn't believe it. "It doesn't feel real that everyone is here for me."

Dean leaned in and pressed a kiss to Kat's head. While those words might have annoyed him from someone else, someone who was just fishing for compliments, he knew Kat too well to think that of her. She really had thought she wasn't capable of this, that she wasn't any good, that no one would care about her if she behaved like herself, if she showed people her real self.

Stupid girl.

A commotion by the door made him frown, drawing his attention there. The moment he spotted it, he cursed softly under his breath. He wanted to escort Kat away from the room, to let her hide again until it was dealt with, to shield her from it, but Kat was too sharp.

She turned and went rigid at the sight of her parents walking into the exhibit.

Well fuck…

"I can't believe how many people are here from Sanctuary," Olin said to Toya as he marveled again at the tight connection between them all.

"That only goes to show you were away too long. We always look out for our own." Toya looked toward Kat, a softness on her face that was rare for the Domme. "Kat is like the heart of Sanctuary. I don't think it would be what it is without her, even if she doesn't realize it."

"Well, I have a feeling she can't pull this whole, 'I am an island,' thing anymore."

"Not with you, Dean and Bradley watching her, at least." Toya let out a soft laugh. "Of course, if you hurt her…" *And* there went that rare sweetness she'd had, bringing her scary side out in force.

It reminded him why Toya ran such a tight ship with Sanctuary, why they had so few problems there. She was ruthless when it came to those she considered herself responsible for, which meant *all* of the people who went. Still, it seemed she had a special place for Kat.

"I wouldn't do anything to hurt her," Olin said instead of making a joke of the threat. "I love her more than anything, and nothing matters more to me than keeping her safe and seeing that mischievous smile of hers."

Toya studied his expression, as if trying to determine the truth, before nodding. "You'd better."

"What are you doing here?" Bradley's angry voice made Olin frown and turn, the way it was lowered but still carried, as if he wanted no one to hear but couldn't quite control it.

Near the front door, Olin spotted the reason. Kat's parents stood there and Bradley blocked their path. Kat and Dean approached from the side, and the pain on Kat's face let Olin understand the aggression in Bradley's voice.

She'd come so far, worked so hard, finally achieved things her parents told her she wasn't capable of, and here they were to destroy it all.

Over my dead body.

"You need to leave," Bradley said, trying to keep his voice low not to attract too much attention. After everything Kat had been through, she didn't need to be humiliated at her own party by the likes of these assholes.

It would have been better for Dean or Olin to deal with them, for the men who had silver tongues and quick wits to smooth things over, but instead it had landed on Bradley's shoulders since he'd spotted them talking to the security at the front door. He knew damned well they weren't on the list, hadn't been invited, so what the fuck were they doing there?

"This is our daughter's party. Of course we're here," Barlow said, playing the part of a loving father.

"You've done nothing but hurt her for years. You've got no place here, and if you think I'm about to stand here and let you hurt her more, you've got another think coming."

Barlow pulled his shoulders back, the look of a man used to getting what he wanted. "You don't scare me. You are some useless backwoods hick and hardly worth my time. We aren't here for you — we're here for Katherine."

"Mom, Dad." Kat's voice had that soft quality it had every time Kat spoke to her parents, as if she turned into a kid around them, no matter what. All that confidence he'd grown used to from her evaporated in front of them. "Why are you here?"

Elizabeth smiled as if seeing Kat were the best thing, but Bradley easily spotted the fakeness of it. "What do you mean, darling? We're here to celebrate your accomplishment."

"You made it clear you don't support my art," Kat pressed.

"Oh, Katherine, that's not true. We're hard on you sometimes so that you do your best, so you can achieve your dreams, but we're always proud of you." Her mother reached out and took Kat's hand as if they were all better, as if none of the things that had happened had actually happened.

It broke Bradley's heart, the yearning in Kat's eyes as if she'd wanted nothing more than that, than the acceptance. Even now, even after everything she'd achieved and suffered and overcome, Kat just wanted her parents to be proud of her.

Kat swallowed hard and pulled her hand away. "Don't try and change history. I know exactly what you've said. You told me I wasn't even invited to the family reunion." Her voice wavered at that, as if it hurt just to admit it, especially with so many others watching.

Which made it pretty damned clear what her parents were doing. They hadn't given a damn about Kat when they thought she wasn't good enough, but now that she seemed to be the talk of the town with her art, they wanted to claim her again. They wanted to use that success for their own means.

Fucking assholes.

Barlow dropped his voice so it didn't carry as far. "We are your *parents*, Katherine. Are you really going to cause a scene and kick us out? You gallivant around with three men and you think they'll be there for you? They will get tired of you and leave, and where will you be then? Alone? We are blood, and that's all you can rely on. Without us, you will be on your own."

Bradley had had more than enough. "That's bullshit. Kat's been alone because of you already. She built herself a life on her own, without your help, so she sure as hell doesn't need your so-called help now."

Barlow rolled his eyes. "Whatever twisted love affair you seem to have with Katherine won't last. She's never managed to keep anyone around long term, and I am certain whatever it is you're getting out of it" — Barlow cast a dismissive and vulgar look between Kat, Olin, Dean and Bradley, as if implying sex was all she could give them — "will get old sooner rather than later. When that happens, she'll regret burning bridges with us."

Bradley went to close his hand into a fist, ready to hit the fucker for making Kat feel that way, but someone got between them.

Ell walked forward, standing up to Barlow as if she were ten feet tall instead of the thin girl she was. She crossed her arms over her chest, meeting his gaze head-on. "Her name is *Kat,* and she isn't alone."

As she said that, Sunny also pushed forward, breaking away from the crowd, along with other submissives from Sanctuary. Behind them stood the others, the Doms and Dommes who all saw Kat as one of their own.

It seemed the two had unknowingly riled up a group they shouldn't have, and Bradley didn't bother to hide his grin because Kat's parents had *no* idea that they'd just messed with the wrong girl.

Kat held her breath as others came to her defense to stand up to her parents. It shocked her the way her friends had stood up, the way they'd backed her even if most of them had no idea if what her parents said was true.

"Who are you?" Kat's father asked Ell, his look dismissive, as if he couldn't believe the woman would even speak to him.

"I'm Kat's friend, and she hasn't been alone in a *very* long time."

"You—"

Sunny spoke up, and despite the fact Sunny tended to be quiet and sweet, Kat knew the woman was tough when it came to protecting others. She pointed her finger at Barlow to silence him. "Quiet. You will not come in here and cause more pain to Kat. She is an amazing, dedicated and loving person who has always deserved so much more than you."

"You don't know anything," Kat's mother added in, though she lacked some of the confidence she'd had before, as if she hadn't expected to have anyone stand up to her. "Friendships fall apart. Family is forever."

"Yeah, family is," Sunny said. "The thing is, Kat *is* family to us. She's risked herself for those she cares about, has given so much to all of us. You won't find a better person, someone with a bigger heart."

Barlow straightened his back, then looked right at Kat. "This is absurd. We are your parents, and you will treat us with the respect we deserve. We raised you, took care of you, and you turn your backs on us when you finally achieve something? Disgusting behavior!"

Kat swallowed hard and closed her hands into fists. She'd run from this for so long, willing to endure whatever her parents said or did to her just because she was desperate for them to finally look at her like she was worth something.

But here they were, doing exactly what she'd wanted. She'd craved them to claim her, to be proud of her, and now they were here ready to do it.

And yet it felt like acid on her skin. It wasn't about her at all, it was about what they thought they could get from her. They *still* didn't give a damn about her, not really. They didn't see her for who she was, but for what she could do for them all of a sudden.

"You abandoned me a long time ago," Kat said, her voice stronger than it ever had been when talking to them. It was the faith of her friends — her *family* — that gave her the strength. "You haven't ever loved me. You've never cared about me — you won't even use the name I go by. It's too late, now. I don't need you. I don't need your approval or your praise or your love, so I certainly don't need your presence here. You need to leave."

Both of her parents widened their eyes, as if those were the last words they'd expected to hear from her. Then again, she'd always been the puppy trailing along behind them, hoping she'd become enough, that they'd throw her scraps of attention no matter how many times they kicked her.

It was enough. She'd finally realized the truth — she had people who actually loved her, who cared about her, who accepted her for who she was, flaws and all.

Barlow leaned in and dropped his voice into a low, angry whisper Kat had never heard before. "You're in the public eye now, and I wonder what your new fans would think if they found out your secrets. I wonder if they'd still support you if they knew you threw away your family when you became famous, or that you seem to be in some weird relationship with three men, or that you spend so much of your time at that disgusting sex club. I wonder if your friends would care about you so much if their secrets were let out because of you."

The color drained from Kat's face. She'd never thought they'd known about Sanctuary. As much as she hated how they spoke about that place, as if it were something filthy and wrong, that wasn't what got to her the most. If they came out with that, if they told the wrong person, it could ruin not just Kat but so many other people.

Kat opened her mouth, ready to make things better, to sacrifice the confidence and independence she felt moments ago in order to keep everyone else safe, but another voice silenced her.

Toya set her hand on Kat's shoulder and squeezed softly before stepping past the other submissives, placing herself between them and Kat's parents. "You will leave, *now.*"

"Who do you think you are?" Barlow asked, staring at Toya as if she were trash. No doubt he thought she were just some dumb girl caught up in whatever he thought Sanctuary was.

"I met Kat a long time ago when she worked multiple jobs to put herself through school because her parents had refused to help despite having the ability to do so. I've been lucky enough to watch her grow into a wonderful young woman all on her own. I can't have children, and my life isn't conducive to it, but I have always thought of her as a daughter and considered myself lucky for it."

"Well, you aren't her mother. I am," Elizabeth spat.

"No, you aren't. Parents love their children—they care for them, want the best for them. Neither of you deserve that title."

"Then we'll tell everyone about her, about that *place*."

"You can do so if you want, but I wouldn't recommend it." She looked right at Barlow, not flinching in the least. "You work as the head of Temon Communications, don't you?"

Barlow nodded. "That's right. It means I have access to several newspapers and TV stations to run this information in."

"Temon is owned by what company again?"

He frowned. "Lacksidy Holdings."

"That's right. Now, ask me who I am again."

"Who are you?"

Toya's grin sent shivers down Kat's spine and reminded her why she was glad to never have been on the receiving end of that look. "My name is Toya Lacksidy, and if you even think about printing slanderous lies for your own benefit, if you consider ruining people for nothing but your own petty wants, if you think for a moment I would allow you to act with so little integrity and keep your position, you are clearly not intelligent enough to keep your job for long."

Barlow's eyes widened, the first sign of real fear on his face as he realized he wasn't the scariest thing in the room. He swallowed hard and leaned in. "I won't," he assured her, his voice having transformed into something entirely different, something Kat had never heard. He was being...respectful? "I swear, I won't say a word."

Toya made a soft huff that implied the man wasn't worth her time or attention. "I suggest you leave now before you make a larger scene. Kat neither needs nor wants whatever you think you can give her anymore. She's turned into the woman she is not because of either of you, but in spite of you. And I am not a woman to repeat myself—I don't give second warnings."

Kat's parents nodded and slunk from the party, leaving an awkward silence behind. So many eyes were on Kat, so many people staring at her after they all witnessed the exchange.

Her eyes burned, but she refused to cry.

Dean laughed softly. "Well, guess they didn't realize the risk of facing off against people who think a fun Friday night involves whips and chains, huh?"

No one responded to the joke at first, as if no one was sure it was appropriate. However, it broke whatever had held Kat back, helped her step forward and away from the pain of her parents.

She laughed, unable to hold it in, until tears ran down her face. Dean wiped his fingers beneath her eyes then pressed a kiss to her forehead. "You did well, Brat."

She offered him a smile before Olin caught her chin and took a real kiss, one that didn't end until a small moan escaped her. "You don't need them—you're way too good for them."

Bradley hadn't moved his arms crossed, his expression guarded and unhappy. Was he angry? Mad that her problems kept getting in the way?

"You really are an idiot, aren't you?" He opened his arms and before she could think twice, Kat rushed into them. He hugged her to his chest tight and whispered into her ear so no one else could hear, "Don't listen to them. You've always got a home and a family, and nothing's ever gonna change that."

Bradley released her, and Kat stepped back, staring at the grouping of friends she'd made, the people who had taken her in, who had given her a place to belong. Maybe they were an odd group, but they were hers and she cherished every one of them.

"Well, I've got another hour I have to hang out here," she said. "But how about we keep celebrating at an after-party?" Kat looked over at Toya in question.

Toya chuckled. "Do you really think you even need to ask? I already have the caterer setting up food. We'll meet you there." With that, Toya nodded and turned on her heel, heading out of the exhibit. The others followed after congratulating Kat. Even the guests cleared out as the event started to wrap up about an hour later.

Finally, Kat stood in the middle of the empty art exhibit, the paintings she'd thought would never see the light of day all hanging on the walls with small 'sold' signs beneath them. Olin, Dean and Bradley stood beside her, and Kat couldn't stop her smile.

"That's not a good thing," Bradley muttered. At Kat's look, he nodded toward her. "That smile means nothing good."

"I'm just happy," Kat argued.

"Yeah, but your *happy* usually means bad behavior," Dean said.

"Don't be so hard on her," Olin pipped in.

"Thank you," she said.

"You're just an enabler," Bradley muttered.

"Not really," Olin said back. "I just like giving her enough rope to hang herself with."

Kat set her hands on her hips and turned to face all three of them. "You know what? I'm going to Sanctuary alone! I don't need this. I am a famous artist now! I'll go find a nice, sweet Dom who knows how to treat a woman." She went to storm past them, but a hand around her arm stopped her.

She found Olin holding her, his honey-colored eyes boring into her. "You're going nowhere without us, Kat. Sorry, but you're about the only thing in the whole world I'm not willing to let go."

Dean ran his finger down her cheek, the nail scraping along her skin in a delicious threat. "You've made your bed, and I plan to spend the rest of my life fucking you in it." His crude, vulgar words were beyond hot, and yet sweet in some weird, twisted way.

Bradley caught her chin, tilting her face up so she was lost in the intensity of his dark eyes. "I may not know how to treat a woman, but I've gotten damn good at taming brats." His expression softened the barest amount, as if he couldn't help it when looking at her, before he added on, "Now, be a good girl and behave."

Kat licked her lip, trapped between wanting to tell them how damned much she loved them and not wanting to say it. They knew, right? They understood how much she needed them, how much they meant to her. They *had* to.

They hadn't fallen for her because she was perfect or obedient or meek. They knew exactly who she was, and they loved her anyway.

So instead of giving in, instead of being someone she wasn't, Kat showed them the woman they said they wanted to spend the rest of their life with.

She smirked before she whispered back, "Make me."

Want to see more from this author? Here's a taster for you to enjoy!

Larkwood Academy: Whispers
Jayce Carter

Excerpt

I never missed my voice more than when Deacon touched me, when I opened my mouth and wanted to moan his name.

Sure, there were other times it annoyed me, when I wanted to tell someone off, when I wanted to explain myself, when I just wanted to *be heard*. Those times irked, but the loss never bothered me as much as when Deacon teased his lips over my breast, when the lack of noise from me made it feel incomplete.

Not that Deacon seemed to mind — or perhaps it was better to say he could make up for it easily. He might not have been the most vocal man usually, but that all changed in bed.

I looked around for a moment, noting the quiet corner of a shed in the yard where we'd tucked ourselves away. *Maybe bed is a stretch…*

We couldn't risk people catching on to us, which had left us finding out-of-the-way spots like this for these little rendezvous. Neither of us wanted to turn into a weakness for the other.

"I missed you," Deacon whispered in his low voice against my skin, his breath warm and rapid.

I loved these moments, how he lost that composure he usually had, how he seemed like anyone else. Normally Deacon was bigger than life, a guard at Larkwood Academy who even the other guards feared and distrusted.

In these moments, though, he wasn't any of that. He was just *mine*.

I set my hand on the back of his neck and brought him closer, pulled him to my body until I could try to tell him the things I couldn't say with my kiss.

He groaned against my lips, then grabbed my thigh to pull it around him. My ass pressed against the small table I sat on, but I didn't care about anything. Not splinters, not discomfort, nothing but drowning myself in these rare moments of happiness.

I'd lived at Larkwood for months, had mostly accepted the brutality that made up my world now, but that made these moments even more important. When Deacon touched me, when he growled into my ear, it made the rest of the ugliness of my life drift away.

He sank his cock into me, and I dug my nails into his back. It was always this wonderful burn when he took me, when I could feel entirely filled by him.

So I lost myself in him, in his strength, in the rough, whispered praise he offered. Too soon, it ended. Too quickly, I wiped off and pulled my sweats back on, brushing my hair with my fingers to appear presentable. We never had much time, never got to indulge in the quiet happiness when normal people could enjoy languid motions and gentle kisses through the night.

Deacon buttoned his pants, his expression having shifted back to the usual closed off one he showed to everyone else. No doubt that was one reason I so cherished the times we had, because it was the only chance I got to really see him.

"You need to be more careful," he muttered.

I turned toward him, furrowing my brows.

The zipper of his pants was loud in the quiet shed. "You've got guards watching you. Warden put out a memo to keep a close eye on you. You think they don't know you've been meeting up with those delinquents you seem to think are friends?"

I pressed my lips together and narrowed my eyes. Of course Deacon didn't care for the other connections I'd made — he considered all the shades dangerous, so he saw any other resident a risk to me.

What he didn't get was that *everything* was a risk to me. The whole damned world seemed to want to take me apart, to pull me to pieces until nothing was left.

He came forward and set his hand on the back of my neck, angling my face so I looked right into those bright purple eyes of his. Those eyes had ushered me into my new life at one time, but they meant so much more to me now. "I don't want to lose you, Hera. You can't trust anyone, can't let your guard down. Whatever they're talking you into, it'll get you killed."

I set my hand on his chest and pushed. He didn't move because of the pressure, but on his own. I could have used my powers, my ability to control sound waves, but I tried my hardest to keep that hidden. I'd finally gotten to where I didn't do it on accident, so I kept it on a tight leash.

"Nothing to say?" Anger flashed across his features, but I didn't fear him. I knew him too well already, knew he'd never hurt me, at least not on purpose. Sure, he was a guard at the very place holding me captive, but he did all he could to keep me safe.

"No one makes me do anything," I signed to him.

"You're too naïve," he snapped. "You think I don't know they're trouble? That they're looking for some magical way out? Look, this place has stood for a long-damned time, and no level one shade has ever escaped. A lot of them have died trying, though. I don't care how good a *friend* you think they are, they'll let you take the fall if it benefits them at all."

Deacon's words were callous but not unexpected.

We'd done this for weeks, ever since I'd left solitary after being caught breaking into that file room. Deacon was smart enough to know I was up to something, but pushing too much might just end up making me a bigger target. It had driven a wedge between us, one that hurt more than I liked to admit.

I hated having to separate my life, to keep things from all the people around me, but I didn't have a choice.

Deacon couldn't find out about the plans I had with Wade, Knox and Brax, and the three of them couldn't know the extent of my relationship with Deacon.

Though I had a feeling all the men in my life had made wrong guesses about each other. It was in the looks, in the aggression they all showed when talking about each other. No doubt each of them assumed I was sleeping with all the others in my life.

Which wasn't true.

Though not because of lack of effort on my side.

It just turned out romance was as foreign a concept to me as the economics of other countries and how football worked. Getting people into bed was much more difficult than I'd have ever imagined. I recalled all the times I'd heard as a teenager how boys were animals who only wanted one thing, how I had to be careful as a woman or I'd get taken advantage of.

Yet most of these men were not taking advantage of me in the way I wanted them to, no matter how I tried to tempt them.

Not that telling them that would matter. Deception was a way of life here at Larkwood, and we *all* had our secrets.

"Don't fight with me. We don't have long."

"I'm not trying to fight," he assured me, despite the aggressive tone of voice that he used almost exclusively for fighting. "I just worry about you. I'm afraid I'll open my email and see your name on the North Tower list. I don't want that."

Which, to be fair, neither did I. Despite the fact The North Tower seemed my only real escape option, I wasn't ready to face that horror just yet. I needed a better plan, more information, anything to give me an edge.

But it wasn't as if I could admit any of that to Deacon. If he discovered any plan for escape I had, he'd just ruin it to protect me.

So I had to keep that all close to my chest. *"You don't need to worry about me."*

He made a soft sound low in his throat, as if he couldn't believe what an idiot I was. "Of course I do. You're trouble, Hera, and you attract trouble like a fucking magnet. Don't forget, I was the one who saved you that night when you changed. I saw it all. I know exactly how much you need someone worrying about you."

I dropped my gaze at the painful reminder, at the fact he was right. If it wasn't for him, I'd have died on that parking structure floor. I'd have bled out from the man who had slit my throat, the one who had taken my voice.

Instead, Deacon had heard my scream, had come and saved me.

Then he'd brought me to Larkwood.

It was a complicated relationship.

He reached forward again, but he didn't touch my cheek. Instead, he touched the scar at my throat, the whole reason I couldn't speak. "You almost died. *This* happened because the world didn't like what you were. I saved you that time, but I'm terrified I won't be able to the next, that you'll do something stupid and end up in a situation I can't do anything about." His words were so soft, so sad that they took me back.

I forced myself to stare into his eyes, to witness the pain and fear there. For all Deacon's faults — and there were a lot of them — he wasn't a bad man. He wanted the best for me.

The problem?

We didn't agree what was best. He wanted me alive even if it meant losing everything else. I wanted freedom, even if it meant risking my life for it.

It was an impasse I didn't know how to fix.

"I don't want to see you get finished off because you want to escape," he whispered.

I forced my hand up so I could sign back. *"I'm not planning anything."*

* * * *

"So, what's the plan for our escape?"

Knox let out a laugh as he read what I had signed. "You really don't beat around the bush, do you?"

I shrugged before reaching into his fridge for a water. It was odd to think that weeks before, I'd been so nervous in his place, so afraid of doing anything wrong, of upsetting him.

Now I treated his space as if it were my own, and each time I did? He seemed to smile a little wider.

I held one water out to him, but he shook his head. It gave me the chance to look at him for a moment, surprised as ever by just how handsome he was.

He had a body that could have tempted me even if he weren't the kind man he was. He was lean but strong, and he kept his hair so short it was basically buzzed off. He had on a T-shirt, and while that wasn't normally the type of outfit to swoon over, he made even it look amazing.

Then again, that was partly due to the general sensuality he had, all thanks to his incubus side. He was a walking billboard offering sex, and while he and I had never fully gone there, it didn't make me immune to noticing.

"How's Deacon?"

I let out an obvious sigh along with an eye roll for good measure. *"Why do you ask?"*

"You're way too casual with him." Knox shook his head, the same argument I'd had with him a few times. I'd had the same fight with Brax as well, though my fights with him were more yelling — at least from him — and always ended up with us having angry sex. Wade didn't bitch, but his snarky comments had suggested he didn't approve.

Knox at least acted nice when we argued.

"It's nothing to worry about."

"You say that because you don't know the real him. If he gets wind of anything, he'll turn you in right away."

"He wouldn't do that."

Knox didn't know Deacon like I did. Sure, I wasn't rushing to tell Deacon everything — that would have been stupid. But I was fully capable of spending time with him without blurting out everything on my mind.

The fact I can't speak helps.

Knox set a hand on my cheek, his palm warm and teasing. He stroked his thumb against my skin. "The fact you can still have some of that innocence after being here is amazing. I just don't want to see it get your killed because you trusted the wrong person."

His words melted some of my annoyance. I understood his worry, especially because if I made the wrong choice, if I trusted the wrong person, if we got caught, Knox and his brother could easily pay the price for it.

Even with that, though, I couldn't just *not* spend time with Deacon. Sure, things would end when I escaped, because what sort of future was there? That should have made it easier to let go now, before I got too attached, but the opposite seemed true.

I just couldn't imagine ending it sooner than I had to.

Knox offered a half-hearted smile, as if I were an idiot climbing too high into a tree and he knew I'd fall and break something. "You are impossible." He leaned in and brushed his warm lips against mine, the touch gentle and sweet.

And it did what his innocent touches *always* did to me. A rush of sensation, like drowning and suddenly being able to breathe all at once. It was his power, that incubus part of him hungry and wanting to feed.

But he'd refused to feed from me or to touch me beyond the bare minimum. I'd been able to touch him, to focus on him, but he never reciprocated. It wasn't selfishness but fear.

As soon as it happened, however, he pulled back and shook his head hard, as though to clear it.

"*It's okay,*" I told him the way I always did, even when his rejection hurt, even when it didn't feel okay at all.

"It's not."

I missed the warmth of his hand when he took it away, when we stood there with this distance between us that I had no idea how to fix. Understanding the reason for it didn't change the hurt. No matter what I did, he didn't trust himself, didn't trust that other part of himself, didn't want it near me.

And there wasn't a thing I could do about that.

Instead of letting him see just how much it hurt, I turned away and brought the water bottle to my lips, trying to let the cold liquid cool my flushed cheeks and slow my racing heart.

Why the hell was my libido like this, anyway? I'd never given a damn about sex before coming to Larkwood, before finding myself tied to a few different men. It hadn't been bad at all, but I'd never cared one way or the other about it. I had to guess my new desires had to do with changing into a shade.

"Hera," Knox started to say, but the opening of his door front saved me.

Sort of.

I wasn't sure if the angry face of a berserker who I felt certain hated me counted as being saved.

"Have you found anything yet?" Brax asked, his tone annoyed.

Was he ever *not* annoyed, though? Maybe, when around others. I had no idea if it was just me or if he was always unpleasant.

Judging from his glare my way, I'd say it was a mixture.

"*Nothing yet.*"

Knox translated for me, since Brax seemed the only person unable—or more likely unwilling—to learn American Sign Language. When it was just the two of us, I used my writing pad, but when others were around, they translated.

"So what good are you? You had this big idea about wanting to escape but then you get nothing over the last month? Fuck, I hate people who are all talk."

And, as usual, I rose to the occasion when it came to his anger. Funny that back when I'd first met him, he'd terrified me. Now? Now I didn't give a fuck about his little hissy fits. If he hadn't killed me yet, he probably wouldn't.

Most likely…

I was pretty sure…

"I'm sorry that I'm not doing enough for you. What exactly was it you've done? Because I figured out about the North Tower and the two projects they're doing there."

Brax narrowed his blue eyes into a murderous glare as Knox translated. At the end, he let out a huff. "Well, don't get sloppy. If you fuck up, we all go down, and I'm not about to let that happen."

I lifted my eyebrow to stare back. What was the point in arguing? Brax only heard what he wanted to hear, and having Knox translate everything made it all take longer.

"Be careful," Knox offered, his voice even gentler than before, as if trying to make up for the attitude of his twin.

Then again, the two were always looking out for each other. Brax tried to protect Knox and Knox made excuses for Brax's horrible behavior.

When I didn't respond, Knox went on. "After getting thrown in solitary, you're bound to get watched more closely. I know Brax is pushing you, but don't do anything risky."

Brax opened his mouth as if to argue that point but snapped his lips together before he could. He let out an angry sound and the edges of his face sharpened the way they always did when his temper got away from him. Berserkers weren't known for their control and calm. Instead of saying anything else, he turned on his heel and stormed out, slamming the door behind him, his exit as dramatic and quick as his entrance had been.

Knox sighed, his gaze pinned to the door as if he could still watch his brother through it. "I swear, his temper is worse than ever."

It seemed the same to me. The only reason he was annoyed there was because he wanted me to do whatever it took, no matter the danger to me, and the fact it was a dick-thing to say frustrated him.

"You don't understand him," Knox said.

"Stop defending him."

"That's never going to happen." Knox gave me a sad smile. "He's not the easiest to get along with, but there's more to him than anyone realizes. Don't take the things he says at face value."

I took another drink of water, mostly to give us a way to end the conversation. I knew what Brax was like, had experienced his brand of asshole behavior plenty of times. The last thing I needed was for Brax's bad behavior to sour my relationship with Knox.

It was already all rather precarious.

Knox glanced behind him at the clock on the wall. "You already had your work detail this morning, right?"

"I have an evaluation in about an hour."

He pressed his lips together, and I knew he was getting ready to lecture me yet again. This time, about Kit.

But what did all these warnings matter? I couldn't just not see Kit since the adjunct professor handled not only teaching lessons but also most of the evaluations. It wasn't like I had an option to not go.

Besides, we hadn't had one since solitary, since I'd gotten caught with files from a restricted room. After spending the time in isolation, I'd had my work details increased for two weeks after. That made this the first eval since that had all happened.

Which meant I'd probably get an earful from him as well.

Why was it that everyone thought I needed their advice? That everyone saw me as a helpless creature who others had to tell how to behave?

Well, I did get caught when I tried stuff on my own.

I cut off his lecture by tossing the now empty water bottle into the recycling bin under Knox's sink. *"I'll be careful, I promise."*

Knox let out a long breath, catching my arm before I walked out. When he tugged me back and pressed his lips to mine in a kiss that stole all my annoyance away, I worried I'd lose myself. Kissing him was like looking over a cliff and down at a body of water. It tempted me to jump, made me want to dive in no matter how deep or dangerous.

As quickly as it happened, however, he let me go, stealing away that warmth. It was like shoving me away from the edge of that cliff. He swallowed hard, his green eyes bright as he stared at me, as if he wanted me to understand something.

What, though?

Maybe he didn't know, either. Maybe it was just hopeless, pointless desire, a drive to have something that wasn't possible.

Whatever it was, he stepped backward, fleeing as he so often did to his room, leaving me there confused and surprisingly cold.

Which felt like a good representation of whatever I had with Knox.

About the Author

Jayce Carter lives in Southern California with her husband and two spawns. She originally wanted to take over the world but realized that would require wearing pants. This led her to choosing writing, a completely pants-free occupation. She has a fear of heights yet rock climbs for fun and enjoys making up excuses for not going out and socializing.

Jayce loves to hear from readers. You can find her contact information, website details and author profile page at https://www.totallybound.com

Home of Erotic Romance

Sign up for our newsletter and find out about all our
romance book releases, eBook sales and promotions,
sneak peeks and FREE romance books!